Ravenous Things

Ravenous Things

Written and illustrated
by Derrick Chow

𝒟𝒾𝓈𝓃𝑒𝓎 • HYPERION
Los Angeles   New York

First Edition, July 2022
10 9 8 7 6 5 4 3 2 1
FAC-004510-22161

Printed in the United States of America

This book is set in 12-point Caslon Pro and Varius/Fontspring
Designed by Joann Hill
Illustrations created digitally with Adobe Photoshop

Library of Congress Cataloging-in-Publication Data
Names: Chow, Derrick, author, illustrator.
Title: Ravenous things / Derrick Chow.
Description: First edition. • Los Angeles ; New York : Disney-Hyperion, 2022. •
Audience: Ages 8–12 • Audience: Grades 7–9 • Summary: "Twelve-year-old Reggie is
still grieving the passing of his father when a strange man promises to reunite the two, if
Reggie only follows him deep into an underground subway system where horrors worse
than Reggie ever imagined lurk around every corner"—Provided by publisher.
Identifiers: LCCN 2021027091 • ISBN 9781368077637 (hardcover) • ISBN 9781368078498 (ebook)
Subjects: CYAC: Horror stories. • LCGFT: Horror fiction. • Novels.
Classification: LCC PZ7.1.C5426 Rav 2022 • DDC [Fic]—dc23
LC record available at https://lccn.loc.gov/2021027091

Reinforced binding
Visit www.DisneyBooks.com

For Baba

ONE

Happy Birthday

The cemetery was an in-between place. The sort of place that barely existed at all unless you were looking for it. It was a small patch of land, with only a dozen gravestones poking out of the yellowing grass. It was bounded on one side by a highway overpass and on the other by a cookie factory, which loomed like an enormous metal fortress. This meant the air was always filled with the roar of passing traffic and the smell of chocolate-chip cookies.

Reggie Wong knelt before a bronze plaque set into the ground. When he'd first seen it at the funeral two years ago, it was as shiny and brilliant as a new penny. Now it was tarnished with green-and-black grime, and its edges were overgrown with grass. Even so, when he leaned over the plaque, he could see his reflection peering back: a twelve-year-old boy with a thin, tanned face, black spiky hair, and a pointy chin he secretly hated. Sometimes he found himself pretending that it wasn't a reflection, but some poor boy buried down there in place of his father.

"Happy birthday, Dad!" exclaimed Reggie, holding up a gift that was wrapped in the comic pages from last Sunday's paper. "Sorry 'bout the wrapping. The only paper we have at home is covered in Santas."

Reggie imagined his dad smiling in response, the way he used to when he was watching reruns of *Star Trek* on Saturday mornings.

"Hope you like it. Made it myself in art class when we were supposed to be painting self-portraits. Got in trouble with Mrs. Pasternak, but it was totally worth it."

Beside the plaque, nestled in a cluster of dandelions, was a blue biscuit tin wrapped in twine. Reggie smiled fondly at it and reached out, brushing it clean of dirt and fallen leaves. This was the very first gift he had brought here to the cemetery.

Then he placed his dad's birthday present on the plaque and tore off the paper, revealing a handsome clay sculpture. He held it up against the sky, which was streaked red and orange by the October sunset. The sculpture was a flat disk the size of a dinner plate, with two oblong shapes stuck on one end. He grinned proudly at his creation. It was pretty darned good.

"It's the starship *Enterprise*! Sorry, I know the color's all wrong," he said, referring to its distinctly pink hue. "It was

Gareth Flanagan's fault. He dipped his red brush in my white paint. That jerk totally did it on purpose."

Raucous honking began ringing out as a flock of geese flew by overhead in V-formation, no doubt headed south for the winter.

"I wanted to add blue lights to the engines to make it even cooler, but I didn't know how."

Reggie tried to blink away the telltale stinging in his eyes. If his father were here, he'd open up his shiny red toolbox and pull out exactly what was needed to make those engines glow. That toolbox was somewhere at the back of the hall closet now, under a stack of moldering boxes, dusty and forgotten.

He set the spaceship down atop the plaque, just below the words:

In Memory of Arthur Wong, beloved husband and father.

"Mom says Happy Birthday too," lied Reggie as he tore up a fistful of dead grass. "She couldn't come today because..."

Because what? How was he supposed to end that sentence? Anger welled up inside of him when he considered the possibilities.

Reggie picked up a small rock and hurled it viciously at the nearest gravestone. It ricocheted off the mossy limestone surface and smashed into the clay *Enterprise*. He couldn't have done better if he'd painted a big red bull's-eye on it.

"Nooooo!" He picked up the spaceship gingerly. One of the engines toppled off and pinged hollowly on his dad's plaque. A bubble of regret floated up into Reggie's throat and came out as a long, quivery sigh. He peered down at the broken spaceship in his hands—this gift he'd made for his dad, that he spent hours on—and the stinging in his eyes blossomed into tears. "I'm so sorry, Dad. I'll take it back home and glue—"

Reggie stopped when he glimpsed his own reflection on the plaque. He looked completely ridiculous, sitting here in an empty graveyard, talking to thin air, crying over things that could never be undone. These visits were pointless. His dad couldn't hear him. Not now, not ever.

With hot, bitter blood racing through his veins, Reggie vowed never to come back. He shouldered his knapsack and stormed off toward the gate.

* * *

The tallest and grandest gravestone in the cemetery was capped with a stone angel. Her arms were outstretched in a pose of permanent blessing, and her face was carved into an expression of serenity. But at the moment, maybe because of the deepening shadows brought on by sunset, her eyes seemed much wider than usual, as if she was frightened of the man standing behind her, cloaked in her shadow.

As soon as Reggie left, the man stepped out from his hiding place. He crossed over to Arthur Wong's plaque and grinned at the blue biscuit tin and broken spaceship the boy had left behind.

Then he pressed a wooden flute to his lips, took a deep breath, and started to play. A strange tune sputtered out, filling the air and echoing hollowly off the huddled gravestones. It sounded almost like laughter, but not the pleasant kind. It sounded like the choking, mirthless cackle of someone up to no good.

TWO

Subway Rats

Reggie stood on the platform of St. Patrick subway station (his favorite in all of Toronto, because the tiled walls were the exact same shade of green as his toothpaste). He usually took the bus home from the cemetery so that he could watch the sun setting behind the distant skyscrapers, but he wasn't in the mood today.

All around him were men and women in business suits. Some texted on their cell phones, some read newspapers, and others stared down the tunnel, as if that would somehow make the train appear faster. Each and every one of them looked completely miserable. You'd think they were headed to the dentist's office and not home to their nice, hot dinners.

Reggie stepped toward the edge of the platform, onto the yellow safety strip, and glowered down at the tracks below. Although the tracks themselves gleamed silver, the floor was blackened with years of accumulated grease. Against this, a discarded orange peel stood out like a bright flower in a charred field.

A small, round shadow scrambled up to the peel and nudged it curiously. It took Reggie a moment to figure out that it wasn't a shadow. It was a rat. Its entire body was black, except for its tail, which was pink and fleshy, wriggling to and fro like a fat worm.

The rat flicked its sharp head up toward Reggie. A pair of black, shiny eyes fixed on him. Reggie had never tried to decipher a rat's expression before, but if he had to, he'd have said this one was hungry. Very hungry. Hungry enough to eat a twelve-year-old boy standing in the middle of a crowded subway station.

Thankfully, the rat returned its attention to the orange peel, snatching it up in its mouth and skittering off along the tracks toward the tunnel at the other end of the station.

That's when Reggie noticed the strange man. He wore a bright crimson blazer that made him stand out like a neon sign against the drab business suits all around him. A row of shiny brass buttons ran down the front, glinting keenly in the fluorescent lighting. Resting atop the man's head was a conductor's cap, its brim angled low enough to conceal his eyes. A leather satchel hung from his shoulder, so overstuffed that its seams were coming loose. And he wore no shoes, exposing the ugliest feet Reggie had ever seen—big and flat as paddles, with yellow toenails long enough to qualify as claws.

He was walking toward Reggie along the very edge of the platform, with his arms flung out to either side like a tightrope walker. As the man drew closer, Reggie could hear the sound of his gnarly toenails scraping against the floor.

He was holding something long and thin in his left hand. A stick? Or maybe a toy wand? When he lifted it to his mouth and danced his fingers up and down the knobbly surface, Reggie realized that it was a flute. He was playing a cheerful, peppy tune, the sort you'd hear on a merry-go-round at the fair. And yet something about those bouncing notes made every inch of Reggie's skin tingle with alarm.

Curiously, no one else on the platform paid the slightest bit of attention. It was as if Reggie was completely alone with this creepy man stepping delicately toward him.

Fear traced a tickly, little path up his spine. He took a few steps back, bumping into a lady behind him.

The man stopped playing his flute abruptly. He removed something from his satchel and held it up in the air. A sculpture. It was a light shade of pink and shaped like the starship *Enterprise.*

Reggie's fear melted into anger. *That creep stole my dad's birthday gift!*

Although his teachers were always scolding him for his hot

temper, he was pretty sure grave robbery warranted a heated response.

"Hey, jerkface! Give that back!" he shouted.

The man looked up. Reggie could see his eyes now. They were black and beady, like pinpricks of night. He flourished the *Enterprise* through the air, grinning all the while. He winked at Reggie. Then he turned on his heel and darted off through the crowd, moving surprisingly fast for a man with no shoes.

Reggie tore after him, but immediately tripped over a pair of suitcases, tumbling head over heels to the floor. He spluttered an apology to the owner of the luggage, but the woman seemed strangely oblivious. Not once did her eyes stray from the subway tunnel, almost as if Reggie wasn't there at all.

After scrambling to his feet, he spotted the thief barging up the crowded escalator to the level above. Surprisingly, no one objected to the man's line cutting. Instead, they swayed out of his way, like reeds parting in a stiff wind.

Reggie ran onto the escalator, but his journey up wasn't quite as smooth. All those thick bodies shifted back into place, becoming still and immovable. Which meant he had to push and shove his way through.

He arrived at the upper level, panting and out of breath. He doubled over with his hands on his knees, sucking in air. That creep was probably long gone by now.

But when Reggie looked up, he was surprised to see the man waiting for him. He was perched atop one of the turnstiles, twirling the clay *Enterprise* above his head. He kicked his hairy feet back and forth delightedly, and grinned at him.

Reggie's entire body shook with rage. He clenched his fists, marched right up to the man, and said something he'd always wanted to say to a grown-up. "I'm gonna punch your lights out!"

"Not a very nice greeting. Next time try a hello or a how-do-you-do," said the man, his smile growing. His teeth were small and sharp.

"Give it back to me. Now!"

"This? Is this what you want?" The man pointed at the *Enterprise* and narrowed his tiny, black eyes until they nearly disappeared.

"Yes!" said Reggie through gritted teeth.

The man stopped twirling the toy spaceship and dangled it just out of Reggie's reach. "But this isn't what you *really* want, is it?"

He hopped off the turnstile so suddenly that Reggie startled backward. The man bent over, thrusting his pale face closer to him. The wooden flute dangled from a cord around his neck, swinging back and forth hypnotically.

"I ask you again, little nibbly," said the man. He wasn't smiling anymore. "If you could have anything in this whole crusty world, what would it be?"

Reggie knew the answer to that question. It's what he thought of every morning while he ate his cereal and every night just before falling asleep. More than anything, he wanted his dad back.

"Perfect," said the man, as if he'd read his thoughts. His sharp smile returned. "Come here tomorrow at midnight, and you'll get what you want, little nibbly."

Reggie felt like the wind had been knocked out of him. He stared in astonishment as the man doffed his cap and tucked the *Enterprise* under his arm.

"What do you mean?" Reggie asked weakly.

"You'll get what you want. Tomorrow at midnight," the man repeated, before letting out a thin, squeaky laugh. Then he was off, scuttling toward the stairs that led to the trains below.

THREE

Peephole Peril

The next day, Reggie was delighted to hear that school was canceled. Mrs. Maloni, the secretary at Our Lady of Sorrows Middle School, had called to inform him that none of the teachers had bothered to show up. Each and every one of them had claimed *parental emergencies . . .* whatever that meant.

And so, Reggie planned to spend his day carving jack-o'-lanterns, making paper ghosts, and festooning his room with fake cobwebs. Halloween was three days away, and it was, hands down, his favorite holiday. But things didn't go as planned. Every time he began a project, his thoughts would wander, and he'd either forget what he was doing or lose all interest. Today his brain was like a badly trained puppy that had broken free of its leash.

He finally abandoned his plan to spook-ify the apartment. Instead, he flopped down on the couch to watch a boring nature show about killer whales. Anything with the word *killer* in it shouldn't be boring, but this was. Just as he was about to change the channel, an emergency news bulletin came on. A very serious-looking anchorman with very plastic-looking hair appeared. He gazed solemnly into the camera and warned viewers about food shortages all across the city, caused by looting gangs of kindergartners.

Kindergartners? Had Reggie heard right? He turned the volume up but was too distracted to follow the rest of the story.

Try as he might, he couldn't stop thinking about that creepy man in the subway. The guy was obviously a crackpot. Not someone he should be giving a second thought to. Still, his words continued to echo in Reggie's head.

You'll get what you want. Tomorrow at midnight.

What had he meant? Reggie knew what he *wanted* it to mean. But that was ridiculous. There was no way he could get what he really wanted. Was there?

"Zane isn't Zane anymore," announced his mother mysteriously. She'd appeared next to the couch and was peering down at him with wide, terrified eyes.

Reggie turned up the volume on the TV, fully prepared to

ignore whatever fresh batch of *weird* his mother was cooking up this morning. His mom wasn't having any of that. She took his hand and pulled him off the couch, leading him toward the front door of the apartment.

"Cool it, Mom!"

"The kid next door—Zane Kembhavi—he's changed!" she exclaimed, staring warily at the front door. Her long, black hair hung in greasy tendrils over her bathrobe. Reggie wondered when she'd last washed it, but he figured it didn't really matter. It wasn't like she ever left the apartment anymore.

"Changed?" said Reggie, rolling his eyes.

"He's not *him* anymore. He's something else." Seeing he wasn't convinced, she added, "And he's not the only one. The little girl in A-34 with the lazy eye. She changed last week. Saw her walking down the hall while I was paying the grocery man. It was her, except it wasn't. She was all wrong."

Reggie sighed and shook his head. His mom had always possessed a *big, beautiful imagination* (or at least, that's how his dad had always described it). Unlike most moms, Reggie's was a believer in anything and everything fantastical. Woodland fairies, time travel, guardian angels, mind reading—it was all possible. This used to be his favorite thing about her. It meant she was silly and loopy and fun. He never knew what magical paths she'd lead him down. But ever since his dad died, all those paths seemed to lead to someplace dark and scary. Suddenly everything was a catastrophe, or a conspiracy, or a threat.

Suddenly it was like she was a prisoner of her own imagination, instead of its conjurer.

"Mom, remember last month when you thought a tornado was coming because your knee started acting up? And that time you told me to stop drinking milk because the government was poisoning the cows?"

He turned to leave, but his mom grabbed him by his shoulders and spun him around. Her eyes were wild with fear, and her skin was pebbled with sweat.

"Please, sweetie. Just take a look," she pleaded.

"Fine!" he said, shrugging his mother's hands off him. "But only to prove you're wrong."

He hefted up the footstool they kept by the hall closet and placed it before the front door. He stepped up onto it, looking through the peephole.

As always, the hallway was meagerly lit with greenish-yellow light, like at the bottom of a murky lake. At first, all he could make out was the door of the apartment across the way, and the expanse of beige wallpaper covering the lumpy walls like a great, dirty Band-Aid.

Then he saw it. A figure crouched on the floor, facing away from the peephole. It was the curved shape of someone on his haunches and bent over in a very strange position, with his face nearly planted on the grimy carpet. Reggie knew it was Zane from the neon-orange sneakers on his feet.

"So what, Mom? He probably just dropped something."

Just as Reggie was about to move away from the peephole, Zane shifted around, like a crab turning in sand. That's when Reggie saw the pink flash of a tongue, and he suddenly understood. The kid was licking the floor. Lapping eagerly at it, as if the filthy green carpet was the tastiest thing ever.

"What the . . ." breathed Reggie.

In the half light of the hallway, it was hard to get a good look at Zane's face, but from what Reggie could see, it looked . . . *off.* As if all his features had been taken apart and put together again in slightly different positions. His smile was a bit too wide and toothy, and his cheeks looked unusually hollow. His nose also looked much pointier than Reggie remembered.

But his eyes were, by far, the worst part. They seemed too close together, too small and piercing, like eyes you'd see stalking you in the dark corners of a forest.

Zane snapped his head up, a sudden motion, like an animal sensing food. He sniffed sharply at the air, then flicked his eyes upward.

Reggie's stomach lurched. The boy was peering straight at him.

FOUR

The Bear Whistle

Reggie jerked away from the peephole so fast that he lost his balance, nearly falling off the footstool. His mother rushed to catch him.

She read the fear on his face and said vehemently, "You saw him. You know I'm right."

He scrambled back to the peephole. Zane was gone. In his place was a dark, round stain on the carpet. It occurred to Reggie that this was where he'd spilled a can of cherry cola last weekend. In fact, the entire hallway still reeked of sugar (on top of its usual funk of wet dog and soured milk). Zane had been licking that nasty stain like some kind of freak. What the heck was wrong with the kid?

There was another possibility, one that gave Reggie the chills. What if his mother was right? What if that wasn't Zane at all? Maybe it was someone or something else entirely....

Reggie turned to his mother. She looked frantic with fear and worry. It was a familiar expression. The same one she wore every time a new, kooky conspiracy theory overtook her.

And just like that, he knew exactly what was going on. Zane wasn't a big, bad monster. He was just a goofy kid acting weird. After all, this was the same boy who once filled a washing machine with beef jerky and chocolate bars (a failed attempt at making chocolate milk). He wasn't exactly the sharpest tool in the shed.

Nope, the problem wasn't Zane. The problem was Reggie's mother. For a few moments there, her paranoid ideas had infected him, filling his mind with shapeless fears.

"No, I didn't see anything!" he shouted, hopping down off the stool. "It was just Zane goofing off."

"But you saw his face, didn't you? It's all wrong!" pleaded his mother, clutching at his shoulders.

"It's dark in the hallway. Hard to see anything." He tried to ignore the shudders passing through him as he recalled Zane's cold, black eyes. "This is just another bogus reason for you to never leave this stinking apartment."

"His eyes. Didn't you see his eyes?" exclaimed his mother.

"You missed Dad's birthday yesterday!" hollered Reggie, shaking with rage. "Do you even care?"

His mom looked like she'd been slapped. She looked down at her slippers and said quietly, "Of course I care, Reggie."

"Then why don't you act like yourself anymore? All you do is hide out in your room, thinking up wackadoo reasons why everything is out to get you!"

She was quiet for a long time, with her hands clasped before her face, and her eyes closed, as if she'd turned into that sad stone angel in the cemetery.

Finally, she gazed up at Reggie with a very determined look on her face. "Let's go to Centre Island."

"What?" said Reggie, feeling like his mom was a television and someone had just flipped the channel.

"Don't you remember that time your dad and I took you there? We stayed on the beach until sunset, and you spent the whole time trying to find green pebbles in the water."

Reggie remembered the sunlight and the creamy air and being happy.

"Yeah, and Dad spent so long in the sun he looked like a lobster the next day," he said, smiling.

His mom nodded, smoothing greasy hair off her forehead. "It was great, wasn't it? Let's go there right now!"

"Really? But it's raining."

"So what?" replied his mother, grinning. "The ferries still run in the rain, don't they? Anyways, that's what umbrellas are for."

She stalked decisively over to the hall closet and flung it open. As she searched inside on her knees, she said, "Go get ready, sweetie. Or do you want to spend the whole day watching whales on TV?"

Reggie leaped to his feet and headed to his room. He stopped after a few steps and turned to his mother. "Mom, are you sure?"

She met his eyes. "Yes, sweetie."

A few minutes later, Reggie and his mother stood side by side in the narrow foyer of their apartment. He'd pulled on his yellow rain boots, and his mother was holding a see-through umbrella big enough to keep both of them dry.

His mother just stood there, staring at the front door, as if waiting for it to swing open on its own. Reggie watched her anxiously and twisted the bottom of his jacket, but he didn't reach for the door handle. He knew that she had to do it herself. She had to be the one to take the first step.

As the minutes passed, he felt his hopes deflating. "You can do it, Mom."

"I know, sweetie," said his mother breathlessly. She sounded like she'd just gone for a jog. "I can go through that door and down the elevator and out into the world and have a fun day with you."

But she still didn't move a muscle.

"There's nothing out there," urged Reggie. "Nothing's out to get you."

"I know, sweetie," said his mother, tears wetting her eyes.

He knew instantly from her voice that they wouldn't be

going to Centre Island. Before he had to listen to yet another of his mom's excuses, he threw down his knapsack, ran to his bedroom, and slammed the door.

*   *   *

Later that evening, Reggie heard a soft knock at his bedroom door. "Can I come in?"

He didn't answer, but his mom barged in anyway.

"I know you don't want to talk to me," she said gently. "So all you have to do is listen, and your old lady will do the talking."

Reggie was sitting on his bed, playing with his Nintendo Switch. He kept his head down and pretended he was too busy with the video game to notice his mother.

"I've not been the best mom lately, have I?"

Reggie mashed the buttons on the controller even harder.

"I want to promise you I'm going to get better. But you're probably sick of hearing me make promises I can't keep," said his mother, crossing over to the bed and sitting down.

"So I'm not giving you any more words. I've got something better. Something you can hold in your hands."

Reggie could see from the corner of his eye that his mother had pulled something from the pocket of her bathrobe. He resisted the urge to look up from his video game.

"Your father gave this to me."

He sucked in his breath at the mention of his dad.

"We'd just gotten married, and we had nothing—no money, nowhere to live. So for our honeymoon, we went camping in Algonquin. He bought this silly little thing at a gas station and gave it to me. Only cost him a dollar, but I wouldn't trade this for all the gold in the world."

She tipped her forehead against the side of Reggie's ear and whispered through her tears, "And I want you to have it, my baby boy."

She set the object down on the bed between them. "Just give it a blow when you're feeling down. It's always helped me."

Then she kissed him on the top of his head and left the room.

Once the door had shut, Reggie put his game down and picked up the small gift his mother had left him. It was an orange, plastic bear with a snarling face and paws stretched over its head. There were flat, rectangular openings on either end of it.

"It's a whistle," Reggie realized.

He turned it over in the palm of his hand and saw faded blue lettering on the bear's back. It read:

KEEP BEARS AT BAY! Blow in case of bear attack.

Reggie scrunched up his face and shook his head. Why had his mother given him this piece of junk? He wasn't going camping anytime soon. And the last he checked, there weren't any bears stalking the streets of Toronto.

He stuffed the whistle into the pocket of his jeans and started up the video game again.

That night, Reggie dreamed he was camping with his father in a dark forest. The trees were taller than skyscrapers, and there were beasts moving in the shadows. Reggie wasn't scared, though. They were safe, because they were together.

FIVE

Night Music

R eggie awoke with a jolt. He'd been dreaming about
something, but it evaporated the moment he opened
his eyes. He sat up in bed and winced at his digital
alarm clock: 11:40.

He'd only been asleep for two hours. What had woken
him up?

Then he remembered—music had reached him in his dreams,
a tune that was slow and sad and made his molars itch. He lay
perfectly still and listened, but the only thing he heard was the
deep rumble of a subway train. Their apartment building sat
right above one of the transit lines, so he was used to hearing it,
had grown to like it even. It was comforting, like distant thunder
on a summer afternoon.

After the train had passed, he heard it again: a flute song, echoing up from the street outside, slithering through the night air like a wily snake. He bounded out of bed, went over to his window, and peered into the night.

Three stories down, a man stood on the deserted sidewalk. He was playing a flute as the streetlight above him flickered like a candle about to go out. It was the weirdo from the subway. Had he followed Reggie home?

The man's promise rang through his head, loud and clear, as if the man was standing right behind him, breathing down his neck.

You'll get what you want. Tomorrow at midnight.

Reggie spun around, but of course, the only face he saw was that of the footballer Cristiano Ronaldo smiling at him from a poster on the wall. He thought of what would happen if he did the *smart* thing, the mother-approved thing. What if he crawled back under the covers, plugged his ears, and went to sleep? He'd wake up in the morning and nothing would have changed. Not his mother, and certainly not the knot of sadness inside him that refused to untangle.

But what if he followed that flute song out into the night? Maybe that man was telling the truth. Maybe he really *could* give him what he wanted.

A happy memory came to Reggie, one he hadn't dusted off in a while.

On a sticky-hot Sunday in August, the whole family had

piled into the car and headed out of the smoggy city. They eventually found themselves surrounded by rolling green farmlands and endless forests of sweet-smelling trees. After cruising down dusty back roads for hours, they stopped at a meadow overgrown with goldenrod. The perfect place for an extraterrestrial test flight. Reggie and his father had fashioned a UFO out of a balloon and a pair of glow sticks. They'd struck onto the idea after watching a creepy TV show about alien abductions.

But the UFO wasn't quite the success they had hoped. Weighed down by those glow sticks, it couldn't float very high; and it only stayed up for a few minutes at a time. It also made the funniest sound when plummeting to earth—not unlike a donkey letting out a killer fart.

Reggie's mom thought it was hilarious. She couldn't stop laughing about it the whole ride home....

That was the last time Reggie had seen her laugh. Not a nervous giggle or a sad smile, but a gut-busting, really-for-real laugh.

His mother had been so different back then. She hummed cheerfully in the shower and talked to friends on the phone, scolded Reggie when he failed his math quizzes, rode her bike to the market, and collected little porcelain dogs . . . she used to *do* things.

Reggie blinked away the memory of that perfect summer's day. He suddenly knew he had to do it. He *had* to take the risk.

If it was true, if that man could somehow grant Reggie's deepest wish, then he'd not only get his dad back...but his *mom* too!

Reggie hurriedly pulled on his purple hoodie, jeans, and grass-stained sneakers. He stuffed a handful of coins into his pocket, along with a packet of gum. Then he slipped out the front door of his apartment as his mom tossed and turned in bed, dreaming of happier days.

SIX

The Midnight Train

Out on the street, the strange man was nowhere to be seen. But his flute song lingered faintly in the chill night air, like the last wisps of smoke from a dying campfire. Those delicate, fluttering notes slipped into Reggie's ear, chasing away his worries, urging him to take those first few steps toward his heart's desire. And so, he pulled on his hood and stepped confidently into the wind.

The walk to the St. Patrick station was very different at night. It was oddly quiet, as if every person in the entire city had taken a deep breath and held it. He could hear his own footsteps and the sound of traffic a few blocks over, but that was about it.

The city *looked* different as well. The streetlights tinted everything the color of dried apricots, so that Reggie felt like he was walking on the surface of Mars, or an alien planet with two suns and three moons. It made him feel sort of lonely, like he was far away from anyone he ever knew. But it was exciting too.

By the time he arrived at the station, he'd decided that if his dreams of soccer stardom didn't work out, he would become an astronaut.

As Reggie dropped coins into the fare box, the man in the booth eyed him suspiciously through the glass.

"Is there a lunar eclipse?" asked the man.

"Huh?" grunted Reggie.

"You going stargazing?"

What an odd thing to ask. "No. Why?"

"Only reason I can think why you and all your little friends are out so late."

Reggie looked around him at the empty station. "What friends?"

"Whatever, kid. Don't tell me. See what I care." The man returned his attention to the sudoku puzzle book in his lap.

Reggie decided the man was making one of those nonsensical jokes that only adults thought were funny. He pushed through the turnstile and headed for the stairs. Upon arriving at the level below, he realized that the man in the booth hadn't been joking. There were hundreds of kids waiting along the platform. They didn't seem to know each other, though. Everyone stood slightly apart, and no one was talking. A few of them had turned to eye Reggie when he'd come down, but now they were all staring expectantly at the entrance tunnel.

"Excuse me, is this the right place?" asked a small girl, sidling up to Reggie. She had brown skin and the ridiculously huge eyes of a cartoon princess. Her black braids were pulled back into a long ponytail fastened with a gold hair tie.

"The right place for what?" said Reggie.

She glanced nervously from side to side and whispered, "The man. He said I'd get what I've been wishing for."

Reggie's skin prickled all over. He thought of the dream he'd had of camping with his father in a forest, of feeling safe and happy again. "What did he promise you?"

The girl opened her mouth to answer, but then she shook her head. "Maybe we're not supposed to say it out loud. Like birthday wishes."

Reggie glanced at the television suspended from the ceiling overhead. Along with the week's weather forecast, it displayed the time. Quietly he said, "Three minutes and thirty-two seconds till midnight."

"My name's Chantal, by the way," said the girl, giving him a lopsided smile.

Reggie suppressed an urge to roll his eyes. This was a subway platform, not a birthday party. Why on earth would he want to know her name?

Chantal was staring, her enormous brown eyes fixed on him like wet spotlights.

He shook his head at her. "Something wrong with my face?"

She let out a high-pitched, breathy laugh that would have been cute coming from a pixie-dusted fairy. But since it came from her, it was just plain annoying.

"Aren't you going to tell me *your* name?" she said primly.

Reggie decided to lie. But what name should he use? The only one he could think of was Brutus. He'd always liked the name because it sounded tough. People knew not to mess with a Brutus. But at the last second, he changed his mind. He didn't want to waste a perfectly good fake name on her.

"I'm Reggie."

"Nice to meet you," replied Chantal. She furrowed her brows curiously at something behind him. Then she tipped her head to the side and pointed down the platform. "Do you know that guy?"

Reggie turned his head. A tall boy with dark, curly hair and freckles all over his pale face stood halfway down the platform. He was staring straight at Reggie with the kind of look you give a really smelly dog.

Reggie clenched his fists. What on earth was Gareth Flanagan doing here?

"He one of your friends?" asked Chantal.

Reggie gave Gareth his best Stare-at-Me-for-One-More-Second-and-I'll-Come-Over-There-and-Make-You-Stop glare. It worked. Gareth jutted his chin out at him, then turned away.

"That's Gareth. He's in my class."

"Let's go talk to him," said Chantal eagerly.

"Not a good idea. Last time we talked, I punched that jerk right in the gut."

Chantal made an O with her mouth, then asked, "Why?"

"He dipped his brush in my paint jar."

"That's not a very good reason to punch someone."

"He's the reason my *Enterprise* is pink instead of gray."

Chantal wrinkled her chin. "Still not a good reason."

Reggie decided to leave out the part where Gareth had called him a butt-faced geek for liking *Star Trek*. He also didn't mention that his punch had swiftly escalated into an all-out brawl in the middle of the art room. That had earned Reggie an entire month of detention and a phone call to his mother. She hadn't answered the phone, though. She never did. She was afraid the sound waves would give her brain tumors.

Reggie got into lots of fights these days. Lately, his anger seemed to live right up under his skin, where it could burst out at a moment's notice. This totally sucked. He hated feeling like he wasn't in control of himself.

"Well, what would *you* know about punching people?" challenged Reggie.

Chantal's gigantic eyes narrowed to a normal size. "I know plenty of things about plenty of stuff. My psychiatrist says I'm mature beyond my years."

He rolled his eyes. "Whatever."

At that moment a gust of greasy-smelling wind rushed down the platform, sending a whole bunch of litter tumbling toward him. Then the curved green tiles of the station began to vibrate with a deep rumbling. All eyes were fixed on the tunnel now.

The first blush of white headlights appeared in the blackness. Reggie watched the lights grow bigger and bigger like a pair of glowing balloons swelling with air.

Seconds later, a perfectly normal-looking train emerged from the darkness. It thundered into the station, becoming a blur of silver. The brakes shrieked loudly, and the train shuddered to a stop at the end of the platform, right where Reggie and Chantal were standing.

The doors chimed open, but no one stepped out. The train was completely empty. Reggie glanced at the clock again. One minute past midnight.

"Where is he? He's still coming, right?" said Chantal anxiously.

The little square window of the driver's cabin flicked open. A man in a red conductor's cap angled his head out. He winked an eye as small and black as an obsidian marble at Reggie.

Then he smiled delightedly at the sight of all the waiting children. It was the very man they'd been waiting for. His outfit made a whole lot more sense to Reggie now. He was the conductor of the train.

"All aboard!" he hollered, as if this was an old-time steam

engine and not a subway train in the middle of the city. When he saw that no one was moving, he added, "Quickly, my nibblies. Mustn't keep them waiting."

All up and down the platform, heads turned this way and that to see what everyone else was doing. No one wanted to make the first move.

Reggie's eyes met Gareth's. The freckle-faced boy arched an eyebrow back at him, as if issuing a challenge. Then he squared his shoulders and sauntered right through the nearest door of the train. He took a seat by the window and glowered at Reggie through the dirty glass.

That was all it took. Everyone else began to board the train, filing inside without a word. Reggie had never seen so many kids make so little noise.

Chantal tugged on his sleeve and said, "Come on, let's get on!"

But suddenly Reggie wasn't so sure this was a good idea. The skin on the back of his neck was crawling with invisible bugs, and his stomach felt like it was filled with small, cold pebbles.

The last time he'd felt like this was three summers ago, when he snuck inside a huge drainpipe in the ravine near his school, just to see how far he could go. He walked exactly fifty steps inside that rusted pipe, until there was more darkness than light around him. Suddenly he started thinking about every scary story he'd ever read and every scary movie he'd ever seen. Bad idea. Soon he became convinced that something was hiding in the darkness.

Something big and evil and hungry. Something that wanted to drag him deep into the gloom. Reggie had panicked and run as fast as he could, not stopping until the sunlight had scorched away the darkness that seemed to cling to him like spiderwebs.

And right now he felt just like he did on that summer afternoon. He wanted to run all the way home, until he was safe under the covers of his bed.

Chantal hurried onto the train. She turned around and shrugged. "What's wrong? Aren't you coming?"

The Conductor leaned out the window of the cabin. He smiled at Reggie, showing off his tiny, sharp teeth.

"Good-bye, little nibbly. Sad you won't be joining us. Really too bad. Too, too, too sad. He *loved* your birthday present. Wanted to thank you himself."

Reggie's mouth dropped open, and the air rushed out of his lungs. Had he heard right? Was his impossible wish really coming true? There was no time to think. He hurried aboard just as the doors were closing. They thumped shut behind him.

Then the train grumbled into motion, carrying him away from the brightness of St. Patrick station and into the darkness of the tunnel.

SEVEN

Wild Tunnel

The train picked up speed as it pulled away from the station, its entire frame rattling like a tin can filled with marbles. Reggie sat down on one of the hard red seats. Even though there were plenty of empty spaces, Chantal came over and sat right next to him. He was too caught up in his own thoughts to be annoyed at her.

He loved your birthday present. Wanted to thank you himself. That's what the Conductor had said, wasn't it? There was only one person he could be referring to. But that was impossible. Reggie didn't know a lot about dead people, but he knew for certain they couldn't open birthday presents.

He glanced around at the other kids in the train car. They

were all sitting quietly, watching the tunnel zoom past the windows.

Chantal got up and crossed over to the rectangular window at the very front of the train. She pressed her hands on either side of it and peered through the glass. "This is so cool!"

Reggie joined her to take in the view. The tunnel rolled out endlessly before them, like the repeating background of a video game. Fluorescent lamps were spaced regularly along the blackened, concrete walls. They looked like an endless fleet of UFOs hurtling toward the train.

"Hey, what's that?" said Chantal, jabbing her index finger at the glass.

Way up ahead, there was a small patch of bright light. It was expanding quickly, taking up more and more of the dark tunnel.

"It's the next station. Maybe that's where we're getting off," said Reggie.

Without warning, the train swerved violently to the left. He was thrown against the wall, his forehead smacking against an ad for chocolate bars. Twinkly blue lights shimmered before his eyes. But he had at least managed to stay on his feet. The same couldn't be said for Chantal. She was sprawled on her back in the middle of the aisle.

"You okay?" Reggie knelt down and took her hand.

He helped her up, led her to the nearest seat, and plunked himself down beside her. Some of the other kids were picking themselves up off the floor. But at a glance, it didn't look like anyone was seriously hurt. Just a lot of bruises and dazed expressions.

"Now I know why my parents don't let me take the subway," said Chantal, touching the back of her head gingerly.

"Been taking the subway since I was nine, and I never saw a train do a turn like that before," said Reggie, shaking his head. "It was kinda cool. Well, except for the part where I went *splat*."

There was the sound of rushing wind as someone slid open the door at the very back of the train car. Gareth Flanagan had entered. He strode up the aisle and took a seat directly across from Reggie and Chantal. Then he crossed his arms, stretched out his long legs, and smirked at them.

"No one wants you here, Gareth. Go back to your own car," said Reggie, narrowing his eyes.

"I can sit wherever I want to." Gareth's smirk turned into a grin. "What's wrong? Want some one-on-one time with your little girlfriend?"

"She's not my girlfriend!" shouted Reggie, jumping to his feet. But the train shuddered over a rough bit of track, and he toppled back into his seat.

"Exactly!" agreed Chantal. "We're just friends."

Reggie scowled at her. "No, we're not friends! You're just an annoying girl who won't quit talking to me." He leveled his glare at Gareth. "And you're just a ginormous jerk who's been bugging me since second grade! What's your problem anyway?

Why can't you just leave me alone? And just so you know, there's nothing wrong with liking *Star Trek*!"

Reggie was out of breath. And his cheeks felt so hot he wondered if they might burst into flames.

Chantal crossed her arms and lifted her chin haughtily. "Maybe you need to see my psychiatrist. She could help you with your ... *issues*."

Reggie wanted to say something really smart to wipe that look off her face, but all his words were tangled up inside him.

"Okay, okay, relax. I didn't come here to tick you off," said Gareth, holding up the palms of his hands. "Some kid just threw up all over the place. Stinks like rotten pumpkins back there."

Reggie's anger cooled enough for him to think straight. "Fine. You can stay. But no talking."

"Whatever," said Gareth, shrugging. "Not like I actually want to talk to you."

"Great. Glad you agree."

Chantal looked from Reggie to Gareth before saying, "And I don't want to talk to either of you."

"Good!" exclaimed the boys in unison.

The silence lasted for only about thirty seconds.

"Ummmm ... guys ..." said Chantal.

"I said no talking," snapped Reggie.

"Look outside. Where are we?" she said, almost in a whisper.

Reggie and Gareth glanced around at the windows. Gone were the smooth, concrete walls of the subway tunnel and the cheerful safety lights that lit the train's path through the darkness. Instead, craggy dirt walls scrolled past the windows. Every now and then, lengths of something twisty and pale flittered in and out of view. Reggie recognized them as tree roots. The tunnel no longer looked like something that had been carved out by big machines. Now it was wild and rough and strange.

"Don't think we're in the subway tunnel anymore," said Gareth. He pushed his eyebrows way up, making the freckles on his forehead squish together.

Chantal's eyes widened with panic. "Then where are we?"

"Looks kinda like a gopher hole," said Reggie.

Gareth made a face. "Don't be such a noob. Gophers can't make holes like this."

"Well, *something* made it."

All three of them fell into a nervous silence as they tried to imagine a creature big enough to dig a train-size tunnel. Reggie didn't like the possibilities. All he could picture were monsters with sharp teeth and very nasty tempers.

"Gophers," said Gareth resolutely. His face looked very pale. "Let's just say it's gophers."

Chantal and Reggie nodded their heads in agreement.

EIGHT

Impossible Reunions

As the night stretched on, the train sped deeper into the earthen tunnels. Its route was filled with so many twists and turns that Reggie found it impossible to keep track of which direction they were headed in.

Sometimes the tunnel shrank so tight that the walls brushed up against the windows of the train, leaving chocolate-brown streaks on the glass. Then, moments later, it would open up, becoming as cavernous as a baseball stadium.

At some point, the motion of the train lulled Reggie to sleep. He had strange dreams about gigantic, floating mouths chewing on a never-ending pile of food. He woke up feeling very confused. It took him a whole minute to remember why he was on a subway train instead of at home in his comfy bed.

Gareth was slumped over in his seat, fast asleep. A line of drool stretched from his mouth to the collar of his leather jacket.

"Regardez la bête sauvage!" muttered Chantal, shaking her head at him in disgust.

The Conductor's voice suddenly screeched out from the speakers overhead. Gareth jolted awake, and startled gasps rose up from the kids around them. "Attention, little nibblies. Our journey is almost through."

Gareth stretched out his arms, yawning. He said groggily, "Did I miss anything? We there yet?"

"Shush!" said Chantal. "Don't want to miss the announcement."

"Keep your wet jellies wide open, little nibblies," continued the Conductor, his voice squeaking like a rusty door hinge. "Wouldn't want to miss your stop . . ."

Reggie hurried over to the window at the front of the train. He cupped his hands around his face and peered through the glass. The headlights picked out the rough, dirt walls of the tunnel for a short length. But beyond that, there was only darkness as thick and velvety as the center of a chocolate cake.

A pinprick of yellow light appeared far ahead in the tunnel. It grew bigger and bigger, until Reggie could make out the hard, clean edges of a platform.

"See something?" said Chantal, clasping her hands.

"Yeah, dude. What is it?" said Gareth.

Reggie returned to his seat and said excitedly, "I think there's a station up ahead."

The windows across from him were completely black, like a row of wide-screen televisions that had been switched off. He counted down in his head, knowing that the station was about to appear. Five, four, three, two...

He let out a small gasp when he saw the brightly lit room slide into view, like a television channel being summoned into existence. The train stuttered to a stop, and all was quiet. Gareth twisted around in his seat to gawk at the view through the windows.

"C'est pas vrai!" exclaimed Chantal.

The room was about as big as a subway platform, but it wasn't like any subway station Reggie had ever seen. It looked like a perfectly normal room in a perfectly normal house. And that was the very last thing he expected to find inside this dark, twisting tunnel, deep below the city.

It was a cheerful room, the sort of place you'd find in the house of a Great-Aunt Ingrid or an Uncle Fujiwara. There was wallpaper with bright blue flowers and a tatty Persian carpet that a cat probably loved to take naps on. The furniture looked old but very comfortable. A clarinet rested on a music stand, before a curtained window with yellow sunshine pouring through it.

An old woman in a green dress stood by this window, with

her back turned to the train. Her mass of curly, white hair wore a halo of sunlight.

"This is bizarro," said Reggie, crossing the aisle and sitting next to Gareth. "How can there be sunlight underground? And isn't it, like, the middle of the night still?"

Gareth didn't answer—his eyes were as wide and bulgy as tennis balls, and his lower lip was trembling in a very odd way. He stood up and walked to one of the doors of the train, never taking his eyes off the woman in the green dress.

"What's wrong?" said Reggie. "You look totally wiggy."

Then Gareth did something that Reggie had never seen him do. His face scrunched up, and his eyes began to leak with tears. The guy was actually crying!

The doors of the train chimed open.

"Grandma!" called out Gareth, emotion making his voice croak. He ran out of the train and into the sun-filled room.

Just as he reached the woman in the green dress, the doors slid shut, and the train lurched into motion. The windows went black with the inside of the tunnel as they sped away from the happy, little scene.

Reggie and Chantal looked at each other with eyes as wide as Gareth's had been.

"That was his grandma?" said Chantal in a small, awed voice. "But is she . . ."

She didn't finish her thought. A secret smile curved her lips as she gazed out the darkened windows.

Reggie scrutinized the other kids in the train car. He wondered if each and every member of this ragtag group had one thing in common. Were they all hoping for impossible reunions?

Ever since his father died, he had felt very much alone—like he was the only kid in the whole world who'd lost someone. He knew that couldn't possibly be true. But it sure *felt* like it. After all, it's not like anyone ever talked about death. Not any of the annoyingly cheerful kids in his class. And certainly none of the guys on his soccer team, whose biggest problems had to do with skinned knees and charley horses.

He always thought he could tell how a person was feeling just by looking at them. But now he wasn't so sure. If that were true, wouldn't he have guessed the truth about Gareth long ago? Wouldn't he have known that the boy had lost someone too?

Over the next hour, they made many stops. Every time the doors of the train slid open, another ordinary-looking room appeared. And inside each of these rooms, someone was waiting. There was a woman doing yoga in front of a television; a little boy playing with a wooden train set; a man cooking up a storm in a sun-drenched kitchen. . . .

At every stop another kid would leave the train. Sometimes in tears and sometimes in slack-jawed silence. Then the doors would snap shut, and the train would trundle onward.

Reggie knew his stop was coming, so he tried to think up questions he should ask and things he should say. He'd been wishing for a chance like this ever since his father died. But now that the moment was about to happen, his mind felt like a chalkboard that had been scrubbed clean of words.

Chantal pulled out a small notebook from inside her coat and opened it on her lap.

"What's that?"

"My journal," she said, running her eyes over the tight, loopy handwriting that filled the pages. "It's got everything I'm gonna talk to my sister about. Funny things that happened to me since the car accident. Names of all the boys I have crushes on. Movies I saw she would've liked. All the gossip she's missed at school. And a whole bunch of other stuff."

"Oh," said Reggie. "I wish I'd thought of that!"

But then he realized how silly it was. How could he have prepared for this? How could he have planned for the impossible? Up until the moment Gareth stepped off the train, it had all felt like a cottony dream, like something much too *good* to be real.

The train eventually came to a stop. Through the windows, Reggie could see a pink room with sloping ceilings and walls covered in posters of horses. A triangular window showed neat rows of rooftops against a hazy blue sky. Twin beds were pushed up against opposite walls. They were covered with so many stuffed animals there was barely enough room for anyone to sleep.

A girl with the same braids as Chantal's sat on one of the beds with her back to the train. She wore blue pajamas with ice cream cones on them, exactly like the ones Chantal had on beneath her yellow pea coat.

The doors of the train chimed open.

"Is that your sister?" said Reggie.

Chantal was grinning so hard it looked like her face was about to explode with confetti. She raced toward the doors but stopped halfway through.

She turned to Reggie and said, "Good luck. And don't worry about not knowing what to say. I'm sure you'll think of the perfect thing right at the last second."

She darted off into the pink bedroom, her braids swinging behind her.

The doors slid tidily shut before Reggie had a chance to see Chantal's sister turn around.

Then the train lurched into motion once again. Reggie glanced around him and realized he was completely alone. He walked to the back of the car and peered through the window in the connecting door. He could see all the way down to the very end of the train. As far as he could tell, no one was left.

The speakers crackled, and the Conductor's voice blared out. "Last stop of the journey, little nibbly. Your guts are just b-b-bustin' with excitement, I'm sure!"

His squeaky, skin-prickling laugh echoed through the empty train car. It was quite possibly the worst sound Reggie had ever heard. It made him want to roll up into a ball and stuff chewing gum in his ears.

The train turned sharply to the left, making all the overhead lights flicker as if in protest. The brakes squealed like angry pigs. Then the train rattled to a stop.

Reggie stared in disbelief at the view through the windows. It was something he hadn't seen since his mom sold their house over a year ago. A cluttered backyard with a maple tree at its center. He remembered that its wide branches and thick canopy of leaves always cast a perfect amount of shade on summer afternoons.

On moving day, Reggie had hidden up in the tree house nestled in its lowest branches. He figured that as long as he stayed up there, the new owners of the house couldn't move in. His mom had found him eventually, though. She promised that one day, when things got a bit better, they could move back there. He knew it was a lie, but he came down from the tree anyway.

Reggie brought his face right up to the window of the train and blinked in astonishment. A dented table saw was set up beneath the big maple. Power tools and wooden planks littered the grass.

A man stood amid this mess with his back turned to the train. He was studying a big, white sheet of paper that had blue markings all over it. He wore a red, plaid shirt and blue jeans that had been washed so many times they looked almost white. His hair was black, but streaked with a bit of gray, just how Reggie remembered it.

The doors of the train car chimed open.

Reggie never had a wish come true before. Not a really important one that lived deep down inside his bones. And now that it was actually happening, he felt like one of those people on TV game shows who win a car or a big boat for answering a question right. Except a thousand times better than that.

He stepped off the train. His feet landed on shiny green grass that was almost as stiff as the bristles of a toothbrush.

Chantal was right. He thought of the perfect thing to say at the very last second.

As he walked up to the man in the plaid shirt, he called out, "Dad, I'm home!"

NINE

The Tree House

As soon as Reggie stepped off the train, its doors snapped shut, and it shunted backward into the black tunnel. A quiet voice in his head wondered when it would return for him, but he was too excited to listen to it.

The backyard was exactly as it should be. The tall, wooden fence was festooned with fairy lights and red lanterns. The blue swing set that Reggie hadn't used since he was six squatted next to a toolshed painted with zebra stripes. He even spotted his mother's little tomato garden. And just as he remembered, the soil refused to sprout anything other than spiky weeds and dandelions.

"Dad! It's me, it's Reggie!"

His father laid the big sheet of paper onto the table saw, bowed his head over it, and began circling things with a stubby carpenter's pencil. He still hadn't turned around. Reggie figured the screech of the departing train must have drowned out his voice.

His stomach fluttered with butterflies. It had been two years since they'd seen each other, and he was worried things might be different between them. What if his dad thought Reggie had grown up funny-looking? What if he hated the way Reggie's voice had gone all croaky in the last few months? *What-if*s marched through his mind like an endless line of toy soldiers.

His dad perked up his head, as if finally sensing Reggie's presence. He put down the pencil and turned around. His face was full, tanned, and healthy.

A lump the size of a grapefruit formed in Reggie's throat, and his vision became smeary. He ran up to his dad and hugged him, pressing his head against his chest. He smelled of sawdust and freshly cut grass, just as Reggie remembered.

Reggie didn't want to let go. The last time they were together was inside a hospital room with ugly yellow walls. It had been filled with machines that were constantly beeping and wheezing, as if trying to chase away the silence that hung in the air like a thick fog. He'd wanted to hug his dad then, but he couldn't bring himself to do it. His dad had looked so small and thin in that hospital bed that Reggie was sure a good, tight hug would crumble him into a million pieces.

Now here he was, hugging his dad so tightly that his arms ached.

"We better get started if we're going to finish," said his dad, pulling away.

"Get started on what?"

He jabbed a thumb at the maple tree towering over them. "The tree house, silly bones. It's all you've been talking about the whole week!"

Reggie wrinkled his forehead. "But we already built it years ago. . . ." He looked up at the maple and was surprised to see that the tree house wasn't there.

His dad turned around and drummed his fingers on the sheet of paper. "Sketched out some plans. I think we can get this thing to look just like Notre-Dame Cathedral. Gonna take loads of elbow grease, though."

Reggie joined him by his side. He recognized the blueprints. His dad had first drawn them up two summers ago in this back-yard (or some other version of this backyard that wasn't deep underground and at the end of a dark, winding tunnel). It had taken them all summer to finish the tree house.

"The key to making this work is the flying buttresses. And I think we can do those with the jigsaw. I'll need your help to cut it, Reg," his dad said, his eyes sparkling.

He fetched a spool of brown paper leaning against the trunk of the maple. He rolled it open on the grass and sketched out a whole bunch of squares using a ruler. Then he passed Reggie a heavy pair of scissors and told him to cut the shapes out carefully.

"Ummmm, Dad? Didn't you want to talk about stuff first?"

"Like what, silly bones?"

"Well…" Reggie crinkled the brown paper in his hands. "Don't you want to hear what I've been up to?"

"Sure I do," said his dad cheerily. He knelt on the grass and started measuring out lines on a piece of plywood.

"Oh, okay." Reggie suddenly couldn't think of anything to say. If only he'd made a list like Chantal. He stared down at the too-green grass until he thought of something.

"Well, we had to sell the house. Our new place is kinda small. Guess it's okay for just the two of us. But there's no place to put a tree house or anything."

Reggie's father was heaving a sheet of plywood onto the table saw.

"But I'm doing real good at soccer. Regional championships are coming up, and I think our team has a shot."

His dad flicked a switch, and the saw started up noisily. Its buzzing sound echoed back from the tunnel.

Reggie shouted over the noise, "Maybe one day, if I get good enough, I can play for Manchester United. But Mom probably won't let me."

His dad eased the piece of wood forward, until the spinning blade ate through it, spraying sawdust everywhere. A smile was fixed on his face, and he nodded as Reggie spoke.

"Could you fetch my goggles, Reg?"

Reggie rummaged inside the huge red toolbox until he found a pair of safety goggles. He reached up, slotting them onto his dad's face. Once the plank of wood had been cut into four triangles, his father powered off the saw and brushed all the sawdust onto the ground.

"Um . . . wasn't there anything you wanted to tell me?" said Reggie hesitantly.

His dad went over to the toolbox and began searching through it. Without looking up, he said, "What do you mean, Reg?"

Reggie knew he wanted his dad to tell him *something*, but he wasn't really sure what that something might be. Kind of like when he was super hungry but couldn't find one thing in the fridge that he actually wanted to eat.

"Well, did you think about me and Mom a lot?"

His dad got up from the toolbox with a sanding block in his hand. He was still smiling, but his eyes seemed a bit too wide. "Think about you?"

"I mean, well, did you . . . you know . . . did you miss us?"

His dad picked up one of the wooden triangles from the grass and began sanding down its edges. "But how can I miss you when you're right here?"

"I don't mean now. I mean these last two years. Did you miss me and Mom? Were you worried about us?"

The corner of his dad's mouth started to twitch like a malfunctioning clock hand, whereas the rest of his face became as unnaturally still as a movie that had been paused. His arms dropped to his sides, and he let go of the wooden triangle and sanding block. They thumped onto his boots.

"Dad? What's wrong?" Reggie began to panic. He'd somehow managed to say the exact wrong thing to his father.

"It's okay if you didn't really miss us," he lied. "I mean, you were probably super busy, right?"

His dad's mouth stopped twitching. An odd, rolling shudder passed from his legs right up to his shoulders. And just like that, he snapped out of his strange fit.

"We better get started before it gets too late, Reg," he said cheerily.

"Sure you're not mad?"

"Of course not, silly bones. Why would I be?" He gave Reggie a reassuring wink. Then he looked down at his empty hands, and his face went slack with confusion. "Reg, do you know where my sanding block went?"

Reggie smiled and pointed at his dad's feet.

"Now, isn't that strange," said his dad, bending over to pick it up. "How'd these suckers get down here?"

Under the blue-green shade of the maple tree, Reggie and his father spent the rest of the day (or was it really night?) making the walls of the tree house. It took a while because they had to cut out lots of finicky, little holes for the stained-glass windows. Reggie remembered doing all of this two summers ago, but he didn't mention it to his dad. He had a definite feeling it would've been another wrong thing to say.

As the hours passed, a constant sound could be heard beneath all their hammering and sawing—the distant shriek of a train barreling through those twisting tunnels. Was the Conductor collecting even more hopeful children, whisking them away to make their dreams come true too? Reggie certainly hoped so.

As he hammered two wooden beams together, all his worries seemed to evaporate. This was the most fun he'd had in a long, long time. Sunlight, sawdust, and silly jokes. His father had always said those were the only things a person needed to be happy. And for the first time, Reggie understood what he'd meant.

"Come on, Reg," said his dad, clapping him on the shoulder. "Let's take a break. Don't want to burn ourselves out on the first day."

Reggie put down his hammer and followed him over to the pair of wooden Muskoka chairs next to the tomato garden.

"Gorgeous weather. A sunny-side-up kinda day," said his dad, sitting down on one of the chairs. The peeling green paint crackled as he leaned back into it.

Reggie plunked himself down in the other chair and gazed up at the sky. "Yeah, it's really nice today."

It was one of those perfect, cloudless skies that looked like a fresh coat of blue paint. But something about it was strange. It seemed too close. Reggie felt sure that if he climbed to the top of the maple, he could reach out and touch it. He imagined that a blue sky would feel soft and satiny like peach fuzz.

"You're getting pretty good with the tools," said his dad. He put his hands behind his head and cracked his knuckles.

Reggie put his hands behind his head and cracked his knuckles too. It was good to have someone to copy again.

"But I'm not as good as you, Dad. Still can't hammer without bending the nail!"

"But you're much better than me in lots of ways, Reg."

Reggie turned his head to look at him. "Really? How?"

"For starters, you got lots more imagination up there than I ever had. And that's really the best tool of all. Came up with the rad idea to make a tree house that looked like Notre-Dame Cathedral, didn't you?"

Reggie smiled. "Yeah, guess I did!"

His dad sighed contentedly and closed his eyes. "You're made of good stuff, Reg. I couldn't be prouder of you."

Reggie was filled with so much joy that he thought he might burst like a water balloon. He wanted to tell his dad how much he meant to him, how much he loved him, but he was never any good at picking out the right words to say. Instead, he went over and hugged his father.

His dad hugged him back tightly as a chilly breeze reached them from the darkness of the tunnel.

Reggie felt so happy that he paid no attention to the strange sounds coming from inside his dad's chest. Rustling sounds. Restless sounds. Like thousands of small, frenzied things trying to escape.

TEN

All Finished

R eggie and his dad stood beneath the shade of the maple
tree looking up at their creation. It was a thing of beauty.
The tree house looked every inch the old cathedral it
was modeled after. Dozens of tiny, arched windows glinted with
yellow sunlight. Miniature clay gargoyles sneered down from
the rooftop. And all the walls looked just like stonework, thanks
to the gray paint Reggie's dad had daubed on with an old sponge.

"Gotta admit, it looks even better than I imagined," said his
dad, wiping sweat from his paint-streaked forehead.

"I kinda knew it'd look this cool," said Reggie slyly.

He remembered how proud he had felt when they finished
the tree house on a very hot Labor Day two years ago. He invited
all his friends (and even some enemies) to come and see the

Most Amazingly Awesome Tree House That Anyone Anywhere Has Ever Built. But this time around, he didn't have even the tiniest urge to show off. All he wanted was to spend time with his father.

"Been thinking about what we could make next," said his dad, crossing his arms and nodding his head.

"Really? What?"

"The bridge of the starship *Enterprise*," he said, grinning. "We'll make all the little details. The control consoles, captain's chair, even a view screen that actually works."

Reggie felt a small, sharp twinge in his heart. They'd made the same plan two years ago, but his dad had gotten so sick they never had the chance to start work on it.

"Let's get started right now," said Reggie determinedly. This was their second chance, and he intended to make the most of it. "I'll draw the stencils, and you—"

"Whoa, hold up there, Reg! There's always next weekend. It's getting pretty late anyways."

Reggie suddenly realized he didn't know what time it was. Exactly how long had he been down here? He looked up at the perfect blue sky. It hadn't changed color at all since his arrival. But how could that be? They couldn't have built the entire tree house in just a few hours, could they?

"Dad," said Reggie. "What time is it?"

His father glanced at his wristwatch. "It's a quarter past."

"Quarter past what?"

"Quarter past the hour, silly bones."

Reggie was starting to get worried. What if it was already morning in the world above? His mom would have a fit if she found out he'd been out all night.

"Dad...uh...you don't happen to know when the train's coming back, do you?"

"Train?"

"Yeah, the one that dropped me off."

"Dropped you off where, Reg?" His dad walked over to the Muskoka chairs, sat down, and stretched his arms over his head.

"Here. In this backyard," said Reggie. A sharp note of worry vibrated through his skull.

"Tell me about it after my nap, Reg," said his dad, yawning. "Afternoon heat's getting to me."

Almost instantly, his dad fell asleep. His snores echoed back from all directions, reminding Reggie that this place was more cave than backyard.

He walked away from his father until he reached the very edge of the grass. It was much darker and cooler here. Across from him was a wall of damp earth. Below him, the train tracks rolled off into the black tunnel, like ribbons of silver.

He sat down at the edge of the too-green grass, with his legs dangling over the tracks. Cold air streamed out of the tunnel, making him goose-pimple all over.

He planned to wait right here until the train came to fetch him. He'd hurry home and tell his mother what had happened.

Then he'd come back to visit his dad the very next day. Maybe his mother would come too. This was the perfect thing to coax her out of the apartment.

But a quiet voice in Reggie's head was wondering what would happen if the train never came back. Would he be stuck down here forever? Stuck deep underground, where no one would ever find him. Stuck beneath an unchanging sky that was always a perfect shade of blue. Stuck with a father who didn't seem to know he was dead.

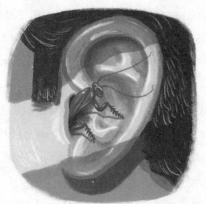

ELEVEN

A Day Replayed

Reggie waited a long time for the train to return. He was exhausted, so he lay down on the grass and rested his eyes, just for a moment.

In his experience, sleep could be a very tricky thing. When he wanted to fall asleep really fast (like on Christmas Eve or the night before a big soccer game), he'd spend half the night tossing and turning. But when he wanted to stay up late, he was always out like a light in five seconds flat.

Well, in five seconds flat, Reggie was fast asleep.

He woke up with a painful crick in his neck and one side of his face completely numb from being slept on.

The tunnel was black and empty. Not a train in sight.

He got up from the bristly grass and turned to face the backyard. It still looked as warm and bright as a Sunday in July. The sky was pristinely blue, and the grass was still a few shades too green.

His dad stood before the table saw with his back to the tunnel. He was busy making notes on a sheet of blueprints.

"Dad? I didn't miss the train, did I?" said Reggie as he walked up behind him.

His dad turned around, flashed Reggie a big smile, and said, "Better get started if we're going to finish."

"Get started on what?"

His dad jabbed a thumb at the maple tree. "The tree house, silly bones. It's all you've been talking about the whole week."

Reggie felt his stomach drop to the ground when he looked up at the maple. The tree house had disappeared.

"But we just finished building it! For the *second* time!"

His dad drummed his fingers on the blueprints. "Sketched out some plans. I think we can get this thing to look just like—"

"You really don't remember?" exclaimed Reggie, cutting him off.

"Remember what, Reg?"

"I came here on a subway train, and we built the tree house all over again, and this backyard isn't really our backyard, even though it looks exactly like it," said Reggie all in one breath.

His dad was still smiling, but the corner of his mouth had started to twitch again.

"I don't want to freak you out, but there's something I have to tell you," said Reggie, looking his dad in the eyes. "You died. Two years ago."

The twitch spread quickly from his dad's mouth to his entire body, until he was shaking like a washing machine filled with too many clothes.

"Dad, are you okay?"

"Better get started if we're going to finish. Better get started if we're going to finish. Better get started if we're going to..." His dad continued on, like a song playing in a loop. His smile had become alarmingly wide. It looked like all the skin on his face was stretched too tight.

Something black and shiny, about the size of an almond, wriggled its way out of his dad's ear. It had a bunch of thin, little legs and two antennae twitching to and fro.

Reggie's mouth fell open, and he backed away. Then he said something he hoped he'd never have to say to anyone ever again: "A cockroach just crawled out of your ear!"

The cockroach skittered all the way down his dad's body. When it reached the ground, it waggled its antennae in Reggie's direction, as if thanking him. Then it darted across the grass toward the darkness of the tunnel.

To Reggie's horror, another cockroach emerged from his dad's ear. Then another, and another. Soon hundreds were pouring out of him. It looked like a stream of thick, dark molasses dripping down his body. Somehow his dad never stopped smiling, as if there was nothing strange at all about insects crawling out of his head.

The cockroaches made a beeline (or in this case, a roach line) toward the tunnel, leaving father and son behind in the sunny backyard. Reggie wasn't sure if he was more terrified or grossed out. So he decided to feel brave instead.

He stepped cautiously toward his dad and whispered, "Are you okay?"

His dad was as still as a mannequin in a shop window.

Reggie reached out to touch him. As soon as his fingers brushed against his arm, his dad toppled backward, as stiff and unmoving as a plank. He hit the ground with a hollow, metallic *clang*.

"Dad!"

Reggie knelt down, pressed his hands on his dad's chest, and shook him. But he didn't so much as blink.

Reggie narrowed his eyes at a thin crack running across his dad's forehead. That certainly wasn't there before. It was a perfectly straight line, like the opening of the battery compartment on a TV remote.

On a hunch, he hooked his fingernails into the crack and gently pulled. The top of his dad's head popped clean off like the lid of a cookie tin. Reggie jumped away and let out a shriek that echoed back from the tunnel.

But he reminded himself that he was trying to be brave. And brave people didn't scream and run away from things that scared them (even though that was probably the smart thing to do). He got down on his hands and knees and peered inside his dad's head. To his relief, there was nothing that looked like slimy noodles or raw hamburger meat. Instead, it was filled with shiny gears and cogs of all different sizes, like the inside of an old-fashioned clock.

Something twitched deep inside his dad's head. Reggie squinted into the darkness until he spotted a cockroach poking its head out from behind a silver cog. It flicked its antennae worriedly and seemed hesitant to move any farther into the light. Once it was sure that Reggie wasn't any danger, it crawled out onto the grass and hurried off to join its many brothers and sisters.

"He isn't really my dad," said Reggie aloud, his eyes widening. "It's just a robot! A cockroach-powered robot!"

He stood up and surveyed everything in the backyard with new eyes. The towering maple tree, the sagging fence, the two Muskoka chairs by the tomato garden. And of course, the clockwork dad lying motionless on the ground.

Someone had gone through a lot of trouble to make all this stuff. But why? The answer came just as a gust of cold wind reached him from the tunnel.

It's a trap!

TWELVE

A Favor Gained

The Conductor had lured Reggie down here with a lie. His father was still dead and buried in that scrubby cemetery under a highway overpass, and nothing was going to change that.

Reggie was used to losing his temper, like the time he punched a hole in the classroom wall because Gareth ripped his Commander Data trading card. But this felt different. It was like a sturdy, wooden door had creaked open deep inside him, letting out a monster that had been locked away for a very long time.

He picked up the red toolbox and hurled it at the maple tree. It crashed straight through the trunk, making an impressive hole. Turned out the tree was made of plaster and chicken wire. Like everything else in this stinking place, it wasn't real.

He let out a scream, ran full tilt toward the table and upturned it, sending tools and paper flying. Reggie's next targets were the Muskoka chairs. He attacked them with a hammer until they were reduced to a heap of splintered wood. He splashed black paint all over the fences. He stabbed at the too-green grass with scissors. He tore up the tomato garden with his bare hands until clumps of soil littered the entire yard. He tore his dad's blueprints into confetti and tossed them in the air.

The monster in him wasn't quite satisfied yet. He picked up a wrench and whipped it at the tallest branch of the tree. He missed. The wrench went sailing toward the perfect blue sky. . . .

The sound of breaking glass was deafening. Transparent shards the size of pizza slices rained down from above. Reggie dove for cover under the tree, skidding across the grass on his belly. But almost as quickly as it had started, the freakish glass storm was over.

He stepped out cautiously from under the maple. His heart was still beating a mile a minute, and he was panting hard. The rage monster living under his skin had burst free once again. As always, once its reign of terror was over, Reggie felt about as foolish as a dog chasing its own tail. At least no one was here to see his freak-out this time.

Reggie crossed to the center of the yard. His feet crunched

on pieces of glass as thin and brittle as frost. He tossed his head back, peering upward.

The sky looked very odd. It was rippling like the surface of a pond. Then, without warning, it exploded into millions of tiny blue dots. The dots swirled about chaotically, creating a dense blue mist. Beyond this mist, only a ceiling of dark, crumbly dirt remained. Reggie realized that the perfect blue sky had only been an illusion.

"They're bugs!" he cried out in amazement. "The sky is made of bugs!"

Without warning, the cloud of blue insects dove straight for him in a huge, spinning column.

Reggie shrieked. He'd seen enough nature shows about deadly insects to have developed a healthy fear of anything that swarmed.

He tried to run for cover, but in an instant he was surrounded. The bugs whirled around his body so closely that he could feel the wind from their tiny wings against his face. It was like being caught at the center of a very gentle tornado.

As they whizzed past his eyes, he caught glimpses of iridescent blue shells and bellies that gave off a soft, buttery glow. Their wings were a blur of dazzling opal. Reggie was pretty sure they were some kind of beetle. He breathed out a sigh of relief. These were clearly *not* insects of the killer variety.

As if he'd passed an inspection, the beetles suddenly rose into the air in a giant corkscrew formation. They alighted on the dirt ceiling, filling up every inch of it, until the perfect blue sky had returned.

Then the most remarkable thing happened. The swarm re-arranged itself into shapes. The shapes became letters. The letters became words.

THANKS TO THE BOY

Reggie stared in awe at the glowing letters on the dark ceiling. He shouted up at the swarm, "Are you talking to me?"

The beetles shifted themselves around, and new words appeared.

BREAKS THE GLASS CAGE

BOY GIVES FREEDOM

Reggie didn't know how to decipher this. But then he spotted the wrench he'd thrown. He walked over to it, picked it up, feeling its weight in his hands.

"You're thanking me for breaking your cage? For *freeing* you?"

The swarm didn't answer. Reggie took this as a yes.

"Who trapped you here?" he said, even though he was sure he already knew the answer.

The swarm spelled out another sentence.

MAN WITH THE SILVER CATERPILLAR

"Silver caterpillar?" said a confused Reggie. He thought this over for a moment. "Oh, you mean the subway train! That's the Conductor. He's the same creep who trapped me here."

Reggie dropped the wrench onto the grass and called out

to them, "You don't happen to know the best way out of here, do you?"

New words appeared.

SQUARE DIRT IS THE DOOR

Reggie flicked his gaze around the backyard until it landed on the tomato garden. Square dirt.

He gently picked off all the broken glass that had landed on the garden. Then he knelt down in the wet soil and started digging with his bare hands. It wasn't long before his knuckles scraped against something that was hard and flat. A few more minutes of digging and he'd uncovered a red wooden door. It had a brass knocker shaped like a lion's head and a plaque that read: *S.S. Enkrad*.

If today had been yesterday, Reggie would have been very surprised to find a door at the bottom of a tomato garden. But since today had included robot dads and talkative beetles, this seemed downright ordinary.

He gripped the knob with both hands and lifted the door open.

A flight of stairs ran down into the ground. The light barely reached beyond the first few steps, so he couldn't tell how far down into the darkness it went.

"Well, thanks for your help," called out Reggie to the beetles overhead. "But I gotta go now. My mom's probably—"

The swarm hurriedly assembled one last message.

THE DARKNESS IS ANGRY

He screwed up his face and said, "What does that mean?"

But no answer came. The beetles took flight, flowing down toward Reggie in a great, luminous wave. They swirled around him once, as if to say good-bye. Then they disappeared into the subway tunnel, taking their daylight glow away with them.

In the pitch-black, Reggie scrambled on his hands and knees toward the plaster tree. He reached into the gaping hole in the trunk and groped around until he found the toolbox. He lifted it out, unlatched it, and searched blindly inside until he felt the cylindrical heft of the big flashlight his dad always kept there. Thankfully, it clicked on.

Figuring it was best to be prepared for whatever lay ahead, he picked through the contents of the toolbox, looking for useful items. He considered bringing either the hammer or the mallet, but he needed his hands free to hold the flashlight. And so he settled on things that fit inside his pocket: a stubby piece of blue chalk, a box of staples, and a roll-up measuring tape.

He aimed the white beam at the uneven dirt stairs in the tomato garden. Then he treaded cautiously down into the earth.

On the fourth step, the beam flickered and died, causing him to lose his footing. He tumbled head over heels down into the darkness.

THIRTEEN

The Darkness Is Angry

Reggie once asked his father how big the universe was. They'd just finished marathoning through a whole season of *Star Trek: Voyager*, and they were lounging on the couch, snacking on popcorn.

His dad pinched up an unpopped kernel from the bottom of the bowl and held it up against the flickering light of the television.

"If this is the earth," he said, rolling it between his fingers, "then the solar system is as big as this room. That would make our neighborhood the galaxy. And the entire world is the parts of the universe we can actually see. Hard to wrap your head around, eh, Reg?"

Reggie had lain awake in bed that night trying to picture just how vast the universe was. He imagined what it would feel like to travel past planets, stars, black holes, and nebulas. To travel so far into space there was nothing left to look at. Only darkness. A darkness so endless that you got dizzy just looking at it.

And that's exactly how dark it was where Reggie had landed. It was like he'd tumbled down the stairs and ended up in outer space, at the very edge of the universe.

He lay on the ground for a full minute, wondering if he'd died. But once he grew bored of lying there and doing nothing, he figured he must be okay after all. He patted the cool, damp earth around him until he found the flashlight. It refused to turn on. He got unsteadily to his feet and turned in a slow circle. Blackness all around. His eyes might as well have been closed.

"Helllllooooo!" he called out. He listened for his echo. It came from somewhere far ahead, which meant that this was a tunnel.

That was a good thing. Tunnels always led to somewhere. And hopefully this one would lead to the world above. He marched forward with his hands stretched out before him so that he wouldn't stumble into a wall.

As he walked, he congratulated himself for being so brave. Here he was, strolling through a pitch-black tunnel, and he wasn't even the least bit scared. He wasn't letting his imagination conjure up all the monsters and ghosts and demons that might live down here. Evil things that might be watching his every move. Waiting for the right moment to pounce...

Reggie was breathing very fast, and beads of sweat had formed on his forehead, even though it was very cold down here.

He decided to start singing, because it was hard to feel scared while doing something as silly as singing to yourself in the dark. But what song? It had to be something goofy, something preposterous, something the very definition of *un-scary*.

Reggie recalled a trip to Disney World with his family. Toward the end of an exhausting day at the crowded park, Reggie and his parents were desperate to escape the Floridian humidity. That's how they made the foolish mistake of riding It's a Small World. Reggie's mother had gaped in disgust at the countless singing dolls surrounding their boat and declared, "This is the most annoying song I've ever heard!" Seemingly in response, their ride vehicle had promptly broken down, stranding them in that musical nightmare for a whole hour.

And so, Reggie sang "It's a Small World (After All)" loudly and off-key as he walked steadily through the darkness, treading on dirt as hard-packed as concrete. The path was mostly straight, but every now and again he bumped into a wall where the tunnel curved. All the while, he kept singing the song over and over again, as if he were an animatronic in that theme park ride, stuck in an endless loop.

It's a world of laughter,
A world of tears,
It's a world of hopes,
And a world of fears.

Reggie stopped singing abruptly. He halted in his tracks, his eyes wide. His own shaky voice echoed back at him from far down the tunnel, like a ghost issuing a dire warning: . . . *a world of fears . . . fears . . . fears . . . fears . . .* All the hairs on the back of his neck stood on end, and an icy shiver rolled through his body. He suddenly felt sure that someone was staring at him. He could feel their gaze fixed on the back of his head like a hot, burning laser.

He spun around. But of course, he couldn't see anything.

Don't be such a baby! he scolded himself. *There's nothing down here.*

But there *was* something down here with him. Something that had followed him every step of the way. Something he could see with his own eyes.

The darkness.

Reggie sucked in his breath when he remembered what the beetles had told him.

THE DARKNESS IS ANGRY

But that didn't make any sense. Darkness couldn't feel angry. It couldn't *feel* anything. It wasn't alive.

Reggie heard something that made his stomach do a

somersault. A wet and oily sound. Like something licking its lips right next to his ear.

Then something cold and wet traced a delicate circle around his neck.

Reggie screamed. He sprinted blindly through the tunnel, his heart thumping like a stampede of elephants. As his feet pounded against the dirt, he could hear the whoosh and roar of something enormous following right behind him. The darkness thickened, like a room filling with black, tarry smoke. It was getting harder to breathe.

Then the hands came for him. Dozens of them, reaching out of the nothingness, clutching at his clothing, his hair, his flesh. Except these weren't really hands. They were far too thin and insubstantial, like something made up of shadows and night-mares instead of flesh and bone. He ran faster, but they grabbed him firmly, pulling him backward.

As he was swallowed up by the slithering void, something worse than panic overtook his senses. It was the certainty that he'd never feel sunlight on his skin, or his mother's kiss on his forehead, or happiness in his heart. Maybe it was best if he just stopped fighting. Maybe he should simply let himself disappear into the darkness.

He hadn't felt this hopeless since ... since the day his dad died. . . .

The thought of his father made him remember what was inside his left pocket. The bear whistle his mom had given him.

His *father's* whistle. He hurriedly stuck his hand into his pocket, his fingers closing around the small, plastic object.

An icy hand seized his wrist, tugging his arm away so that he almost dropped the whistle. He struggled against the not-quite-hands holding him in place, thrashing about wildly. The darkness around him was so thick now it felt like a scratchy wool blanket pressed up against his face.

With his last bit of strength, he wrenched his arm free. He raised the whistle to his lips and blew as hard as he could.

A sour note echoed through the tunnel.

Then, far off in the dark, one small pinprick of light appeared. It bobbed gently up and down, like a boat on water. He could tell it was coming closer, because the light was expanding quickly.

As the hands continued to claw and scratch at his flesh, he kept his eyes on the glowing orb, which was almost close enough for him to touch now. It was about the size of a basketball and gave off a ghostly green glow that picked out the rough walls of the tunnel in either direction. It floated to a purposeful stop right over Reggie's head.

A chilling shriek cut through the air, like the cry of an injured animal. He felt the not-quite-hands release their grip on him. There was a rush of air as something enormous sped away down the tunnel. Then, just like that, he felt like himself again.

Reggie stared at the mysterious, glowing orb as it bobbed before his eyes. He shook his head and let out a disbelieving giggle. It was a plain, old balloon with two glow sticks inside.

This was the UFO he'd made with his father. But how in the world did it get all the way down here? He'd last seen this balloon on the day of the funeral, when he'd packed it up carefully inside a blue biscuit tin. Then he'd bound the tin with twine and placed it atop his dad's plaque in that scrubby cemetery. He wasn't sure what, if anything, happened after death, but he figured something to light the way might be helpful.

Reggie gasped. When the Conductor stole his dad's birthday present, he must've taken this too. But why? And how was this balloon up and about, floating around like it had a mind of its own?

Reggie looked down at the whistle in his hands. The bear seemed to be smiling knowingly. He thought of what his mother had said when she'd given this to him.

Just give it a blow when you're feeling down.

"You came to rescue me," he said to the balloon. "You came 'cause I blew the whistle."

The balloon wobbled in place, and Reggie could almost imagine that it was nodding in agreement. He gave the whistle an appreciative squeeze, then slipped it back into his pocket.

"Come on, let's get out of here."

The path ahead was as dark as ever, but Reggie felt a bit less scared, knowing he wasn't completely alone.

FOURTEEN

Found Friend

R eggie trudged through the seemingly endless tunnel. He'd been walking for so long he was starting to suspect he was lost. But the balloon seemed sure of the path. It floated ahead at a quick, steady pace like a faithful dog leading him through a black forest.

When Reggie's shoelace came undone, he knelt down wearily to tie it. He didn't notice the balloon drifting farther and farther ahead, its green glow seeping away like the tide on a beach. He also didn't notice the shadows creeping up behind him, slithering across the ground like snakes on the hunt for food.

Fingers as thin as matchsticks darted out of the Darkness

and clawed at his backside, trying to grab hold of him. He yelped and scrambled forward into the green light.

The Darkness let out a frustrated hiss, and it retreated into the depths of the tunnel. From then on, Reggie was sure to stay well inside the friendly glow of the balloon.

After taking a sharp turn to the right, he reached a long stretch of tunnel. All along its length, staircases spiraled up into the gloom. Each was carved from dirt and looked just like the one he'd tumbled down.

As Reggie passed the first staircase, something caught his eye. He knelt down and picked up a small, flat object on the bottom step. It was a notebook decorated with sparkly hearts. It looked awfully familiar.

The balloon continued to drift ahead, eager to complete their journey. Reggie lunged, grabbing on to its rubbery surface with his free hand.

"Hey! You can't keep leaving me behind like that!" he exclaimed. "Come on, I wanna find out where this book came from."

He crept warily up the steps as the balloon trailed behind him. There was a door at the very top. White light showed through the cracks. He gave the balloon a wide-eyed glance, then turned the doorknob and pushed the door open.

Reggie stepped over the threshold into bright white light and blinked until his vision came into focus.

He was in a pink bedroom. Posters of galloping horses covered the walls, and the air smelled sweet like candy.

A girl sat cross-legged in the middle of the room. She was swaying back and forth with her eyes closed, like she was listening to music. She had on a pair of blue pajamas with ice cream cones on them.

"Chantal!" Reggie called out, stepping deeper into the room. "We gotta get out of here!"

She stopped swaying, opened her eyes, and stared right at him. Then she started to sing a cheerful, little song. It was French and sounded a bit like "Twinkle, Twinkle, Little Star."

"I'm being serious," shouted Reggie. "This place is really dangerous."

A smile formed on her face. But it was too big and too wide. It looked like it had been drawn on with a big, fat marker.

She's not real, thought Reggie. Every muscle in his body tensed up. *It's just another robot.*

He backed away slowly, as the not-quite-Chantal reached the end of her song and rose to her feet. She kept her eyes fixed on him. Her smile had turned into something sharp and angry.

As soon as he backed through the doorway, small fingers clamped on to his shoulder. He let out a blood-curdling scream and whirled around.

Standing behind him on the stairs was the real Chantal. She looked like a ghost in the pale green light from the balloon.

Her eyes were wide and starry, and a smile was stretched across her face. She threw her arms around Reggie and hugged him.

"*Génial!* You came to rescue me!" she squealed delightedly.

"No, I didn't!" Reggie protested. He tried to wriggle out of the hug, but the girl was much stronger than she looked. "I just came to—"

"To make sure I was okay?"

"No!" said Reggie, finally breaking away. "I just came to warn you this is a trap."

"Well, duh! Figured that out myself." Chantal glared at the girl who looked just like her. She stood at the center of the room, swaying slightly, grinning at them. "That thing is definitely not my twin sister."

"But how'd you figure it out?"

"A twin always knows," she said mysteriously. "No impostor could fool the likes of Chantal Pelletier."

Reggie rolled his eyes.

"And once I knew she was simply an impostor, I did what my psychiatrist always tells me to do."

"What's that?"

"Write down my feelings in my journal," said Chantal in exasperation, as if the answer was glaringly obvious. "So I sat down and did just that. Almost used up all the pages. I had lots of conflicting emotions to get down. I'm very complicated, you know. At least that's what my psychiatrist says. But I think I made a breakthrough about why I'm so jealous of—"

"But how did you find your way out?" exclaimed Reggie. One minute with this girl, and he already wanted to dunk his head in a bucket of ice water.

"I felt a draft coming from the wall. That's how I found this door hidden behind the wallpaper. I went down into the tunnel, but it was so dark I dropped my journal and had to come back."

Chantal spotted the notebook in his hands, and her eyes lit up. "You found it! I thought I'd lost it forever! You really are *mon chevalier blanc*!"

Reggie was suddenly very glad he couldn't understand French.

"Come on, let's get out of here," he said, shaking his head.

They followed the balloon down the stairs and into the lightless tunnel. As they walked, Chantal held his hand firmly. He usually pitched a fit when a girl tried something like this on him (Cindy Lupeebles was the worst offender. She even liked to spring surprise kisses on boys who strayed near the baseball diamond during recess). But down here, in a place more dangerous than a thousand Cindy Lupeebleses combined, Reggie was secretly glad to have someone's hand to hold.

"I think something's following us in the dark," said Chantal in a whisper. "I can hear it. Sounds kinda like breathing."

"It's not *something* in the dark. It *is* the Dark," said Reggie.

"How do you know that?"

"Bunch of beetles told me."

Chantal stopped in her tracks and gave him a weird look.

"It's a long story," he said, tugging her forward. "Don't slow down. We have to stay in the light. It'll keep us safe."

They walked for a while in silence. The air was cold and smelled like earthworms and wet socks.

Then Chantal said haughtily, "My psychiatrist says monsters only exist in the imagination."

"Well, I bet your psychiatrist hasn't ever been in this tunnel. Things that make sense up there don't have to make sense down here."

"I guess she was wrong, then," Chantal said disappointedly. "Is your psychiatrist ever wrong about stuff?"

"Don't have one," answered Reggie, keeping his eyes on the dense gloom ahead of them.

"Really? Then who do you talk to?"

"Talk to about what?"

"Feelings and stuff."

"I got plenty of people to talk to," said Reggie. He was about to list off his buddies on the soccer team. But their conversations usually revolved around soccer and video games and teachers they hated. They never talked about *feelings*.

"I got my mom to talk to," said Reggie. It was a complete lie, of course. But he had to say something to shut Chantal up.

"Oh, that sounds nice," she said genuinely. "My parents are too busy to talk to me about stuff. I think that's why they got me a psychiatrist."

Chantal was staring at him with those big cartoon eyes of hers.

"Something on my face?" said Reggie.

"No. I was just wondering something."

"What?"

"Who did you lose?"

Reggie shrugged. "My dad."

"Oh, sorry about that," she said quietly. "Do you think about him a lot?"

"Yeah." Reggie slid his free hand into his pocket and held on to the bear whistle.

"Same here. I think about my sister all the time, even though it always ends up making me feel sad."

"I know how that feels," said Reggie, nodding his head. "It sucks, doesn't it?"

"Totally," agreed Chantal.

They both nodded their heads and fell silent.

After a few paces, Chantal stopped walking and snapped her fingers in the air. Then she flipped open her notebook and started to write something.

"What are you doing?"

"Checking off something from the list!" she said enthusiastically, her voice going all high and squeaky. "That's two in one night!"

Reggie was about to ask what list she was referring to, but he suspected her answer would be more of her usual psychobabble. And so, he simply said, "Uh . . . good, for you, I guess."

He grinned, shaking his head. Chantal was still the most annoying girl he'd ever met, but he was glad she was here.

FIFTEEN

Keepsakes

"Is this tunnel ever going to end?" Chantal sighed.

"It's got to. Everything has an end," said Reggie.

"Not everything."

"Name one thing."

"A circle!" replied Chantal triumphantly.

Reggie frowned, worried. "Well, we better *not* be going in circles."

After a long trek, they had finally cleared the last of the staircases. They were now traversing a gently curving stretch of tunnel where the walls of black dirt were dotted with white pebbles. The air was getting warmer the farther they walked. And the tunnel *smelled* different too. Instead of damp socks and worms, it smelled of grease and stale smoke. Reggie took this to mean they were drawing closer to the city above.

"Got a feeling we'll be home real soon," he said, quickening his steps.

And sure enough, not twenty paces later, the tunnel came to an abrupt end. The dirt walls narrowed into an alcove about the size of Reggie's bedroom closet.

Two small doors just big enough to duck through were set into the wall. The one on the right was red with a brass knob, just like the one he'd discovered at the bottom of the tomato garden. The one on the left wasn't a proper door. It was a piece of corrugated metal with a purple smiley face painted on it. Yellow light leaked through the cracks.

"Which one's the way out?" Reggie asked the balloon.

It bobbed three times and drifted back up the tunnel. It stopped a few yards away so that its pale glow formed a barrier between them and the waiting Darkness.

"It doesn't know?" remarked Chantal worriedly.

"Well, at least it got us this far," said Reggie. "Guess it's up to us to do the rest."

He knelt down on one knee and gripped the knob of the red door. It felt warm to the touch.

"Wait!" exclaimed Chantal. "How do you know that's the right one?"

Reggie shrugged. "Looks just like the one I opened to get down here. That must mean it's the way out."

Chantal gave him the very same look his mother used to give him when he did something especially foolish. Like the time he put his Ensign Harry Kim figure into the dishwasher after the neighbor's dog slobbered all over it.

"Are you really that gullible?" said Chantal, shaking her head.

"I conned my teacher into letting me skip gym for a whole month," Reggie protested, his cheeks growing hot. "Gullible, I am not!"

"Don't you see? It's probably a trick. We shouldn't choose the one that looks like the way out. We should choose the one that *doesn't*."

Even though she was a complete know-it-all, Reggie had to admit she had a pretty good point. "Maybe you're right."

He took his hand off the brass knob and placed it on the edge of the metal door instead.

"But if you're wrong..." he said, looking over his shoulder at Chantal.

"Dr. Peregrine says there's no such thing as a wrong choice, so long as you learn a lesson from it." She saw the face Reggie was making and added, "And I'm almost never wrong about things."

"Riiight," said Reggie dubiously.

The door hinge was tight with rust, so it took a few good, firm tugs to open it wide. The tunnel beyond was narrow and curved sharply to the left. Flickering yellow light danced along the walls.

"Unto the breach!" declared Reggie as he crawled into the cramped tunnel. The ground was soft and warm, covered with a layer of dirty sand. He could hear Chantal following behind him, muttering nervously in French.

"Something wrong?"

"I don't like tight spaces," she said. "And I just saw a cockroach."

"Just think about your nice, warm bed. You'll be there before you know it."

"I'll need a long bath first. My jammie bottoms are filthy!"

Just after the curve, the tunnel opened up into a massive, circular room. Reggie got to his feet and looked around in amazement.

Hundreds of colorful paper lanterns hung from the ceiling high overhead. They looked like glowing fruits dangling from the branches of a tree. Mirror shards flecked the dirt walls, allowing the lantern light to bounce all around the room. Because of this, the space was about as bright and cheerful as an underground lair could get.

"Holy mackerel!" uttered Reggie, when he caught sight of a towering pile of objects in the center of the room. It was easily as tall as a two-story house.

"*C'est ouf!* What in the world is that?" exclaimed Chantal.

As they walked toward it, Reggie sensed movement at the corner of his eye. He turned his head in time to see a figure with a misshapen head charging at him, wielding a long black spear of some kind.

Chantal screamed and flung her arms around Reggie. They backed toward the tunnel, their eyes wide and mouths hanging open.

"I'm gonna knock your roach-filled heads right off!" shouted a voice that was muffled, but surprisingly familiar. The stranger halted his charge and pointed the spear at Reggie's chest. On closer inspection, it was clear that his oddly shaped head was just a football helmet studded with old tuna cans. And the spear was only an umbrella.

"I mean it!" warned the figure, swinging the umbrella menacingly. "I'm not afraid to use this!"

"Gareth?" said Reggie, stepping forward. "Is that you?"

"Of course it's me. Now get back!" Gareth's hands were shaking so much that the umbrella suddenly popped open, eliciting a startled shriek from him.

"Stop clowning," said Reggie. "We have to find a way out of here."

"How do I know you're not one of those... those roach-bots?" responded Gareth, his voice cracking.

"Would a roach-bot know that you put goose poop in my knapsack at the planetarium field trip last year?"

"Well, maybe..."

"Come on, Gareth! We don't have time for this."

Gareth lowered his umbrella and lifted off his helmet. And there was his freckled face, shiny with sweat.

"So I guess you figured out this is all a trap, eh?" said Reggie.

Gareth nodded. "Clued in when a roach crawled out my grandma's nose. I tried finding my way to the surface, but something chased me down the tunnel. Something in the shadows."

He paused, his eyes glittering with fear. "I couldn't see it, but I could tell it was big and nasty. Thought I was a goner until I found this place."

"Where'd you get that?" asked Chantal, pointing at his helmet.

"From the mother lode," he said with a grin. Then he darted over to the enormous pile at the center of the room.

Reggie and Chantal exchanged surprised looks before following him. They all stood at the base of the colossal mound and gazed up in awe. It was a teetering pile of junk, or maybe treasure, depending on who was looking at it. Its contents ranged from keepsakes like teddy bears and porcelain dolls and jewelry boxes to slightly odder items like a rusty bicycle and a hula-dancer lamp.

As Reggie passed his eyes over the junk heap, something caught his attention at the very top. It was pink and round and very familiar. He scrambled up the pile, grabbing hold with his hands. He almost slid down several times as objects gave way underfoot. When he had nearly reached the top, he dug his fingers into a clump of old shoes with one hand and reached up with the other.

Feeling sort of like the Grinch stealing an angel off a Christmas tree, he took the object sitting on the very top of the pile.

"What's that?" asked Chantal once Reggie had climbed back down.

"Something I made for my dad," he said, narrowing his eyes at the clay *Enterprise* in his hands. "The Conductor stole it."

"But what's it supposed to be?"

"A spaceship. The USS *Enterprise*. Galaxy Class, NCC-1701-D."

Chantal giggled hysterically, as if Reggie had just told the funniest joke she'd ever heard.

"What?"

"Nothing," she said at the tail end of her giggling fit. "Just that your face looks so serious when you're talking about imaginary spaceships."

Gareth laughed and slapped Reggie on the back. "See. That, right there, is why I put goose poop in your bag."

Reggie was sure his face had gone so red that he could be mistaken for a stop sign. He scowled at Gareth, gearing up for a fight, when Chantal suddenly clapped her hands in surprise. She went to the junk heap, stooped over, and tugged something free from the bottom—a small, stuffed unicorn.

"Mr. Winkle!" cried Chantal, dusting it off and hugging it tightly. "I thought I'd lost you!"

A troubled expression appeared on Gareth's face. "This doesn't make sense. Why would the Conductor steal our stuff?"

Reggie looked at the clay *Enterprise* in his hands, then at the pile of random keepsakes. He thought of the green balloon, which was floating out in the dark tunnel. The answer was suddenly there before him, like a magician reappearing at the end of a disappearing act.

"It's because these things are full of memories," he said slowly. "*Our* memories."

"I don't get it," replied Gareth, shaking his head. "How can a bunch of junk have our memories in it?"

"Mr. Winkle isn't junk!" exclaimed Chantal, hugging her stuffed unicorn protectively.

"Exactly!" agreed Reggie. "And what makes that unicorn special to you? What's the difference between Mr. Winkle and some other stuffed toy?"

Chantal's eyes widened, and she gasped. "My sister gave this to me. She won it at the carnival!"

"So, every time you look at it, you think of her, right?" said Reggie. "Just like how every time I look at this spaceship or at that balloon, I think of my dad. These things are filled with our memories of the people we lost."

Chantal glared at her stuffed unicorn, as if it had betrayed her. "That's how that horrible man did it! He used my memories to make a robot copy of my sister!"

Gareth crinkled up his face in thought. "But how did he get the memories out? I mean, what did he use? A magic wand or something?"

"I don't know," said Reggie, glancing worriedly at the junk heap. "But this must mean the Conductor is more powerful than we thought."

"And more dangerous," added Gareth, raising his dark eyebrows.

Reggie thought again of that glowing balloon, which had shepherded him safely through the gloom. Had the Conductor really extracted happy memories from it? Using magic? If so, maybe there had been an unexpected effect. Maybe a bit of that magic had rubbed off on the balloon, puffing it up with both light and life. Anything seemed possible in this strange underworld.

Chantal took a step away from them and cocked her head to the side. After a few moments, she said, "I hear something."

From somewhere, a ways off, a thin, wavering note could be heard. It grew louder and more confident as its source neared them.

Chantal's eyes widened. "Someone's coming!"

SIXTEEN

Transforming Tune

The three of them rushed over to the pile of keepsakes, ducking behind it just as the music stopped. It was replaced by the unmistakable sounds of someone crawling through the entrance tunnel. Then the music started up again—a flute song that sounded like clear water rushing over pebbles in a stream. It filled the cavernous space, echoing off the mirror-flecked walls.

Reggie slowly peeked around the pile. The Conductor had entered, and he was stealing lightly toward them, like a cartoon Santa sneaking out of a fireplace. He held a wooden flute to his lips, his fingers moving nimbly across the dark wood. Reggie glared at the man who had lured him down here, who tricked him into believing he'd see his dad again. Anger flashed through him, and without even thinking, he stepped out from behind the mound. A split second later, a firm hand pulled him back. It was Chantal's. She shook her head at him and pressed her finger to her lips.

"What the heck, dude?" whispered Gareth. "You're gonna blow our cover!"

"Well, he needs my fist in his face," grumbled Reggie through gritted teeth.

"I don't think he spotted you," whispered Chantal, craning over his shoulder. "I wonder what that terrible man is up to?"

"Whatever it is, it can't be good."

Gareth watched the Conductor play for a moment, then shook his head, saying, "He's got horrible breath control."

Reggie and Chantal turned to look at him with their eyebrows raised.

"What? I play the clarinet," Gareth said, running a hand through his curly hair. "Well, I used to anyway."

Suddenly more notes joined the fluttering tune. A symphony of shrieking violins, cutting through the air, making Reggie's molars ache. But as small, dark shapes streamed into the lair, he realized that it wasn't violins he was hearing. It was rats. Hundreds of them, chattering in their high-pitchy, nerve-jangling voices. The rodents pooled around the Conductor, becoming a roiling sea of furry bodies and wriggling pink tails.

The Conductor's fingers went still, and he lowered the flute. He looked around at the gathered rodents like a proud father. Remarkably, they ceased their squeaking. They were watching him, waiting for him to speak.

"Welcome to this room of light, to this place of fake sunbright," boomed the Conductor, gesturing up at the glowing lanterns overhead. "Feels spiffy, doesn't it? To be bathed in the shiny yellow?"

Squeaks of agreement swept through the furry crowd.

"Soon you will feel *real* sunbright on your fur. Up there, where it's warm and bright and sparkly. No more scuppering around down here in the blickity-black. No more surviving on paltry scribs and scrabs."

His small, dark eyes beamed at the attentive rats.

"Time to join your brothers and sisters. It's a different world up there now. I've twisted it around, made it ours. Made it *home*. Yes, my dearies. You finally have a home. A place where you'll be tucked in, where you'll be scrubbed from your twitchy-gitchy ears down to your flickity tails. A place where you'll be *loved*. Doesn't that sound as nice as mice?"

The air erupted with excited squeaks and the clacking of tiny teeth.

"I don't like the sound of this one bit," Chantal whispered into Reggie's ear.

He didn't like what he was hearing either. Dread washed over him like ice water.

The Conductor snapped his fingers, and the ratty throng fell silent.

"Enough of this gib-gab, my dearies. Time to become *new*. Time to become *chosen*. Perk your ears up and let the music into your bones!"

He took a deep breath and raised the wooden flute to his lips. His fingers began their spidery dance, filling the air with a new tune. The notes were quick and pointed, sounding like sharp instruments stabbing into something soft and vulnerable. The Conductor's fingers slowed, and so did the rhythm. The song was transforming into something shapeless and terrible, like the tail end of a nightmare forgotten in the morning.

Reggie's skin prickled, and his teeth vibrated in a funny way.

The lantern light above was guttering and fading, as if a stiff breeze was sweeping through the space. Shadows leaped and flittered about the room, making the scene strange and otherworldly.

Reggie squinted into the gloom at the congregation of rats, and a small yelp escaped him. Even through the shifting shadows, it was clear that something bizarre was happening to them. They were *changing*. Growing. In the blink of an eye, tiny rat paws were shooting up and out into long, thin limbs. Dark fur melted away to reveal skin as smooth as frog bellies. And narrow, ratty heads were ballooning out, becoming rounder, more *human*.

As the Conductor's tune grew more frantic, it became painful to hear. Reggie clutched his ears, as did Gareth and Chantal. They fell to their knees as the horrible tune filled their heads and burrowed right inside their brains. Tears leaked from Reggie's eyes, and he shook his head to rid himself of the flute song.

And then, abruptly, it stopped. The sudden silence was like being dropped from a great height. The lanterns above stopped guttering, and the leaping shadows went still.

Reggie lowered his hands from his ears and looked up. The Conductor stood with his arms poised in the air, his motionless fingers keeping the flute aloft. A tendril of blond hair escaped his cap, falling over his right eye, and a satisfied grin stretched across his wide face. Shockingly, there were no rats in sight. Only children. Hundreds of them, gathered around the Conductor and his wooden flute. Naked and dirty, the children looked like odd potatoes that had just been dug up from the earth and exposed to the sun for the first time. They let out strangled sounds of awe as they examined their new limbs.

The Conductor pointed his flute over their heads, and all those slight figures turned to peer behind them. Reggie's eyes followed theirs, and he noticed, for the first time, a gargantuan heap of clothes next to the passageway.

"Go on, dearies," said the Conductor expansively. "Fresh threadies for the taking!"

All at once the children descended on the clothing pile, like vultures attacking a carcass. They scrambled over one another, jostling for position, seizing whatever they could reach with their small hands. First, they would sniff and nibble at a find. Then, if it didn't pass muster, up it would go, tossed into the air, only to be caught instantly by another pair of hands. This flying blur of hoodies, jogging pants, skirts, sweatshirts, overalls, button-ups, and even some school uniforms was like watching a washing machine explode.

"*Étonnant,*" breathed Chantal. She clutched at the lapels of her pea coat, as if fearful one of those strange kids would snatch it off her.

Putting the clothes *on* seemed a trickier feat. The newly formed children twisted and tugged at the unfamiliar fabrics, turning them about in their hands, trying to figure out which bit went where. But eventually, after a lot of trial and error, they had managed to dress themselves... technically speaking. Reggie spotted quite a few backward shirts, socks on heads, tights wrapped around necks, and inside-out jeans. Despite these beginner's mistakes, the overall effect was impressive. Suddenly they looked like the real deal, like *real* kids.

"And now, my ratty-tatties, you are ready!" announced the Conductor. He swept his arm over the children, who let out excited squeaks and chitters. "It's time to join your brothers and sisters up there in the sunbright!"

He raised the flute and played the same jaunty tune he'd used to summon the rats. Then he turned on his heel and marched happily out of the lair. The peculiar children trailed after him, a troop of obedient changelings.

The Conductor's flute song thinned into silence as he led the new children away, through the tunnels, toward the world above.

SEVENTEEN

The Way Out

"Holy crud!" exclaimed Gareth, pointing a shaking finger at the entrance tunnel. "Did you see that? He turned those rats into kids! That's, that's—"

"Impossible," interjected Chantal.

"But it happened," said Reggie, striding over to the very spot where the Conductor had played that beguiling tune. "Right before our eyes."

Chantal shook her head adamantly. "But the lights were flickering, and it was kinda hard to see clearly. It must have been an optical illusion. A trick of the brain."

"Oh, come on!" said Gareth, kicking at the dirt. "That was definitely magic or voodoo or pixie dust or...something. But whatever it was, it happened."

"*C'est impossible,*" said Chantal, more to herself than to anyone else. She chewed on her lip as she stroked the stuffed unicorn.

"We have to go after the Conductor. We have to stop him from doing whatever he's going to do," declared Reggie as his dread started edging into panic.

"No way," said Gareth incredulously. "Did you see how many rats . . . kids . . . rat-kids there were? We're totally outnumbered."

"Well, we have to do something. He's obviously up to no good."

Gareth scowled intensely at the pile of junk, as if he were about to tunnel inside like a frightened rabbit escaping into its warren. Then he shook his head, let out a long sigh, and said, "Fine, let's do this. But if I die, I'm haunting both of you. And I can be real frickin' scary when I want to be."

One by one, they each climbed up into the cramped entrance tunnel. Chantal in front, Reggie in the middle, and Gareth bringing up the rear. They crawled slowly, for fear of making too much noise.

"I never knew about your dad," whispered Gareth.

Reggie blinked, distracted by the cockroach skittering between his knees. "What?"

"I mean, I never heard that you lost him," explained Gareth, suddenly sounding sheepish.

"Well, it's not like I was gonna make a big announcement in front of the whole school."

"Yeah, I see what you mean."

Reggie cleared his throat. It felt strange having a conversation with Gareth that didn't involve curse words or flying fists. "So, you play the clarinet, eh? That's news to me."

"My grandma taught me," said Gareth enthusiastically. "She was amazing at it. Toured all across Europe when she was younger. And she was first-chair clarinetist for the Toronto Symphony Orchestra."

"Why don't you play anymore?"

Gareth was silent for a long moment before mumbling, "Dunno. I just don't."

Chantal had reached the end of the tunnel. She pushed open the metal door and poked her head through, glancing left and right. "I don't see them."

After hopping down out of the passageway, they found themselves shoulder to shoulder in the low alcove that featured two small doors. On the left was the metal door they had just come through. And on the right was the only door they had yet to try—small and red, with a brass knob. Hopefully, this was the way out.

The balloon had waited patiently for them. It hovered protectively between them and the long, dark tunnel beyond, keeping all three of them safe with its ghostly green illumination. The Darkness was there also, crouched just beyond the glow. Reggie knew it was there because he could hear it—a slippery, slimy sort of sound, like a toothless mouth slurping up intestines.

"I think they went through there," said Chantal, pointing at the red door, which was now ajar.

Reggie narrowed his eyes at it. His heart was racing, and sweat dotted his forehead. What was waiting on the other side? More roach-bots? More tunnels leading to more doors? There was only one way to find out. He placed his hand on the knob and tugged the door open quickly.

Directly behind the door was a curved panel streaked with rust. Reggie puffed out his cheeks with disappointment. Just a crummy dead end. But a mixture of stubbornness and hope made him reach out and knock his hand against the panel. It swung outward with a creak.

Bright, artificial light poured into the dark tunnel, making him squint. He heard the sound of a subway train screeching to a halt and a canned announcement about some sort of delay. These were the sounds of the city. The sounds of home.

EIGHTEEN

Splitting Up

Reggie ducked his head through the door. On the other side was a short drop to the subway platform. He steadied himself against the frame and hopped down onto the checkered tiles.

Chantal tossed her stuffed unicorn to Reggie and climbed down after him.

"Home at last!" hollered Gareth as he leaped down with an impressive crack of his knees.

All three of them looked around at the brightly lit subway station in amazement. It was hard to believe they'd finally made it out of that tunnel, which had stretched as long and dark as a bad nightmare.

Reggie turned around to examine the door they'd just come through. He was surprised to see that it was simply a large green tile on a hinge.

Inside the tunnel, the balloon shone weakly against the blackness. It looked so small and alone that Reggie felt a strange pang of guilt for leaving it behind. He was about to thank it for helping them, but he stopped himself. Now that he was above-ground, in a world filled with mundane things like triple-beef hamburgers and dentist appointments, the idea of talking to a balloon seemed a silly thing to do.

The balloon bobbed three times at him, bidding him good-bye. Then it floated off into the depths of the tunnel until it was nothing more than a speck of green.

Just then a vicious gust of wind blasted out of the tunnel, making Reggie's eyes water and his skin goose-pimple. He could hear a throaty growl echoing from the blackness. It was getting louder, as if something big and angry was barreling toward him.

He rushed forward and slammed the tile shut. Then he backed away slowly, keeping his eyes on it. Words were carved in its bottom right-hand corner: *S.S. ENKRAD.*

"Come on, let's get out of here," said Reggie, turning his back on the sealed passageway and everything that lay beyond it.

"I couldn't agree more," replied Chantal.

The trio climbed the flight of stairs leading out of St. Patrick station and emerged into the dull light of a cloudy afternoon. The sidewalk was curiously empty except for a shabbily dressed man huddled against a newspaper box. His eyes were obscured by dark sunglasses, and he was beating a cane against the box, as if keeping time to an unheard song.

A solid plane of dreary, gray clouds seemed to press down on the skyscrapers overhead. It made Reggie feel claustrophobic, like he was still underground. Even though everything looked just as he remembered it, he felt sure that things had changed somehow. It was like the entire city had been taken apart brick by brick and then put back together again.

"The Conductor is up here with all those rat-kids," he said, eyeing the quiet street suspiciously. "What's he up to?"

"I got a feeling it's not a surprise party for sick orphans," said Gareth, zipping up his leather jacket to ward off the biting wind.

Reggie contemplated something the man had said to all those gathered rats: *It's a different world up there now.... You finally have a home.* What did that mean, exactly? And why did those cryptic sentences make him feel nauseous with fear?

Home. That's where his mom was right now. Alone and scared, unaware that danger might be headed her way....

"I need to go home. Make sure everything's okay," Reggie said decisively, trying to keep the fear out of his voice. "You guys should too."

Chantal's eyes widened. "But what if I run into the Conductor? Or those rat-kids? We should stick together."

"Well, I could go with you. We'll hit up your place first, then mine," offered Gareth.

"Good, you two stick together," said Reggie, nodding. "Then we should meet back up later—figure out how to stop whatever the Conductor's planning."

Gareth gestured up the road. "Let's meet at that old church on Bloor and Spadina, the one across from the supermarket. It's near my house."

A siren wailed in the distance, and all three of them tensed up like jumpy house cats sensing an intruder.

"Well, I guess we have a plan," said Chantal, seeming less than confident. "Dr. Peregrine says that plans are the antidote to chaos."

There was a long pause as they stared at each other awkwardly, hesitant to break up their unlikely trio. They weren't exactly the most compatible of teams, or even a good fit as buddies. And yet they had escaped those treacherous tunnels together. That had to count for something.

"The old church. One hour," said Reggie finally. "And keep your eyes open."

He turned around, striking off on his own down the wide avenue. Just as he rounded the corner, Chantal's worried voice rang out, "Be careful! Don't do anything foolish!"

NINETEEN

Message in Red

The streets were oddly empty as Reggie made his trek home. He saw a lady pushing a shopping cart piled high with canned food. She seemed so exhausted and hollow he wasn't sure if she counted as a person at all.

About a block away from home, he spotted the first signs of life. Two people were waiting at a bus stop. An old lady in a fluffy pink bathrobe that made her look like one of those fancy poodles with skinny legs and cotton-candy puffs for fur. And a tall man in a business suit who looked like an oh-so-serious exclamation point.

The two of them were scrutinizing the poster on the side of the bus shelter. It was an advertisement for Reggie's favorite breakfast cereal. On it, two kids with chubby cheeks grinned at a giant bowl of rice puffs and rainbow marshmallows.

Then, as if it were a perfectly ordinary thing to do, the poodle lady extracted a can of spray paint from her handbag, gave it a good shake, and swept it carefully over the poster.

Reggie stopped in his tracks and goggled at her. He'd never seen anyone making graffiti before. And never, in a million years, would he have imagined a little old lady doing it.

Once she was finished, Poodle Lady stepped back and admired her work with a wistful sigh. Mr. Exclamation Point seemed to appreciate it too. He nodded his head and gave a solemn grunt.

The freshly sprayed words read:

Love Your Children. Feed Them!

"Oh, I almost forgot," said Poodle Lady with an embarrassed titter. She went to work again, spraying red whiskers onto the plump cheeks of the children in the advertisement. "There we go. Perfect."

Reggie let out an involuntary gasp, and the odd pair turned toward him. All at once their faces went strangely slack, like chocolate sculptures that had begun to melt in the sun. They leveled such vicious glares at him that he felt like a nasty spider about to be stomped on.

Without taking her eyes off him, Poodle Lady began to

hum. A happy little tune that somehow terrified Reggie to his very core. Then the man joined in, humming along in a low baritone that harmonized perfectly with the woman's high, creaky voice. They both kept their eyes fixed on Reggie.

A violent shudder rolled through his body. He backed away from the freaky pair and ran off down the street. As he rounded the corner, he chanced a look over his shoulder.

They were still humming, and still watching him with cold, hateful eyes.

TWENTY

A Nasty Homecoming

R eggie stepped into his apartment and slammed the door behind him. He locked the two dead bolts, slotted in the chain, and let out a moan of relief and exhaustion. He was so happy to be home that he could've kissed every inch of the place, even the patch of mildew on the shower tiles that looked a bit like Marmite.

"Mom!" he hollered as he kicked off his sneakers. "This is going to sound weird, but I think something bad's going to happen. Or maybe it already has. I don't really know. . . ."

He made his way down the hall and ducked into the narrow kitchen. It was like someone had smacked him in the face with a rotting fish that also happened to be stuffed with dirty underwear. He cupped his hands over his nose and swallowed the urge to throw up. What was that nasty smell?

In the sink was a pile of dirty plates so high that it was teetering dangerously to the side, seemingly moments away from crashing down onto the counter. The kitchen table was covered with things that had probably once been food, but were now just a mass of squidgy lumps covered in fuzzy green mold. On the floor, an entire colony of ants marched across a cheesy puddle. (In its former life, it had probably been a slice of pizza, or maybe a hunk of lasagna.)

"Mom?!" Reggie hollered in alarm. "Where are you?"

He padded down the hall and into the living room. The television was tuned to a cooking show hosted by a lady in a flowery apron. She was emptying a box of Halloween candies into a big pot, wrappers and all.

"The secret to a perfect chocolate-coleslaw stew is to leave the plastic wrappers on. Adds to the flavor. My little ones can't get enough of this dish," the television host said with enthusiasm as she stirred a pot that boiled over with lumpy black liquid.

Reggie couldn't see past the tall armchair in front of the TV, but he knew someone was there. He could hear them munching noisily on what was probably a cookie, judging by the empty biscuit packets strewn all over the living room carpet.

"Mom?" said Reggie worriedly as he crept closer.

The lady on the television proudly displayed her completed

dish, which looked about as appetizing as the contents of a toilet bowl.

"Shall I have a taste?" she said, before plunging her entire head into the stew like a ravenous pig.

The person in the armchair seemed to approve. They clapped their hands together and wheezed out an odd, squeaky sound that could barely pass as laughter.

Reggie narrowed his eyes at the chair. It didn't sound at all like his mother.

"Who's there?" he demanded. The clapping and the munching stopped.

"Tell me who you are, or I'm gonna come over there and make you!" roared Reggie, even though he was feeling a lot more like a mouse than a lion at this moment.

There was a long pause, filled only by the slurping noises coming from the lady on the TV. Finally the armchair creaked around slowly. The stranger tossed aside a pack of cookies and stood up to face him.

Reggie gasped. It was like looking at a reflection of himself. The boy standing before him had the same haircut—short on the sides and spiky at the front. He had the same thin face as Reggie (rounded cheekbones tapering to a narrow chin). He was even wearing Reggie's favorite *Star Trek* T-shirt and plaid pajama bottoms.

But it was an imperfect reflection, like one in a fun house

mirror. The boy's eyes were only about half the size of Reggie's, and they were spaced so close together they looked like two black beetles having a conversation. His nose was long and severely pointy, with six black whiskers sprouting from the tip of it. He probably would've been the same height as Reggie if he stood up straight, but his back was hunched over like an old man in need of a cane.

Reggie saw flashes of that lantern-lit scene in the Conductor's underground lair. He heard the beguiling flute song that had coaxed rats into new forms, into something almost human....

His mouth had gone so dry he could barely stammer out, "Y-y-you're one of them. One of those rats! What are you doing here?"

The rat-boy looked him up and down. His long nose twitched, and his beady eyes twinkled with interest. He sniffed at the air between them, as if smelling something delicious.

A wide, terrible grin split his face in two, and he leered at Reggie hungrily.

Not keen on becoming some rodent's afternoon snack, Reggie spun around and sprinted down the hallway. He veered into his bedroom and tried to slam the door shut. But something was in the way. He looked down and saw a wide, hairy foot shoved between the door and the jamb. The door crashed open, sending Reggie sprawling backward onto the bed.

The rat-boy tore into the room and leaped on top of him. He

bared his teeth, which were as small and sharp as bits of glass. Then he reared up and swiped his claws across Reggie's chest, shredding his hoodie.

That did the trick. Anger bubbled up in Reggie, hot and fierce like a superpower.

"That's my favorite hoodie!" he snarled as he grabbed a handful of the rat-boy's whiskers and yanked as hard as he could. Two of them popped off in his hands. The rat-boy squealed loudly and scrambled away from him.

Reggie rolled off the bed and backed away into the far corner of his room. He waved the whiskers in the air and taunted, "Oops. Guess you'll want these back, huh?"

The rat-boy was standing in front of Reggie's open closet. He'd risen to his full height, with his claws flicking impatiently at his sides.

"Want a taste of me?" Reggie asked as he eyed the soccer ball on the floor by his feet. "Come and get some."

The rat-boy charged forward, gnashing at the air with his teeth. The muscles in Reggie's body clicked into automatic. He pulled back his right leg while flicking his eyes at the rat-boy and imagining that the center of his chest was the center of the goal. Then he kicked the ball as hard as he could. Perfect shot. The ball hit the rat-boy's chest with a satisfying thump. He sailed backward into the closet, landing on a pile of old sweaters.

Reggie sprang forward and slammed the closet door shut. He grabbed the cricket bat from under his bed and shoved its thin edge into the door crack, wedging it tight. And just in time too. A second later, the closet door rattled in its frame as the rat-boy rammed it from the inside. Thankfully, it remained shut. It rattled again, but held.

Reggie gave the door a kick for good measure and shouted, "Serves you right, you dirty rat!"

Then he hurried out of the room in search of his mother.

TWENTY-ONE

Mother and Son?

Reggie opened the door to his mother's bedroom. The drapes were drawn, as always, so it was dark inside. The air was stuffy and smelled of stale sweat. It was more of a mess than it usually was, with clothes and shoes heaped all over the floor, but at least it wasn't in as foul a shape as the kitchen.

He could see the lumpy form of someone lying under the covers on the bed. He crept up to it as dark imaginings of what he might find there filled his mind. Once he peeled away the sheets, he was relieved to see his mother fast asleep.

"Mom! Wake up!" he said, shaking her shoulders gently.

Her eyes blinked open, but she squinted at the bedside table and not at Reggie. "What time is it, honey?"

"I don't know. But we have to get out of here."

"Sorry for falling asleep. Just wanted to rest my eyes a bit. I'll get started on your lunch."

She sloughed off the covers and stumbled out of bed without even looking at her son.

"Forget lunch!" he shrieked. "There's a rat in here! And he tried to eat me. Only it's not just a rat. It's, it's—"

But she didn't seem to be listening to a word he was saying. She shambled down the hall with her arms hanging limply at her sides. She walked into the kitchen and didn't seem even the least bit bothered by the mess in there.

With her eyes half-closed, she pulled a dirty pot out of the cupboard and began to fill it with the contents of every cereal box on the counter.

"Told the grocery man to bring you some ketchup chips, but he said they're all out," she mumbled sleepily. "They seem to be out of lots of things these days."

"Mom, listen to me!" Reggie shrieked. "We have to get out of here. That rat-kid is inside my bedroom. It's all because of the Conductor, and maybe he's headed here right now. I don't really know."

She dropped a slice of moldy bread in with the cereal and continued talking, as if Reggie hadn't said anything at all. "But don't worry, honey. I'll track down some ketchup chips for you somehow. And I'm going to make you a cereal loaf today. That's one of your favorites, isn't it?"

"Didn't you hear what I said?" said Reggie desperately.

She continued to ignore him as she poured a full bottle of orange soda into the pot.

"I could make you a snack while you wait for lunch. How about a plate of Cheez Doodles and chocolate sauce?" she said in a monotone.

Reggie grabbed his mother's hands and spun her around.

Finally his mom looked directly at him. Her reaction wasn't exactly what he'd hoped for. She gazed vaguely at him for a while, as if he was an acquaintance she used to know a long time ago. She seemed just on the verge of recognizing him, when her eyes drifted lazily away, focusing instead on a distant scene he couldn't see.

She started to hum a happy, little song. Fear fluttered in Reggie's stomach. It was the same tune that creepy pair at the bus stop had been humming. His mom's thin, breathy voice echoed in that tiny kitchen, making the distance between them seem enormous.

And then she fell silent, as if suddenly forgetting the tune. Her gaze shifted again to Reggie. All the color drained from her face, and her eyes widened in terror. She grabbed a frying pan from the stove top and angled it at him threateningly.

"Mom?" he said, holding up his hands. "What are you doing?"

"Don't come any closer," warned his mother breathlessly. She backed away with the frying pan still pointed at him. She pawed behind her with her free hand until she found the door for the cupboard under the sink.

She opened it and spoke in a fake cheery voice, as if she were talking to a wild animal that she wanted to keep calm. "That's probably where you came from, right? Why don't you just crawl through the hole and go back to your nest? I promise I won't hurt you."

"My nest?" said Reggie, shaking his head.

The muffled sound of a door rattling in its frame made both of them hold their breath.

"Is that you, Reggie?" she called out.

Reggie furrowed his brow. "Mom, I'm right here."

"Reggie? Are you okay?" she shouted, looking toward the hallway. The door rattled again, even louder.

She leveled a terrified look at Reggie and then dashed out of the kitchen, still clutching the frying pan in her hand. He followed a few steps behind her.

When Reggie's mother entered his bedroom and saw the closet door wedged shut with the cricket bat, she let out a horrified shriek. Then she rounded on him. Her eyes had gone narrow with anger, and her face was flushed red. She was shaking so badly she needed both hands to point the frying pan at him.

"What did you do to my son?" she demanded.

Reggie was so confused that he backed away until he smacked into the hallway wall. His mother smoothed her hand against the closet door and cooed, "Don't worry, honey. I'm getting you out of there."

She knelt on the floor, set the frying pan down, and grabbed the cricket bat with both her hands.

"No!" yelled Reggie. "He's dangerous!"

Once she'd pulled the bat free, the door flung open. The rat-boy skulked pitifully out of the dark and into the waiting arms of Reggie's mother. She hugged him tightly and kissed the top of his head, her shoulders shaking with relief. The rat-boy's nose twitched as he gurgled like a happy bird. Reggie felt like he'd just been punched in the gut. He couldn't believe it. She was actually hugging that freak.

She held the rat-boy at arm's length and scrutinized him from head to toe. "Did that nasty thing hurt you, Reggie? Are you okay?"

The rat-boy stroked the side of his pointy nose. The skin was pink and swollen where the whiskers had been ripped out. He let out a series of squeaks and wheezes that sounded like balloons being rubbed together. It was gibberish. Rat gibberish. And yet Reggie's mother was nodding sympathetically, like she actually understood him.

"My poor, poor baby." She licked her finger and pressed it gingerly against the side of his nose. "I won't let that nasty rodent hurt you anymore."

She picked up the frying pan, stood up, and turned to face Reggie. She glared at him like he was a creature that had just crawled out of a pile of dog poo. The way she was looking at him—her jaw set and her eyes gleaming with rage—chilled him to the bone. For the first time ever, Reggie was afraid of his own mother.

The rat-boy flashed a ghastly grin at Reggie. He raised up his claws and waggled them tauntingly.

Then all the strange, scattered pieces of the last day snapped together in Reggie's head. This had been the Conductor's plan all along. This was why he, and all the other children, had been lured down to those dark tunnels. So that they could be replaced ... by rats!

Reggie felt his stomach drop to the floor. There was absolutely nothing he could do to fix things, to make everything right again. So he did the only thing he could think of. He ran.

TWENTY-TWO

The Stowaway

T he sky opened as Reggie sprinted away from the apartment building. It was a downpour. By the time he
reached the park across the street, he was soaked straight
through. He sat down on one of the benches and watched a
muddy river form on the edge of the pathway. As the river snaked
between his feet, a saying popped into his head: *If a tree falls in a
forest, and no one is around to hear it, does it make a sound?*

His dad had asked him this once. A philosophical puzzle—
that's what he'd called it.

Reggie suddenly felt just like the tree in that puzzle. A tall,
twisted oak in the middle of a sprawling forest. And he was
waving his branches around wildly, trying to get someone to
pay attention to him. But no one was there to hear. Not his dad,

128

who was dead and gone. Not even his mother, who had looked at him like he was some kind of pest she wanted to squish with her frying pan.

He was alone. More alone than he'd ever been in his whole life. A sob burst out of him. Then came the tears. He pulled his hoodie over his head, slouched forward into the rain, and cried like a baby. By the time the storm had let up, so had his tears. The absence of pitter-patter meant the park felt abruptly quiet. That's when he heard a sound that was somehow both small and strangely close. It was a soft rustling, like candy wrappers crinkling together. From the corner of his eye, he saw something skitter from the inside of his hoodie and onto his shoulder, an insect of some sort. He leaped to his feet and shook his body about like a boy possessed, trying to dislodge the unwelcome guest.

He looked down and saw a large blue beetle, flopping around on the grass in a very undignified way. He got down on his knees and pressed his face close to it. It was one of the glowing beetles from the tunnels below! It made little hopping attempts at flight, without much success. One of its luminous blue wings was bent, and its back leg dangled feebly as it walked. No way the poor thing would be up to flying anytime soon.

"Looks like you need just as much help as I do, eh?" commiserated Reggie, feeling suddenly a lot less alone than he had a moment before. He reached into his pocket and pulled out the box of staples he'd taken earlier. After emptying it out onto the ground, he placed the open box next to the beetle. Then he gestured at it invitingly.

"Climb on in, little guy. I'll keep you safe."

The beetle fluttered its one working wing gratefully and pulsed a bright periwinkle before crawling inside this make-shift home. Reggie gingerly picked up the box and slotted it into his pocket. He never had a pet before, not even a goldfish (most likely because his mom knew he was better at punching things than petting them). But keeping this tiny, helpless thing safe filled him with a delightful warmth, as if a cozy bonfire had materialized inside his heart.

That's when he remembered. He wasn't truly alone. He'd made two new friends last night (even though Gareth techni-cally qualified as an old *enemy*). Which meant there were people out there who had his back—his very own crew that he could count on.

Feeling a new sense of purpose, he hunched forward against the biting wind and headed toward the rendezvous spot.

As he walked down eerily empty streets, he kept his eyes peeled for danger. But the only thing that really caught his eye was graffiti. Everywhere. Painted in huge letters on the sides of buildings. Sprayed onto parked cars, on lampposts, tree trunks, and shop windows. Even slanting across sidewalks, like color-ful shadows being cast by invisible objects. Although the graffiti was clearly written by different people in different styles, they all said the same thing:

Love Your Children. Feed Them!

A chill that had nothing to do with the wind cut through Reggie. He thought of the creepy pair at the bus stop earlier. Poodle Lady and Mr. Exclamation Point. He thought about their cold, hateful stares, and that cheery tune they'd hummed. The very same tune that had escaped his mother's lips before she went berserk on him. What did it all mean? His mind spun with possibilities. But the only thing that turned up was a sense of dread as deep and dark as the wild tunnels beneath the city.

As Reggie hurried past a row of darkened coffee shops, his eyes drifted up toward the cloudy sky. Off in the distance, a huge red blimp was floating above the skyscrapers. He had only ever seen one on TV before, circling over stadiums during the World Series. Maybe he'd forgotten about some big game today?

Reggie had just about reached his destination when he stopped suddenly in his tracks. Up ahead, in the middle of the street, was a man. He was splashing about in a puddle, kicking excitedly at the water, like someone who had never seen the rain before. He was wearing a red blazer and a matching cap, and he held a flute carved from dark, knobbly wood. It was the Conductor.

Reggie gasped and ducked behind a parked car. Anger boiled hot and red inside him. He wanted to rush at the Conductor and pound him with his fists, make him pay for everything he'd done. But he'd seen the man do impossible things—transforming subway rats into children using nothing more than a flute and a song. This knowledge held Reggie back.

The Conductor gave the puddle one last playful kick, spraying a gang of feisty pigeons on the sidewalk. Then he started to play his flute. Chirpy notes fluttered out, sounding like mocking laughter, the kind Reggie was used to hearing in the schoolyard during recess. As the Conductor played, he strolled up the street, past restaurants and shops that were shuttered and dark.

Reggie followed his slow, ambling progress for half a block. In order to keep hidden, he darted from one parked car to the next, and threw himself behind lampposts and abandoned hot-dog stands. As the notes fluttered through the air, thick clouds swirled menacingly overhead, like an enormous cauldron being stirred.

They soon arrived at a supermarket with all its lights on, glowing like a beacon against the gray, dismal day. Reggie watched from a safe distance as the Conductor crossed its curiously full parking lot and entered the front doors of the building.

What's that creep up to? he thought, eyeing the cheerful-looking supermarket. *What's going on behind those beady little eyes of his?*

Well, there was only one way to find out.

Reggie approached the front doors, and they slid apart with a comfy sigh.

He wasn't at all prepared for what was inside.

TWENTY-THREE

Anarchy in Aisle Nine

G rocery stores were usually neat and organized places. So much so that Reggie always had an urge to wreak havoc the moment he stepped inside one. Maybe by smushing all the cupcakes or hiding a bunch of watermelons inside the milk freezer. He felt no such urge this time.

Gone were the tidy pyramids of fruits and vegetables. Gone were the perfect rows of cereal boxes along the shelves. Gone were the neatly arranged towers of microwave dinners and biscuit tins.

The only food left was on the floor. Bananas and apples that had been trampled into pulp. Moldy hunks of bread being investigated by curious ants and cockroaches. Empty chip bags floating in puddles of tomato sauce.

Reggie walked gingerly down the nearest aisle, keeping his eyes peeled for the Conductor. With every step, the floor beneath his feet crunched and squished and popped. All the shelves were empty, except for a bag filled with moldy green lumps and a few dented cans that looked like they'd been chewed on by someone very hungry.

That's when he noticed that he wasn't alone. A crowd was gathered at the back of the store. He crept over to them and took a position behind a ransacked shelf to observe. There were about fifty people. They were all staring avidly at a pair of double doors, as if the Queen of England herself was about to emerge and hand out bars of gold.

The doors swung open, and a cart stacked high with cardboard boxes rolled out. Each one bore the words *Grub Pockets* in emphatic red letters. The cart came to a stop, and a skinny teenage boy stepped out from behind. He stared at his feet uneasily as murmurs of excitement rippled through the crowd. The doors swung open again, and a balding man with a nose as plump and red as a strawberry marched through. He stood next to the teenager and glared at the waiting crowd.

"Alrighty, folks," said Strawberry Nose Man. "There it is. All the food we got left in the store."

He looked meaningfully at the teenage worker before continuing. "We're gonna do this in a calm and orderly fashion. So listen up. Only one box per customer. You hear me? One box. No exceptions."

"But my boy goes through five boxes a day!" shouted a lady in a stained bathrobe.

"Think of my children! They need to eat!" pleaded another woman. Three little girls were gathered around her. Identical triplets, each wearing pink overalls.

"Give me twenty boxes or I'll set my lawyer on you!" hollered a man in a rumpled business suit.

Soon everyone was shouting and cursing and shaking their fists in the air.

"SHAAAAADUP!" roared Strawberry Nose Man. He had everyone's attention.

Everyone except the triplets. They had dropped down onto all fours and were scooping up handfuls of rotting food from the floor. As they shoved the slimy glop into their mouths, Reggie's stomach lurched, and he pressed his hand over his lips. He could see their faces clearly now. They each had black, beady eyes and pointy noses with whiskers sprouting out.

"Either my way or the highway," warned Strawberry Nose Man. "So if you don't like my rules, get the heck outta my store."

There was an electric pause, like those few seconds just before a huge bolt of lightning rips through the sky. Then the crowd surged forward, a snarling tide of angry people.

The teenage boy yelped and darted back through the double doors, but Strawberry Nose Man stood his ground. He climbed atop the cart and wrapped his meaty arms around the stack of boxes.

"Back up, you thieving scoundrels! One step closer, and I'm calling the cops!"

The lady in the bathrobe took this as a challenge. She clambered up onto the cart, clenched her fist, and punched Strawberry Nose Man right in his strawberry nose. His eyes rolled back into his head. Then his body went limp, and he fell backward into the crowd.

The lady snatched a box of Grub Pockets from the top of the stack. She raised it up in the air like a triumphant prizefighter and cackled.

A free-for-all ensued. Many hands reached up, tugging on the lady's robe, scratching at her legs. She lost her footing and toppled onto the floor. The entire stack of boxes crashed down after her, scattering all over. This sent the crowd into an even bigger frenzy.

A long, sharp note rang through the air. Everything went still and quiet. People gave up their rioting and looked around, searching for the source of the noise. There, standing among the crowd, was the Conductor.

Reggie gritted his teeth at the sight of him, ducking farther behind the shelf.

"Turn your ears to my voice, silly nibblies!" commanded the Conductor as he shouldered his way through the crowd. He hopped nimbly onto the empty cart and lifted the brim of his red cap so that his squinting eyes were visible.

Then he gazed keenly at the confused faces before him and

said, "You scratch and snatch and fight and bite. Like animals you act. Nasty and trashy. Why?"

The lady in the dirty bathrobe got up off the floor, still clutching a box of Grub Pockets to her bosom, and called out, "There's no food left in the city. It's all gone. And we've got mouths to feed! Isn't that right?" She turned imploringly to her fellow shoppers.

All at once, like students reciting a school creed, the crowd chanted in unison, "Love your children. Feed them!"

The Conductor seemed satisfied with this response. He smiled and patted his flute, which dangled from a cord around his neck. "Good mumsies and daddies. Very, very good."

He twitched a beckoning finger at the triplets in pink overalls. The rat-girls stopped their snacking and hurried over to him. They hugged him eagerly, pressing their strange faces into his bulging belly, as if he were Santa Claus.

"Yes, you need to protect these precious kiddies," he said, patting their blond heads. "And to love them, you must feed them. You must fill them up with crunchy munchies."

His round face tensed into a stern expression. "But you shouldn't be fighting each other. You should be fighting the baddies. Fighting the enemy."

Confused murmurs rippled through the crowd.

"An enemy that chomps and munches on everything in its path," said the Conductor fervently. "An enemy that skittle-skattles in the shadows, right under your nibbly noses. An enemy that's nastier and squabblier than any this fine city has faced before."

The Conductor allowed a dramatic pause as his eyes flashed with unhinged passion. Then he smashed his fist down on the cart handle and shouted, "Rats! Rodents! Voracious vermin! *That* is the enemy. They've munched up all your tasty treaties. Gobbled up all your grubbies."

Cries of shock and horror bubbled up from the crowd.

"And it's not just food these ratty-tatties are after. Once they've eaten up all the nosh, they'll come after your kiddies too. They'll eat them whole!"

The crowd was in a hysterical uproar.

The Conductor locked eyes with Reggie and winked. A chilling grin spread across his face, making Reggie's blood run cold.

The man clapped his hands together and announced excitedly, "What perfect timing! There's a nasty little ratty right now. Come from the shadows to say hello."

Everyone turned around. The very sight of Reggie caused a distinct transformation to sweep through the crowd—eyes widened in shock; mouths curled with disgust; and many gasps sounded out. Then the tide turned from revulsion to anger. All at once, like a chorus of well-rehearsed haters, everyone began to shout and jeer at him, to pelt him with rotten food. Reggie ducked, shielding his face with his hands, but he didn't run.

All those angry, disdainful eyes felt like tractor beams, holding him in place.

"And what do we do to rats that nick our food, that attack our kiddies?" asked the Conductor, like an indulgent teacher teasing out an answer from his students.

"We exterminate the vermin!" shouted the woman in the bathrobe.

"Bash their heads!" shouted the man in a business suit.

"Drown them in the lake!" croaked an old lady at the front of the group.

As the crowd began to swear and shout in a frenzy of rage, the Conductor bent over and whispered something to each of the triplets. They all turned to face Reggie. Three pairs of beady black eyes flashed with malice. Their pointy noses twitched, and their whiskers fluttered like insect legs.

The three rat-girls sprang toward him in a blur of pink overalls and pale, skinny limbs. One vaulted onto his back. Her hands set upon his ears, twisting them so hard he feared they might pop right off his head. He staggered backward, knocking over a display of teakettles.

As Reggie tried to shake the rat-girl off his back, another one dropped down to her knees and swiped at his legs. Her razor-sharp claws sliced right through his jeans and into his skin. He yowled in pain and nearly tripped over his own feet.

The third rat-girl launched at him with her mouth cracked

open wide, like a bear trap with two rows of small, sharp teeth. He caught her around the shoulders and shoved her away just before she could sink those teeth into his neck. He teetered around for a moment under the weight of the rodent on his back. Then his legs gave out, and he face-planted right onto the squidgy floor.

"Leave him alone!" hollered a familiar voice.

Reggie jerked his head up. Standing at the end of the aisle, a look of determination on her face, was Chantal. She held a silver teakettle in her hands.

"What are you doing here?" he said breathlessly.

"Never mind that," she answered. "Duck!"

He threw his arms over his head as Chantal raced forward and swung the kettle at the rat-girl clinging to his back.

THWWWWWWOOOOOOMP.

The rat-girl dropped to the floor like a swatted fly.

The other two gnashed their teeth furiously and rounded on Chantal. They ran toward her, trying to tackle her from both sides. Chantal let out a scream as she swung the kettle to the left and then to the right.

THWAAAAAAAACK. KLAAAAAAAANG.

Each of the rodents had received a face full of kettle. They collapsed, clutching their heads and hissing in pain.

"Whoa! You're like a Klingon warrior," an impressed Reggie told Chantal.

"Well, it's not something to be proud of," replied Chantal,

trying not to smile. "Dr. Peregrine says that violence is never the solution."

"Kill them! Bash their ratty little heads in!" shrilled the Conductor, pointing a crooked finger at them. "Before they get to your kiddies too!"

The crowd surged forward with murder in their eyes. Chantal hastily pulled Reggie to his feet, and they fled down the aisle, running straight through the front entrance of the market. Standing just outside, with his hands shoved into his pockets, was Gareth.

"Did you get the chips?" he said, turning around. His dark eyebrows arched with surprise when he spotted Reggie. "Never thought I'd be happy to see you, man. We figured out what the Conductor's up to! He's replaced us with—"

"Rats! I know!" exclaimed Reggie, rushing past him with Chantal in tow. "Run!"

Gareth's face blanched when he saw the mob tearing toward him.

"Hold up. Wait for me!" he called out as he raced after his friends.

TWENTY-FOUR

Dead End

Reggie, Chantal, and Gareth fled up the street as fast as their legs could carry them. The pursuing mob, all puffed up with rage and fear, seemed greater than its fifty or so members. And, just so there was no confusion about what they planned to do once they caught the three kids, they started up a horrible chant.

Kill them rats. Bash their heads. Drown them in the lake till they're deader than dead!

"They're gaining on us," wheezed Gareth, glancing over his shoulder. The older members of the horde had fallen away. But the younger, fitter ones—the ones who looked like they could do real damage—were hot on their trail, not twenty yards behind. Leading the charge were the triplets in pink overalls.

They moved more like rats than children, galloping along on all fours. Worst of all, they were grinning nastily, clearly eager to finish what they'd started.

"It doesn't make any sense," said a very out-of-breath Chantal, running up alongside Reggie. "They think we're *rats*, but we don't look anything like rodents."

"Well, Gareth's ears do kinda stick out like—"

"Finish that sentence, and I'll feed you to that mob myself!" broke in Gareth. He squinted up at the street sign they were passing under. His eyes glimmered with recognition, and he sprinted ahead. "I know a safe place. This way!"

Reggie and Chantal trailed Gareth as he rounded the corner, turning into a quiet neighborhood with bare trees lining the sidewalk. Looming before them, at the end of the cul-de-sac, was the Smith Library. It was a cheerfully imposing building, covered in gleaming yellow tiles that reminded Reggie of the tidy slices of sponge cake his mother used to put out for him on rainy afternoons. As always, a pair of smiling griffins stood watch at the entrance, their bronze wings supporting the archway above.

Gareth raced to the revolving glass door and pushed. He let out a roar of frustration when he realized it was locked. Reggie and Chantal looked back at the advancing mob, their eyes wide with panic.

"There's another way in, come on!" exclaimed Gareth. He ran along the sidewalk to the edge of the building and veered into an alleyway between the library and a boarded-up shawarma restaurant. Reggie and Chantal hurried after him.

The alley was narrow and shadowy, and stank of rot. It was jam-packed with an obscene amount of garbage bags, piled head-high in columns of sagging and ruptured plastic. Gareth valiantly kicked and shoved his way through the stinking mounds, clearing a path to the end of the alley, where an impassable brick wall rose up before them.

"A dead end!" uttered Chantal, her eyes wide. "What do we do now?"

"Relax, my grandpa's a librarian here, and he always leaves the back door unlocked so he can open it for fresh air," said Gareth, stalking up to a metal door that was well camouflaged beneath layers upon layers of faded posters and graffiti tags. Gareth reached for the edge of the door and tugged. All the color drained from his face in an instant. He tried with both his hands, failed, then started to pound desperately on the door.

"Grandpa! You in there? Open up!"

Reggie was rooted to the spot, staring fearfully at the mouth of the alley. "They're coming. I can hear them!"

Kill them rats. Bash their heads. Drown them in the lake till they're deader than dead.

The three of them exchanged looks of horror as the chanting grew louder. They were trapped. Any second now, the blood-thirsty mob was going to storm the alleyway and make good on their promises.

Chantal leaned back against the filthy brick wall and held herself tightly. She gazed up at the gray sky, where a sliver of blue was peeking through the fast-moving clouds. It looked as if she was savoring one last moment of beauty before the end was upon them.

Then she gasped and said, "Rescue a helpless victim from evildoers!"

She pulled out her journal, flipped it open, and used her glitter pen to scribble a checkmark on the middle of the page.

"What are you doing?" asked Reggie.

"Checking off number nine on the list," she replied, snapping the journal shut and slipping it back inside her coat pocket.

"We're about to be ripped to shreds by an angry mob! This is *not* the time for your shopping list!" he erupted.

"Don't be ridiculous! It's not a shopping list, it's—"

At that moment the metal door swung open with an arthritic creak. Out poked a man's head. His face gave off the impression of a friendly, if slightly confused owl. He had two large, droopy eyes behind gold-rimmed spectacles, and a cute sprinkling of moles on his upper cheeks. Adding to his already impressive height were dramatic puffs of white hair adorning either side of his head.

"Who on Gaia's green earth is making such a ruckus out here?"

Reggie held his breath. He fully expected this man to accuse them of being filthy rodents, and to shoo them away with a broom, or frying pan, or some other object just as suitable for wounding his dignity.

"Grandpa!" cried Gareth, his face suddenly a study in Christmas-morning joy. He launched himself forward like a jack-o'-lantern on a catapult, but instead of a gory puddle of pumpkin guts, the result was a surprisingly sweet hug.

"You're such a softy!" The old man chuckled.

Reggie raised an eyebrow. He could think of many words to describe Gareth's personality, but *softy* wasn't one of them.

"I'm all for healthy displays of affection," offered Chantal tentatively. "But I think we should maybe get inside. Like, right *now*."

"Yes, please," agreed Reggie, bobbing his head anxiously. "Less hugging, more fleeing."

The three kids scrambled inside as Gareth's grandpa pulled the door shut. Just as the clamor of angry chanting echoed through the alleyway, the lock snicked into place.

TWENTY-FIVE

The Familiar Librarian

The three kids followed the old man through a gloomy storage room filled with crates and boxes; down a corridor with bare concrete walls; then up a spiraling staircase. They emerged into a bright, circular lobby that Reggie recognized instantly.

"The library," he breathed, taking in the many rows of bookshelves that fanned out from the central hub.

His mom couldn't afford to pay for internet anymore, so he often came here on weekends to surf the web and do his homework. However, unlike his usual visits, it was completely deserted now. Without people leafing through books at the long tables, or click-clacking away at the computer terminals, this place felt completely alien, like a futuristic cathedral drifting through space.

Gareth's grandpa slipped behind the circular checkout counter. He plucked a handkerchief from under a pile of books and began cleaning his glasses. Pinned to his moss-green cardigan was a gold name tag engraved with the words *Mr. Flanagan, Head Librarian.*

"Now, will you tell me why you were caterwauling out there like a hellcat?" asked Mr. Flanagan, leveling a quizzical glare at his grandson. "I let you skip school today because of your tummy ache, but I'm not okay with you running all over the city."

"Skip school? Tummy ache? What are you talking about? I've been underground!"

"Well, I'm not okay with you fooling about in the sewers either."

"How can you be so calm?" asked Gareth incredulously. "The whole city has gone topsy-turvy!"

Mr. Flanagan cocked his head and jutted his lips out in thought. "Well, yes, things have been a bit strange 'round here lately. Folks aren't coming to the library anymore. More concerned with nourishing their bellies than nourishing their minds, it seems. Even my colleagues stopped reporting to work. Too busy feeding their little ones to do their jobs."

He crossed his arms and waggled his head. "Come to think of it, you've been pretty insatiable with your meals the last few days too. I'm still flabbergasted you ate that entire bowl of haggis. I guess it's this darned food shortage; they keep nattering on about it in the news."

"Haggis? I hate haggis. You're not making any sense!" said a confused Gareth.

"Wouldn't have thought so from the way you inhaled it," returned Mr. Flanagan.

Gareth shook his head incredulously. "Okay, we're totally getting sidetracked. What's important is that something seriously freaky is going on!"

"Leaky? What's leaking? Not those blasted pipes in the basement again? I just called the plumber last week," said Mr. Flanagan, sighing.

"No, not leaky. *Freaky!*" hollered Gareth.

Mr. Flanagan took a moment to process this, then let out a hearty chuckle at his own expense. "Pardon my ears. Took out my hearing aid earlier to change the battery, and now I can't find the pesky thing."

He leaned his elbows onto the countertop. "Anyhoo, you were saying something about *freaky* goings-on?"

"Well..." replied Gareth, looking to his companions for support. "It has something to do with the Conductor... I think."

"The what? The dumb doctor?" said Mr. Flanagan.

"No, the Conductor!" hollered Gareth.

"He's the man who tricked us, sir," chimed in Reggie, stepping forward and giving a little introductory wave. "He tricked all of us. Promised us that..."

He looked at Gareth, then at Chantal. They both turned away as regret swept across their features. "Well, he promised something he couldn't deliver on. Let's just leave it at that, sir."

Mr. Flanagan shook his head in utter confusion. "Some man called..."

"The Conductor!" interjected all three kids in unison.

"This Conductor...he tricked you," said Mr. Flanagan with the air of someone trying to learn the rules of a very confusing board game. "And why, pray tell, did he do that?"

"To *replace* us," said Chantal, her expression suddenly hard and fierce. "To replace all the kids in the city. With rat-kids."

"Rat...kids?"

"They look almost like real kids, except they're butt-ugly when you see them up close," added Gareth helpfully.

"I see," said Mr. Flanagan. "And where did these...these rat-kids come from?"

"The Conductor made them," answered Reggie, approaching the counter. "They were just regular subway rats until the Conductor transformed them."

Mr. Flanagan narrowed his eyes. "Transformed? How?"

"He played a song, Grandpa," said Gareth. "Using that flute of his."

Mr. Flanagan propped his chin in his hand, nodding somberly as he thought over their explanation. Then he smacked his palm on the counter and erupted into laughter. It was such an infectiously jolly sound that, just for a split second, Reggie was tempted to join in. The man's deep, bellowing guffaws filled the quiet library for a good while before finally dwindling to a thin wheeze.

"You gotta stop tickling my funny bone, boy!" said Mr. Flanagan, using his handkerchief to dab tears from his cheeks. "Times like this, you remind me of your dad. He was always clowning around when he was your age too."

Gareth wrung his hands in the air. "But we're not joking, Grandpa!"

"Killer rats and magical flutes. All real!" insisted Reggie.

"I can assure you, Mr. Flanagan. They're telling the truth. I do not tolerate lies," declared Chantal, confident that her stamp of approval would dispel any doubts.

Mr. Flanagan's eyes flicked from one kid to the next, as if he were trying to ferret out another punch line about to be lobbed his way like a water balloon. When he was finally certain that they were as serious as their faces looked, he pushed up his spectacles and rapped his knuckles on a stack of laminated dust jackets.

"These are extraordinary claims you kids are making. And you know what they say: Extraordinary claims demand extraordinary evidence."

"Who cares about evidence!" erupted Gareth. "We just have to find a way to stop the Conductor!"

"To get our lives back!" added Reggie with a determined nod of his head.

"Well, sounds like you kids have a problem that needs solving," said Mr. Flanagan good-humoredly, as if he were playing along with some sort of silly prank. He spread his arms out over his head in a lofty gesture. "Good thing you're standing at the very epicenter of humankind's collected wisdom. You can find the answer to *any* question at the public library!"

Chantal turned to the boys and rubbed her hands together. "He does make a good point. I think it's time we did some homework."

TWENTY-SIX

Kindred Spirits

The three kids installed themselves in the surprisingly grand study room on the top floor of the library. Three of its walls were glass, allowing a clear view of the entire floor. The outer wall consisted of smooth, gray stonework, more like something you would find in a castle than a city library. Punctuating the length of this wall was a series of stained-glass windows framed in Gothic arches. Late-afternoon light streamed through the jewel-toned glass, making every surface shine with the colors of a well-stocked candy shop.

Reggie, Chantal, and Gareth had pulled every book they could find about unusual rodents, subterranean creatures, and magic. Now dozens of thick tomes were piled before them on a long wooden table that seemed more suitable for a medieval feast than reading. Reggie had let out his beetle buddy, and it was currently skittering up and down Chantal's glitter pen on the table, enthralled by its sparkly-ness.

"Bosavi woolly rats grow to be more than two feet long," said Gareth hopefully. He held up a leather-bound book, pointing at a photo of a chubby rodent with sharp teeth. "Check out those chompers!"

"That's just a regular old rat. Nothing magical about it," said Chantal, barely glancing up from her copy of *A Post-Colonial History of Magic Tricks and Illusions*.

"What about you?" returned Gareth. "Any luck?"

She shook her head. "None of these books are about real magic—just pulling rabbits out of hats and card tricks. Not the sort of stuff we've seen the Conductor do."

"This is hopeless!" groaned Gareth, snapping his book shut. "How're we supposed to undo what he did if we don't even know *how* he did it?"

Reggie put down the mind-numbingly dull book he was reading—*Dung Beetles and Other Dirt Dwellers*—and clapped Gareth on his back. "There's three of us, and only one Conductor. If we put our heads together, I'm sure we'll find a way to out-smart him!"

Reggie wasn't only saying this to cheer the boy up. He really was starting to believe that things just might turn out okay. For the first time in a long time, he wasn't facing down his problems all on his own. Now he had backup. Now he had a *team*. And they were going to win, just as sure as the Conductor was going to lose. Just thinking of it made his belly feel warm and full, as if it were filled with the tastiest wonton soup imaginable.

Gareth got up from the table. He stretched his arms over his head and yawned.

"I can't believe I just spent my afternoon flipping through books about rodents. Not my idea of a good time."

Chantal set her book down and rubbed her eyes. "Things could be worse. At least we're not at the bottom of the lake . . . deader than dead."

"Oh, come on. Admit it!" exclaimed Gareth, picking up the glitter pen with the beetle still perched on it. "This totally sucks. Wouldn't you rather be somewhere else right now? If you could be *anywhere*, doing *anything*, what would it be?"

"My idea of the perfect day?" asked Chantal.

Gareth nodded. He brought the pen up to his face and coaxed the beetle onto the tip of his nose.

Chantal slouched, resting her chin in her hands as she thought over his question. Then she sat up straight and declared, "I'd have a picnic! At that pretty greenhouse in Allan Gardens. It's always so warm and bright in there, even in the winter."

She clasped her hands and gazed fondly down at the table, as if hothouse flowers were blooming before her. "I'd sit down on my favorite bench in the orchid room. Then I'd lay out all my treats: strawberry macarons, sugar pies, marzipan fruit, and a bottle of raspberry cordial. I'd stuff my face until the sun went down and the night-blooming flowers opened up all around me."

Gareth went cross-eyed as he tried to watch the beetle scrabbling around curiously on his nose. "Sounds pretty cool! I'm always down for food."

"What about you, Reggie?" asked Chantal. "What's *your* perfect day?"

Reggie leaned back in his chair, linking his fingers behind his head. "Easy. I'd be on the soccer field with my team."

He could almost feel the sun on his face and the freshly cut grass beneath his feet.

"Practicing my footwork and messing around with my boys. Getting so sweaty and tired I can barely walk home. Nothing to worry about, except keeping on top of the ball and sending it to the net. Now *that's* perfection."

Gareth gaped at him. "Dude! You play soccer?"

Evidently losing interest in Gareth's nose, the beetle leaped onto the table and crawled over to Chantal. It bounded right into her palm, pulsing a cool blue.

"Yeah, and my team is fourth in our league," boasted Reggie.

Gareth sat down next to him. "Not bad, not bad! You psyched for the Premier League Championships?"

"Of course! I'm gonna paint my face and watch it with my teammates at the community center. There's a big TV room there."

"Who you rootin' for?"

"Manchester United. Red and yellow all the way, baby!"

"No way! Same here. Remember that amazing header by—"

Chantal started to giggle. Both boys turned to look at her.

"Something funny?" asked Reggie.

"If I didn't know better," she replied with a knowing smile, "I'd think you two were kindred spirits."

"Kindred what?"

"BFFs, buddies, best friends!"

Reggie and Gareth raised eyebrows at each other and shook their heads.

"More like mortal enemies!" declared Reggie, laughing. He glanced over at Gareth and was surprised to see that he wasn't smiling.

"Really? That's how you think of us? Enemies?" asked Gareth, seeming disappointed.

"Well," answered Reggie, shrugging, "we gave each other black eyes last week. Not exactly something best buds do, is it?"

Gareth turned away from him, fiddling with the dog-eared page of a book. "Never mind...."

"Go on. What were you gonna say?" urged Reggie, twisting around in his chair to face him.

"The key to building bridges is communication," chimed in Chantal, nodding encouragingly. The beetle had climbed to the top of her head, where it was twitching its antennae in a most dignified way, like a king surveying his kingdom from a clifftop castle.

Gareth flicked his eyes from Chantal to Reggie. Then he sighed and said begrudgingly, "I know we've had our scrapes . . . but I always thought you were pretty cool. Thought maybe we'd hang out someday."

Reggie's mouth dropped open so wide that the beetle seemed to seriously consider hopping inside to have a good look at his molars. "You don't *act* like you want to be buds! You're always making fun of me!"

Gareth gestured vaguely with his hand. "Because you're a lightning rod."

Reggie stared at him, confused.

"Remember in second grade?" asked Gareth, meeting Reggie's eyes. "Brogan Bradley?"

Reggie squinted as his mind reeled backward in time. Then he said, "That buzz-headed bully?"

"Yeah! Well, I brought my clarinet to school one day. I was showing it off at recess, playing my favorite song—'Clair de Lune.' Thought it went great, until Brogan hunted me down on the way home. He tossed my clarinet into the bushes and emptied my backpack into a puddle."

Reggie let out a low whistle. "Yeah, that kid was a monster. I still can't get over what he did to Dunstan Klebold. I don't think they ever found his retainer. . . ."

"So that's when I learned my lesson: Clarinets are dorky," continued Gareth. "From that day forward, I kept a side of me hidden—the *musical* side."

"*Non, non, non!* That's terrible," uttered Chantal, her face stricken. "You should never be ashamed of your passion! It's what makes you *you!*"

Gareth smiled and locked eyes with Reggie. "Actually, that's why I've always kinda looked up to you. Every chance you get, you're fanboying about *Star Trek* and spaceships and stuff. You don't care who's listening, or if they'll think it's geeky. But that's also what made you an easy target . . . a lightning rod. I figured if I teased you about *your* stuff, people like Brogan wouldn't notice I was just a clarinet-playing dweeb."

Reggie was shocked. All these years, he'd been convinced that Gareth hated his guts. This was even more mind-blowing than witnessing rats magically transform into children.

Chantal clapped spiritedly, as if the climactic scene of a play had just ended. "That was beautiful, just beautiful! This might be the beginning of a lifelong friendship!"

Both the boys crumpled up pages from a notepad and tossed them at her. Chantal ducked just in time. The beetle dove onto the table, scurrying for cover inside the binding of a book.

A moment later, Chantal cautiously poked her head up into view. The boys looked at her, then at each other. All three of them broke into a fit of laughter.

"I declare a cease-fire," said a grinning Chantal as she climbed back onto her chair.

"Probably for the best," replied Gareth, examining his index finger and wincing. "Gave myself a nasty paper cut."

Chantal's gaze drifted up to the elaborate stained-glass window on the wall overhead. She sighed and rested her head in her hands. "They're beautiful, *non*?"

Reggie turned around and examined the window. In all his previous visits to the library, he had never given it more than a passing glance. There was a pretty woman in a wild, rambling garden. Her hand was stretched out, about to pluck a ruby-red rose—a scene from a story that Reggie vaguely remembered. His eyes slid over to the next window, which showed the same woman gazing up in terror at an enormous beast with horns.

"Beauty and the Beast," said Chantal. "It's my favorite fairy tale. *Comme c'est romantique.*"

Gareth had gotten up and was walking the length of the room, examining each of the dozen or so stained-glass windows. He came to a stop at the second-to-last one. After scrutinizing every inch of the colorful imagery, he crossed his arms and glared at the window as if it had challenged him to a fight.

"Hey, guys!" he called out. "I think you better take a look at this one."

TWENTY-SEVEN

The Pied Piper

In the upper left-hand corner of the stained-glass window, a pointy-roofed village nestled atop a grassy hill. A long line of rats stretched out from the village, weaving across a green landscape. They were arranged in single file, whiskered noses to squiggly tails. Heading up the line was the most prominent figure in the picture. A thin man in a peculiar outfit made up of red and yellow squares. He held an instrument up to his mouth. A wooden flute.

Gareth traced his finger over the flute, which was painted with brown and black streaks on the glass. "Look familiar to anyone?"

Reggie cocked his head and squinted at the picture for a

moment. Recognition flashed in his mind like lightning across a dark sky. "The Conductor's flute!"

Gareth nodded and rubbed his hands together. "Exactly! But if all these windows are fairy tales, which one's this?"

"The Pied Piper," replied Chantal, her eyes shining like wet pebbles.

"Sounds familiar," said Reggie. "Think I heard it when I was little."

Gareth frowned. "I don't know that one. What's it about?"

Chantal turned her face to the gleaming window, so that her features were streaked with a kaleidoscope of colors. She pulled herself up to her full (not very impressive) height, tilted her chin up, and poised one hand daintily in the air, like a stage actor about to deliver a dramatic monologue. Reggie rolled his eyes at Gareth, but a sharp clearing of Chantal's throat brought his attention back. When she finally spoke, her voice echoed off the walls of glass and stone.

"I give you: 'The Tale of The Pied Piper'... A long time ago, in a faraway land, there was a small town with a big problem: an infestation of rats. The pests had eaten up all the food and drunk up all the well water, so the townspeople were starving. Something had to be done.

"Well, one day a strange man came to town. Said he could help—for a fee. And help he did. He used his enchanted pipe to play a song the rats could not resist. He led the vermin away and drowned them all in the river."

Chantal turned to the last stained-glass window. In it, the village seemed extra small and vulnerable beneath swirling storm clouds. Once again, the Pied Piper led a twisting procession across the landscape. Only this time he was trailed by children instead of rats.

"But when the townsfolk refused to pay the Piper, he decided to exact a cruel revenge. He played a new song, one the *children* of the village could not resist. He lured them all away, across fields and moorland. Led them into the black caves that tunneled deep into the mountains. Those poor children were never seen or heard from again."

Everyone fell quiet as the sound of a photocopier whirring somewhere down below echoed throughout the empty library.

"But that's just a fairy tale," said Gareth, breaking the silence. "It's not real."

Reggie narrowed his eyes at the triangular piece of glass from which the Pied Piper's pin-dot eyes leered back at him. He suddenly felt as though a dense fog had lifted, giving him a crystal-clear view of things that were only vague shapes before.

"What if fairy tales aren't just *tales*? What if they're *history*?"

"You're saying fairy tales really happened?" said Chantal, hiking up one eyebrow. "But that's ridiculous. Fairy tales have things like enchanted pumpkins and magical spells in them. *C'est impossible!*"

Reggie looked at the stained-glass flute, then back at Chantal. "But you saw the Conductor transform those rats with a song. Before I saw that with my own eyes, I would've said *that* was impossible."

Chantal jabbed a finger into the air, ready to debate him, but then her shoulders slumped, and she gaped at the window in astonishment. "You know what? I think you might be onto something there...."

"Hold up!" declared Gareth, brushing a misbehaving curl from his forehead. "Does this mean the Conductor is actually the Pied Piper?"

"Doubt it," said Reggie. "That happened a heck of a long time ago. The Pied Piper is long dead and buried now, I bet."

"But his flute isn't!" exclaimed Chantal, clapping her hands together. "The Conductor somehow got his hands on the Piper's magical pipe...er, flute...whatever you call it."

"That's it, then! We gotta find out everything we can about that flute," said Reggie determinedly.

The beetle leaped off the table, hopped across the carpeted floor, and scampered up Reggie's body. Once it had claimed a spot on his shoulder, it twitched its antennae with approval.

TWENTY-EIGHT

The Clarinet

The three kids raced down to the first floor. They bounded up to the checkout counter, where Mr. Flanagan was carefully taping stickers onto book spines.

"We need everything you've got on 'The Pied Piper'!" demanded Reggie.

Mr. Flanagan answered without looking up. "That would be in the children's section. Plenty of picture books about that story."

"No, Grandpa," said Gareth, spreading his hands on the countertop. "Not kids' books. We need to know the truth about this Pied Piper and his magic flute. The *real* story."

Mr. Flanagan pulled the corner of his mouth into a you've-got-to-be-kidding-me smirk and chuckled. "I've been a librarian for forty years, and I can tell the difference between fantasy and fact. 'The Pied Piper,' I'm sorry to inform you all, is filed under *fiction*."

Chantal tried a different tack. "Well, are there any books that talk about fairy tales like they're real? Maybe some writer with a wild theory that magic really can happen?"

Mr. Flanagan had already started to shake his head no when his eyes lit up with some sort of memory. He shuffled over to one of three computers on the countertop and began typing away fervently.

"What is it, Grandpa?"

"There was this one book," said Mr. Flanagan, hunched toward the monitor. "A peculiar one. By an author from a very small publisher. All his books are a bit out there. He has lots of theories about things respectable people don't believe in. Things like fairy tales and magic."

The three kids looked at one another hopefully.

"Ah, here it is!" Mr. Flanagan spun the monitor around and pointed triumphantly at the flashing green text on the screen. *Fairy Stories and Folklore: An Exhaustive History of Magical Events and Personages* by Hayato Hoshimi.

"Sounds promising," said Chantal as she picked up a pencil and note card from the counter. "Where is it?"

Mr. Flanagan was already writing down the book's call number. "Cool your heels. I'll fetch it for you kids. It's on a very high shelf, reachable only by head librarians of towering proportions."

As he strode toward the elevator at the far end of the lobby, he called out, "While I'm gone, make yourselves useful and find my dang hearing aid!"

Reggie and Chantal shrugged at each other before obediently rifling through the various books, notepads, and librarian doodads on the countertop. At least it gave them something to do while they waited.

Gareth, on the other hand, headed to one of the tall windows facing out onto the main street. He brought his face right up to the glass and surveyed the empty avenue—the litter drifting lazily in the wind; the traffic lights flashing urgently, despite the complete lack of cars; and the sky darkening from smoky gray to slate.

"It's so calm and quiet out there," he muttered to no one in particular. "Too calm, too quiet. It's like that moment right before a crocodile jumps out of the water and bites your head off. Something bad is coming. I can feel it."

Reggie and Chantal looked at each other, their faces suddenly tense.

"We're okay," reassured Reggie, trying his best to stomp out an ember of worry that started to spark in his chest. "We're safe inside this library. It's practically a fortress. And we have Mr. Flanagan to help us figure out what's what."

Chantal smiled, then busied herself with pouring out the contents of a pencil holder onto the countertop.

After searching in silence for a few minutes, she remarked, "Everything was so simple yesterday. I didn't have to think about magical flutes and real-life fairy tales." A lightness spread across her features, and she let out a tinkly giggle.

"What's so funny?" said Reggie as he got down on his knees, throwing open the many drawers beneath the counter.

"Nothing, really. Just that . . . my sister . . . she *loved* this kind of thing. Mysteries and adventures—anything more exciting than boring, everyday stuff. If she was here, she'd find a way to put the Conductor in his place."

Reggie nodded. With great effort, he steered his thoughts off a path that would lead only to a sunny backyard with a tall maple at its center and a man in a flannel shirt whose smile felt like home.

Chantal took out her journal and set it on the countertop. She opened it up to the middle, smiling brightly down at its pages.

"So, what's this list you keep going on about?" asked Reggie, popping open a tub of printer cartridges. "Is it a hit list? Planning on offing your enemies?"

"Must everything be about violence?" replied Chantal, rolling her eyes.

She stretched over the counter and passed the journal to

him. Reggie looked curiously at a lined sheet of paper that was stapled to one of the pages. It was creased all over, as if it had spent lots of time inside someone's pocket. It was a list, written in glittery green ink. There were purple check marks next to the first, fifth, sixth, and ninth entries.

1) *Learn how to play the harp*
2) *Visit the capital of every country in the world*
3) *Get a boyfriend*
4) *Have my first kiss*
5) *Sneak out of the house in the middle of the night*
6) *Become friends with a stranger*
7) *Lead a revolution*
8) *Perform on Broadway*
9) *Rescue a helpless victim from evildoers*
10) *Pull off a daring heist*
11) *Laugh in the face of danger*
12) *Waltz in the rain while wearing a ball gown*

"What's this?" asked Reggie, wrinkling his chin.

"My sister wrote that on our eleventh birthday last year. All the things she wanted to do before graduating middle school."

He tapped on the check mark beside number nine on the list. "You checked this one off earlier. . . . Excuse me? I wasn't helpless! I was holding my own against those rat-triplets!"

"I'll consider that a thank-you," said Chantal, grinning.

"So, did she do it?" asked Reggie. "Did she do everything on the list?"

Chantal took the journal out of his hands and delicately traced her fingers over the glittery words. "No. She never . . . well, she never had the chance. I know she would've, though. When she put her mind to something, she always made it happen. She was *fearless*. She was my hero."

Chantal's wistful smile faded. She knit her brows together and said resolutely, "It's up to me to finish it for her. I owe her that."

Reggie wondered if his father had made a similar list. Were there things *he* had wanted to accomplish? Things that Reggie could finish for him?

A contemplative silence settled over them. Then they resumed their search for the elusive hearing aid in earnest. But after failing to discover anything other than a chaotic mess inside the drawers, Reggie shut them all and stood up. He was about to call it quits, when it occurred to him that he'd spotted something unusual while rifling down below. Something that stood out like a soccer ball in a pile of hockey sticks.

He dropped back down to the carpeted floor, pushed aside the trash can, and peered into the dark alcove beneath the computer terminal. There it was. He reached inside, pulling out a mustard-yellow suitcase decorated with stickers of orange flowers. This didn't seem at all like something that belonged in a library.

"What's that?" asked Chantal, peeking over the countertop.

"Somebody's suitcase, I guess," said Reggie. He unlatched the metal catches and lifted open the lid. The only things inside were two bundles of sheet music tied with twine, and a long, thin object wrapped in a blue towel. Reggie gently unwrapped the mystery item, revealing a shiny black instrument adorned with white buttons and silver doohickies.

"A clarinet," said Chantal. "Wonder what that's doing here?"

Gareth had crossed the length of the library and joined Reggie behind the counter. He gazed at the clarinet with the oddest look on his face—like an obedient puppy who really wanted to chew on the Sunday roast but knew it would mean a night in the doghouse if he dared. After a moment, his expression hardened into anger.

"Put that back! It's not yours!"

He bent over and snatched the clarinet away from Reggie. But as soon as he looked down at the instrument in his hands, all his bluster melted away like a delicate frost at sunrise. He ran his finger fondly up and down the instrument, and a wistful smile appeared on his face. "It was my grandma's. I haven't seen this since ... well, since everything went wrong."

"Play something for us," said Reggie, hopping up onto the countertop, as if he were taking a seat at a concert.

"Oh, that's a splendid idea!" agreed Chantal. "I love how clarinets sound. So moody and sad. I bet it's what unicorns sound like when they cry."

Gareth shook his head and set the clarinet down on the counter. He took a few steps back, as if resisting its allure by distancing himself from it. "I don't play anymore."

"But your grandma played in the symphony, right? And she taught you how to play?" wheedled Reggie. "That must mean you've got mad skills!"

Chantal suddenly seemed ill at ease, as if she just now realized that this whole conversation was a bad idea. She flashed her eyes in warning at Reggie.

"Oh, come on," said Reggie, plowing on. "Just a short song. How about 'O Canada'? Or 'Yankee Doodle'? Oh, how about the *Legend of Zelda* theme . . . ?"

He trailed off when he noticed that Mr. Flanagan had returned from the stacks above. The man was standing a few yards away from them, staring intently at the clarinet atop the counter. The eyes behind those spectacles no longer glinted with good humor, and his mouth was downturned in a sad grimace. Reggie recognized this expression all too well. It's how his mom looked on one of her bad days, when she was just a thin whisper of herself, rather than the full-throated roar.

"Grandpa!" exclaimed Gareth, hastily scooping up the clarinet and placing it back into the suitcase. "Sorry, I told them not to touch it."

But Mr. Flanagan seemed intent on pretending that whatever had just happened was no big deal. He cleared his throat, rolled his shoulders, and tugged a smile onto his face that wasn't quite big enough to mask the sadness in his eyes.

"I couldn't find that Hoshimi book," he said, pulling a handkerchief from his pocket and swiping at his forehead, which was now beaded with sweat. "No one checked it out, so either it was mis-shelved or some ungrateful lout stole it. But who in their right mind would steal a silly book like that?"

"Maybe the Conductor did," offered Reggie. "If there's something in that book that could help us stop him, you can bet he'd make sure it doesn't see the light of day."

Gareth snapped the suitcase shut and shoved it as far as he could behind the trash can. He got to his feet and cast a worried look at his grandpa.

"*Oh la vâche!*" declared Chantal so loudly and abruptly that Reggie nearly toppled off the countertop. She was crouched down, pinching something off the carpeted floor. "I think I found it!"

She held up a beige object about the size and shape of a cashew.

"Ah, indeed you have, young lady!" said Mr. Flanagan gratefully. He stepped forward to take the hearing aid from her. "A thousand thank-yous. You have rescued me from an eternity of broken telephone."

He promptly slipped the device inside his left ear, tapped

on it three times with his index finger, and said brightly, "That's much better! I can finally hear the...the..."

His eyes went completely blank, as if every thought in his head had leaked out, like sand from a shattered hourglass. His face blanched, and his thin lips began to open and shut mutely. He lifted his hands into the air, paused for a moment, then began to swish them to and fro, as if conducting a silent orchestra.

"Grandpa?" said Gareth, his brow furrowed with concern. "Are you okay?"

But Mr. Flanagan couldn't hear him. He'd slipped away into a world all his own, and there was no telling when and *if* he would be returning.

TWENTY-NINE

Tainted Tea

"What's wrong with him? What should we do?" said Gareth in a panic.

"Splash water on his face, maybe?" Chantal asked.

"Slap him," advised Reggie. "That's what people do in movies."

"I'm not going to hit my grandpa!"

"I said slap, not hit."

Then, just like that, the life and color returned to Mr. Flanagan's features. He blinked his droopy eyes and gawked with fresh interest at the three kids, as if seeing them all for the first time.

"My oh my!" he exclaimed in an unusually high-pitched voice, the type adults use to converse with babies. "You three are something to behold. So very... big! I wonder what species you are?"

Reggie and Gareth exchanged weirded-out looks.

The beetle was suddenly racing up and down Reggie's arm, as if something had upset it. Figuring that it just needed a time-out, Reggie ushered the energetic insect back into the staple box and returned it to the safety of his pocket.

Mr. Flanagan clapped his hands together excitedly. "I know just what you three need. Tea! A nice hot cup of mulberry chai to soothe what ails ya."

"No, I'm good, sir," said Reggie warily. "Not really thirsty."

Chantal leaned on Gareth's shoulder and whispered, "I think maybe he needs a nap or something. He seems a bit... stressed."

"Grandpa," said Gareth, "are you sure you're feeling okay? Maybe I should get *you* a cup of tea, instead?"

But Mr. Flanagan was already on the move, backing away slowly. He kept his eyes fixed on the three kids, his gaze darting anxiously from Reggie to Gareth to Chantal, as if he were worried they might run off and reorganize all the books in the library. After backing into a table and knocking over a stack of comic books, he spun around and practically sprinted toward the staff room door.

"What the heck was that about?" said Gareth, shaking his head.

Reggie shrugged. "Old people are big on tea. My grandma

used to make me a cup every time I visited, even though I always ended up pouring it out in her aloe plant."

Chantal picked up a newspaper from the countertop. As she read it, her eyes grew as big as harvest moons. *"Oh la vâche!"*

"What's the matter?" asked Reggie.

Her hands were shaking as she flipped the paper around to face him. Both the boys stepped closer to read the blaring headline: *Schools Empty Across City: Mysterious Flu or Something Sinister?*

"So what? I already got my flu shot," said Reggie, shrugging.

"No, look at the date!" exclaimed Chantal.

He squinted at the small lettering just below the headline. "Monday, October thirty-first . . . wait, no. That's wrong. Halloween's not for a few days."

"A typo!" proclaimed Gareth excitedly. "My grandpa collects coins, and he says mistakes actually make them more valuable. So maybe this paper is worth some cash!"

"It's not a typo!" insisted Chantal, thumping the newspaper with her finger. "Haven't you been wondering how the Conductor changed everything so fast up here? How, in the blink of an eye, he made this city a comfy home for rat-children and a *nightmare* for us?"

The boys just stared at her, not sure what she was implying.

"We weren't down there just one night," said Chantal frantically. "We were down there three days!"

Reggie's brain juddered, like a bicycle thudding down a flight of stairs. He retraced his steps last night... or what he *thought* was last night. He recalled stepping onto the subway train, journeying into the winding dark, and finally disembarking at a make-believe backyard bathed in the glow of a counterfeit sun.... But how long was he down there? Had he really hung out with a roach-fueled impostor for three whole days? The Conductor's trap suddenly seemed much more horrifying. Reggie felt like he was going to be sick.

"But how?" he said, shaking his head in disbelief.

Chantal glanced down at the newspaper in her hands. Then her eyebrows darted up.

"Maybe it's like *La Rivière des Sœurs Jumelles*."

"The what?"

"Near my parents' hometown in Quebec, there are two rivers. Audrey and Adélie," she said, putting the newspaper down on the counter. "Everyone calls them the Twin Sister Rivers, because they run right up alongside each other. They're identical, but the current in Audrey flows faster than the current in Adélie."

She swept her hands in parallel lines through the air. "So, if I get into a canoe in Audrey, and you get into a canoe in Adélie at the same time, I'd still float to the other end faster."

Gareth shook his head. "Rivers? Canoes? What the heck are you talking about?"

"No, it makes sense!" said Reggie, his eyes widening. "Maybe time somehow runs *slower* down below, in those tunnels. I mean, look at all the stuff we've run into. An invisible monster, talking beetles, rats changing into kids. The rules up here don't apply down there. Not even the rules of *time*."

Gareth puffed out his cheeks and used his hands to mime his head exploding. "Mind officially blown!"

Mr. Flanagan returned from the staff room with three Christmas-themed mugs balanced atop a cafeteria tray.

"Piping-hot cuppas!" he announced, setting the tray down on the counter and beckoning the kids over.

"Grandpa!" exclaimed Gareth. "Have I really been missing for three days?"

Mr. Flanagan shushed him and said, "None of your squeaking. Come, have some tea, you little beast."

Out of politeness, each of the kids went up, claimed a steaming mug, and sat down at a round table with a carousel of bookmarks as its centerpiece. The liquid inside smelled sweet and fruity, with a hint of something sharp that tickled Reggie's nose.

Just as he was about to take a sip, Mr. Flanagan began to hum. A light and cheerful tune that promised summer afternoons and happy memories. And yet Reggie's blood ran cold at the sound of it. He froze, like a rabbit in a meadow suddenly aware a hungry wolf was watching from the tree line. Reggie had heard this tune before. . . . The mug slipped from his fingers and smashed down onto the carpeted floor.

"Stop! Don't drink it!" He dove across the table, knocking the mugs right out of Chantal's and Gareth's hands.

"What's your problem?" cried Chantal.

"That song!" warned Reggie. "We can't trust him!"

"What're you talking about? He's my grandpa!" said an offended Gareth.

Mr. Flanagan stopped humming. He put his hands on his hips and tutted disapprovingly instead.

"Look what you silly rodents have done!" he scolded, wagging his finger at them. "I used up all my rat poison making those. And you lot have wasted it!"

"Rat poison?" exclaimed Gareth, his eyes bulging. "You tried to *poison* us?"

Mr. Flanagan pursed his lips as he tapped a finger against his cheek. His eyes shone with maniacal enthusiasm. "Guess I'll have to conjure up another way to put you rodents out of your misery. . . ."

He ambled toward the staff room, humming merrily and drumming his hand against his thigh. As an afterthought, he singsonged sweetly over his shoulder, "Stay right where you are. I'll be back straightaway with a nice, sharp knife. That'll do the trick."

As soon as he disappeared through the double doors, Reggie, Chantal, and Gareth ran for their lives.

THIRTY

Follow That Beetle

As the three kids fled the library, a bloodred sunset sizzled behind distant skyscrapers on the horizon. Long, spindly shadows stretched from streetlights and trees, like the bars of an improbably large cage. They raced through deserted streets, without any real idea of where to go, frantic with the need to get away, to put as much distance between them and the horrible things they'd seen and heard since returning from the underground.

They finally came to a stop in a small playground that was little more than a sandlot with a swing set and wooden jungle gym. It sat in the shadow of a tall cathedral, its many windows dark and unseeing.

"He was going to poison us!" said Gareth, panting. He collapsed onto his hands and knees on the overgrown grass. "And Grandpa doesn't even like swatting flies!"

Chantal slumped onto one of the swings. She wrapped her arms tightly around herself and looked down at her dangling feet, which were adorned with glittery silver sneakers. She was shivering—whether from the chill night air or from shock, it wasn't clear. When she spoke, her voice was small and shaky: "My parents didn't recognize me."

Reggie shuddered as he recalled the terrible welcome his own mother had given him.

"My dad called me a *diseased vermin*, and my mom threw a shoe at me," continued Chantal, sniffing. "One of those terrible rat-kids was there—sitting on *my* bed, wearing *my* favorite polka-dot dress. *Je n'en reviens pas*, what if I never get my parents back?"

Reggie walked to the far end of the park, where a sagging chain-link fence stood between him and a steep drop-off overlooking a wooded ravine. All the worries and fears he had been shouldering felt impossibly heavy all of a sudden, like he was wearing a backpack slowly filling with rainwater, until its weight threatened to bring him to his knees.

Back in the library, he had felt so sure that a happy ending was just around the corner. But now? All that warmth and hope and fuzzy goodness was gone, as if the stiff October wind had carried it off into the night. He realized now what a big difference Mr. Flanagan's mere presence had made. Having a bona fide adult in their corner, someone who could boss them around, tell them what to do and when to do it, someone who probably had all the answers tucked away in his pocket, *because isn't that why adults are in charge of the world?*

What Reggie really wanted, what he really *needed*, was someone to pull him into a hug and whisper, *Everything will turn out okay*. He had needed that for a long time now. But grown-ups kept on disappointing him. Before Mr. Flanagan, there was his mom, who was much too broken herself to be any good at mending someone else. And before that, there was his father. When he was around, things were great. Better than great, they were *perfect*. Right up until he died, that is. Then, like a great pyramid reduced to rubble by a terrible earthquake, *perfect* crumbled away into *sort of okay* and *I don't want to talk about it*.

Reggie glared at the silhouettes of thin, gangly trees in the ravine below.

"Face it, we don't stand a chance. We might as well just give up."

He turned around and was met with two shocked, disbelieving faces.

"You don't mean that," refuted Chantal. "We have to do something!"

Reggie shook his head. "Rat-kids have taken over the city.

Everyone wants to drown us in the lake till we're deader than dead. And the Conductor has a *magical* flute. What do *we* got? Nothing!"

"Come on, buddy," said Gareth, a hopeful smile on his face. "You told me yourself. There's three of us, and only one Conductor, remember? If we put our heads together, we'll out-think that twisted jerk."

"And what's this grand plan of yours?" sneered Reggie. "Go find a fairy godmother somewhere? Or maybe we can ask your grandpa for help. Oops, already tried that one. Didn't work out so good, did it?"

"You're not seriously suggesting we just give up?" exclaimed Gareth. "Walk away from our families? Let those rat-faced freaks take over our lives?"

The icy pool of sadness in Reggie's stomach had heated to a boil, becoming furiously hot. It coursed through his entire body, threatening to scald anyone within reach. Even those he'd come to think of as his friends.

"Well, it's not like we had such great lives to begin with!" he shouted, his voice seeming extra loud in the quiet park. "My mom is a mess who spends more time crying her eyes out than being a mom! And you won't even let yourself play the clarinet, even though it's so frickin' obvious it's something you love...."

Then he turned his fury toward Chantal. She stared him down, her arms crossed, ready for his worst. "And no one cares about your pointless therapy claptrap. It's total bull! Not like it can bring my dad back, or his grandma, or *your* sister!"

Chantal blinked at him. Then her face crumpled, as if she was about to burst into tears. He didn't want her to cry, because then there was a good chance he'd feel sorry for her. And what he wanted right now was to feel angry.

But she didn't cry, or holler, or repeat one of Dr. Peregrine's maxims. Instead, she twisted around in the swing seat until her back was turned. Then she pulled out her journal and began to write.

As Reggie watched her scribbling away, his anger evaporated, only to be replaced by the achy pangs of regret. He didn't know who he was angriest at—his dad for dying, his mom for letting things fall apart, or the Conductor for promising the impossible. But he knew that Chantal didn't deserve his anger, and neither did Gareth. He should apologize. That would be the right thing to do. Only one problem—dragging the words out of his heart and into his mouth seemed about as impossible as lifting a boulder up Mount Everest.

Gareth shook his head disappointedly at Reggie. He flipped up the collar of his leather jacket and began to tear out fistfuls of grass, letting them scatter in the wind.

Feeling wretched and suddenly very alone, Reggie went over to the jungle gym and sat down on the edge of the dented metal slide. He retrieved the staple box from his jeans pocket, slid it open, and peered down at the only individual in the entire playground who didn't hate him. Seeming to sense Reggie's sullen mood, the beetle's blue illumination pulsed wanly, like a candle flame about to go out.

An image suddenly appeared in Reggie's mind: glowing beetles, a whole swarm of them, forming brilliant blue letters on a wall of rough, black dirt...

He stood up slowly, gaping at the beetle in the box. A thin ray of hope had cut through his stormy mood.

"Maybe this little guy can help us!" he said excitedly. The beetle leaped out of the box and onto his thumb, its tiny legs feeling like eyelashes tickling his skin. "Remember when I said these beetles can spell words?"

Gareth ceased his reign of grass destruction and raised a wary eyebrow at him. "Well, okay. Ask it something, then."

Reggie shook his head. "But they work together, as a swarm. I don't think he can do it on his own."

Chantal walked over to him, gazing at the beetle. It was now flapping its uninjured wing energetically.

"Well, if he can't make letters himself, let's do it for him," she said determinedly. After opening up her journal to a fresh page, she wrote out all the letters of the alphabet in four neat rows using her glitter pen.

"Oh, that's a great idea! Kinda like playing the Ouija board...except with a bug," said Reggie, grinning at Chantal. But he noticed that she refused to meet his eyes.

She brought the open journal up to Reggie's hands, and held it steady. Sure enough, the beetle hopped onto it eagerly. It looped in circles around the page, its wings glowing with the vivid blue of a summer sky.

"What should we ask it?" said Gareth, shoving his hands into his pockets and shrugging.

After thinking it over a moment, Reggie alighted on the perfect question. He snapped his fingers and asked, "The Bad Man, the one who trapped you in the glass cage...how do we stop him?"

The beetle was suddenly very still, as if using every ounce of its energy to ruminate. Then it sprang into motion, skittering around the page. The three kids watched avidly, their eyes darting along with the beetle as it sped from letter to letter. It would pause for a few beats atop each chosen one before flitting off to the next, like a hummingbird zipping from flower to flower in a spring garden.

Chantal spoke aloud the words it had spelled out: "Whistle stick."

"What in the world does that mean?" said Reggie, screwing up his face.

"The flute!" exclaimed Gareth excitedly. "It's essentially a stick that whistles, right? Kinda like my clarinet."

Reggie nodded, returning his attention to the beetle. It was perched on one of the metal spirals of the journal's binding, flicking its antennae back and forth proudly.

"We need to know more about the...uh...whistle stick. Can you tell us anything about it?"

The beetle got to work once again, flitting from letter to letter.

Chantal squinted confusedly as she read aloud its next answer, "Lady with wings."

The three kids fell silent as they puzzled over this. Reggie gazed through the sagging fence at a full moon emerging from the swaying treetops.

When the answer finally came to him, goose bumps traveled up his neck. He knew where they had to go next—to a place he had tried to leave behind forever.

THIRTY-ONE

The Angel's Secret

Reggie opened the squeaky gate and stepped inside. A somber view greeted him—dozens of gravestones sprouting up from a narrow patch of scrubby yellow grass. He had only ever come here during the day, when the air was filled with both the smell of cookies from the factory looming overhead, and the roar of passing traffic from the nearby highway. But right now, in the ghostly moonlight, the cemetery felt eerily hushed and still, like a hunter waiting for deer to amble into his sights.

Reggie would ordinarily make a beeline for his father's grave. In fact, despite his resolution not to, some small part of him still longed to seek out that familiar copper plaque. But he was on a mission. There was *another* grave he intended to visit tonight.

Chantal and Gareth stood on the other side of the gate, seemingly anxious about crossing the boundary. Reggie waved them in, and a few moments later, all three of them stood looking up at the tallest and grandest monument in the cemetery: a life-size stone angel.

"Are you sure this is it?" whispered Chantal, as if wary of waking the dead.

"Lady with wings," said Reggie, gesturing up at the angel's white marble wings. They were spread out like a great bird about to take flight. "And the Conductor was definitely in this cemetery. He stole my dad's birthday present from here."

Reggie looked over his shoulder, toward his dad's memorial plaque, which was just a few yards away. *Was the Conductor watching me all those times I visited? Did he eavesdrop on my conversations with Dad?* The thought made him want to crawl right out of his skin.

At the stone angel's feet, set into the grass, was a small silver plaque, about the size of a postcard. Curiously, it bore no birth dates or death dates. Only eight letters in a simple font—*S.S. Enkrad.*

"I've seen this before," said Chantal, staring intently at it. "It was on the tile door in St. Patrick station, remember?"

Reggie nodded. "Yeah, I saw the same thing when I escaped from my robot dad—on a door in the bottom of the garden."

"So, who is this S.S. Enkrad?" mused Gareth, crossing his arms.

"Whoever it is," replied Chantal, shaking her head, "must be someone important."

Her gaze shifted from the plaque to something sitting right next to it on the grass—a short length of rope. She bent over and took hold of it. But when she straightened up, it snapped back, flying out of her grasp. It was suddenly quite clear that the rope wasn't *on* the ground at all. It was *in* the ground, coming up through the grass, rooted to the earth below.

All three of them looked wide-eyed at one another as its meaning dawned on them.

Reggie bent over, grabbed the rope with both hands, and tugged as hard as he could. A square of grass—about the size of a school-bus window—swung open. It revealed a set of dirt stairs spiraling down into whatever dark realm lay beneath the moonlit cemetery.

"Just like the door in the garden," uttered Reggie as he examined the trapdoor. It was made of wooden planks, overlaid with sod as camouflage. "Guess we're heading back underground...."

"Whoa, hold up!" said Gareth, waving his hands before him. "You sure that's a good idea? What if you-know-who shows up?"

Reggie scanned the huddled shapes of gravestones all around them. He couldn't shake the feeling that someone was watching, just out of sight. "You're right. Someone should stay up here, as lookout."

Gareth shot his arm up in the air like an eager student. "I volunteer!"

"We should hurry," interjected Chantal, her face tense. "I don't want to be in this place any longer than we have to."

"Keep your eyes peeled," said Reggie, gripping Gareth's shoulder. "And scream like a banshee if you need our help."

Reggie gazed at the stairs leading down into the waiting darkness. Was returning to the world below really such a good idea? Wasn't it safer up here, where he knew his bearings, where he was surrounded by unchangeable things he could depend on—the starry sky above, the grass beneath his feet, the city streets as familiar as the back of his hand? But things that seemed familiar and safe no longer held protection in this bizarre new world in which the Conductor was king, and the rat-children were his minions. Bravery and wit were the kids' only weapons to defeat that man. And this was the time for both.

Mustering his resolve before it melted into fear, Reggie gave Chantal a determined nod and began his descent into the earth. She followed closely behind.

THIRTY-TWO

The Black Stone

The dirt steps were soft and squishy underfoot, like treading on grass after a heavy rainstorm. After a few minutes of walking down the corkscrewing stairs, they could no longer navigate by the light of the moon. It was so dark that Reggie could barely make out his own feet.

He hurriedly pulled the staple box from his pocket, sliding it open with his thumb. The glowing beetle hopped out, scrambling up his arm and onto his shoulder. Its calming blue illumination seemed extra vivid in the gloom.

Reggie glanced over his shoulder. Chantal's face was set in grim concentration as she stepped carefully down the stairs. She trailed one hand along the dirt wall, which was flecked every so often with pale, twisted roots and flinty rocks.

"You okay?" he asked.

She ignored him, jutting her chin out and averting her eyes.

Maybe it was the fact that they were quite possibly marching toward their doom, but Reggie was finally able to say what had felt impossible earlier.

"I'm sorry for biting your head off back there. I know I was kind of a jerk."

Still more silence.

"Okay, I was a super-big jerk," admitted Reggie, coming to a stop and turning around. "Such a big jerk they should name an overflowing Porta Potty after me."

Chantal halted, five steps above him. The beetle's blue light cast jagged shadows across her face, making her furrowed brows appear quite alarming.

"You know you have a problem, right?" she said, her arms crossed.

"You mean . . . the rats and the Conductor and—"

"No, not that. You have an *anger* problem." She brushed past him and continued down the stairs.

As Reggie followed her, he rolled those words around in his head, like an old pair of dice he had never paid close attention to before. Anger problem. Was she onto something there? Maybe. He was always getting into fights at school, and even on his best days, it was like he was only a moment away from blowing up like a raging volcano. And the worst part? He didn't really know *why* he was so angry. Was he mad at his father for dying? At his mom for falling to pieces afterward? Or at himself for not spending more time with his dad before it was too late?

Reggie suddenly felt deeply embarrassed, as if Chantal had acquired X-ray vision and could see right through his clothes.

"When you get back home, you and your mom should talk to someone," Chantal suggested.

Reggie chuckled. "Lemme guess, someone like Dr. Peregrine?"

"Yes, someone like her can help diagnose your problems," she said matter-of-factly. "After all, Dr. Peregrine says the only way to tame a problem is to name it."

Reggie smiled. He was super glad to count Chantal as a friend. Most of the guys on his soccer team would have decked him in the face for acting like such a jerk earlier. They certainly wouldn't have given out useful advice.

"Well, I guess it's not such a bad idea," he acknowledged.

Chantal grinned at him over her shoulder. "I am full of not-bad ideas, just so you know."

That's when Reggie noticed they'd reached the bottom of the stairs. Straight ahead was a low, round passageway carved out of dirt. A shimmering glow was visible on the other side. They leveled anxious looks at each other before ducking under and awkwardly maneuvering through.

On the other side, they straightened up and gasped in awe at their surroundings. They had entered a rocky cavern as enormous as a domed stadium. The rockwork was so remarkably black and shiny that it didn't look at all like something you'd find underground, more like shattered chunks of the night sky that had been assembled into a craggy patchwork. Twelve gigantic columns of black stone stood at regular intervals along the walls of the cavern. Each of these soaring structures was decorated with the same unsettling image in white paint—a serpentine monster with dozens of bony arms poking out of its sinewy body. It wound its way up each column, cracking open its impossibly huge mouth, baring row upon row of sharp teeth.

But the most unexpected feature of this massive space was spread out before them, taking up the entire floor of the cavern: a field of pretty purple flowers.

Chantal leaned forward and ran her hands back and forth through the dense floral growth. Teardrop-shaped petals fluttered to the ground as she did so.

"They look sort of like forget-me-nots," she said, plucking a flower from its stiff green stalk. She brought it up to her face and inhaled. "Smells lovely. Like cotton candy."

Reggie took a deep breath. A candy-sweet scent hung thick in the air, reminding him of suffocating hugs from aunties wearing too much perfume. But there was something else under it. A musky, wet odor that filled his head with thoughts of rotting fruit and dead things in dark places. The first scent was a *welcome*, but the one skulking underneath was a *warning*.

"Something's over there," said Chantal. She pointed toward the center of the cavern, where a rectangular slab of black stone stood. It was just tall enough to be glimpsed above the tops of the flowers.

Although every square inch of Reggie's body was warning him to get out of there, he forced himself to say the brave thing instead: "Let's check it out."

They strode side by side into the field, tramping through the waist-high flowers. As they headed toward the center of the cavern, Reggie's eyes were drawn to the imposing columns around him. He noted the creeping vines and gnarled roots that snaked up the base of each one.

"This place looks ancient. I bet it was here long before the city above ever existed," he said in a hushed tone. The beetle had settled on his left shoulder, becoming still and dark, as if wary of this place.

It suddenly occurred to Reggie that it was strangely bright in here, although he couldn't pinpoint the light source. Everything was bathed in a thin, silvery glow, allowing him to take in all the details around him quite well—the glossy black stalactites hanging high overhead; the expanse of flowers as still as a painting (none of the swaying in the breeze you'd see in an *above*ground field); and a dark passageway at the other end of the cavern that probably led to wild, winding tunnels beyond.

As they walked, the ground underfoot changed from the spongy feel of wet dirt to something else entirely—it crunched and popped and shifted with every step. What was it they were treading on? Was it gravel? Rocks? Snail shells? Reggie glanced down, but it was impossible to discern even his shoes, let alone what was underneath. All he could see were those lovely flowers, their purple petals shuddering gently as he passed.

On closer examination, he noticed that each petal was embossed with delicate silver veins that gave off the faintest glow, like slivers of glass catching light on a cloudy day. *This* was the source of light, he realized. The soft glow from all these flowers was keeping the gloom at bay.

Chantal suddenly stopped in her tracks and threw an arm toward Reggie. Her brown eyes were wide, and she was gazing slowly about her at the rocky black walls of the cavern. "Did you hear that?"

Reggie held his body very still and listened as hard as he could. But he heard nothing. "No, what was it?"

Chantal took one last suspicious glance about her, before replying, "Not sure . . . Probably just our footsteps."

They trudged onward, their crunching footfalls echoing back from all around, until finally reaching a circular clearing. They could now see that the ground was a mixture of what appeared to be oddly shaped white stones and chalky grit.

Rising up at the center of this clearing was a cube of gleaming black stone. It was about the height and size of a kitchen table, but probably a thousand times heavier. Reggie circled it slowly, marveling at the chaotic images that had been carved into its sides. There were people in long robes kneeling before an altar; crying women holding babies up toward the sky; and hundreds of little figures fleeing from the same snakelike monster painted on the columns.

They stepped up to the strange cube and peered down at its top face. Two Y-shaped silver prongs jutted out of the black stone, about six inches apart. Below this was an inscription. The letters were written in such an extravagantly curly style that it took them a few moments to decipher exactly what it said. But even then, the *meaning* of the words remained a mystery.

> *You Always Have Been. Always Will Be.*
> *Accept Our Gift of Harmonious Wind.*
> *Forgive Us the Cage We Trap You In.*
> *Your Name Is Mightier Than Iron or Stone.*

Reggie's face crinkled with confusion. "I hate riddles. Why can't people just say what they mean?"

Chantal's gaze lingered on the inscription for a good, long while.

"*Harmonious Wind...*"

She trailed off, licking her lips in concentration. After a moment, she goggled excitedly at Reggie and ran her finger over the second line. "Harmony! As in music! This part is about an instrument."

Reggie narrowed his eyes at the two silver prongs, which looked strangely naked and incomplete. Almost as if they were intended to hold something up. Something long and thin...

"It's supposed to be here!" he said, pointing at the prongs. "This thing was built to display a flute. The Pied Piper's flute!"

"I think you're right!" said Chantal, nodding. She tapped her index finger on the inscription. "*Accept Our Gift.* That must mean the flute is a gift... but for who?"

"Well, it must be for someone super important. Like a king or a pharaoh or something," said Reggie, glancing around at the towering columns. "I mean, look at this place!"

The beetle scurried down his arm and onto his hand. It was pulsing a periwinkle blue and flapping its wing steadily.

Chantal frowned at the inscription and bit her bottom lip. "I haven't the foggiest what these last two lines mean."

"We should figure it out when we get back to the surface," said Reggie, shrugging. "Gareth acts tough, but he's probably freaking out, all alone in that cemetery."

After one last look, they struck off toward the passageway, turning away from the gleaming black cube and all the archaic secrets it held.

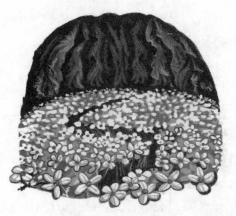

THIRTY-THREE

Beneath the Purple Flowers

They strode once again into the field of purple flowers. Reggie dangled his arms loosely as he walked, enjoying the velvety caress of those petals against his skin. Chantal had fallen into a thoughtful silence. She was no doubt puzzling over everything they'd just learned.

Reggie's foot caught on something rather large, and he tripped, nearly falling over. Peering down into the cheery flowers, he spotted something round and white, about the size of a soccer ball.

Chantal had stopped as well, and she was watching him curiously. "What's wrong?"

Reggie's brain hadn't quite processed what the object was, but the rest of his body already knew it was bad news. With his heart beating a steady tattoo and his hands shaking, he crouched down, scooping up the mystery object.

He was holding a human skull! It was white as chalk, as if it had bleached in the sun for many years. Most of its teeth were missing, and dozens of thin fracture lines zigzagged across its smooth surface. Now that Reggie's brain was fully up to speed, he yelped, and his grip faltered. The skull smashed into countless brittle pieces.

Chantal shifted her focus from Reggie to the field under her own feet. She went down on one knee, scooping up a handful of the grainy mixture covering the ground. After she'd examined it closely, her mouth dropped open, and she looked like she was either going to faint or throw up. When she was finally able to speak, her voice came out in a stammer. "B-b-bones. We were w-w-walking on bits of bones all this time!"

Reggie gazed in horror around him, at all those purple flowers. Who would have guessed those colorful blooms concealed a field of death? Then his eyes swept from one column to the next, taking in those strange paintings of a razor-toothed monster. His stomach flipped. This was a killing ground, a place where *something* hunted and devoured its prey. . . .

"We need to get out of here right now!" he exclaimed.

They hurried toward the passageway. With every step came the unsettling popping and crunching underfoot. Reggie tried his best not to think of what they were walking on. Tried only to think of—

Chantal's shriek made him stop in his tracks. She was panting and staring straight ahead at something Reggie could not see. She slowly turned her head toward him and mouthed, "There's something in the flowers."

Reggie's eyes swept across the field. But he saw nothing. Only those deceptively pretty flowers. Then there was movement. Straight ahead, about ten yards. A swaying of green stems and purple petals fluttering through the air. Reggie caught the briefest glimpse of something sickly pale emerging just above the flowers, like a deep-sea creature surfacing, before disappearing again into the depths.

A football field's distance stood between them and the passageway. But it might as well have been a hundred miles of shark-infested waters, because something was clearly lying in wait for them.

Trying his best to stay calm, Reggie locked eyes with Chantal. He mimed his plan at her, sweeping both his hands in opposing arcs. They should split up—she to the right of the figure's hiding spot, he to the left. Chantal's features became wild with panic at the notion of separating. But then she squeezed her eyes shut and took a series of deep breaths, gathering her courage. When she opened her eyes again, she gave him a shaky thumbs-up.

Keeping his attention on the motionless field ahead, Reggie held his hand in the air. He counted down silently with his fingers. Three...two...one. They resumed their advance as planned—he veered to the left and she to the right. He walked gingerly, like someone treading on literal eggshells, trying not to make a sound. But this was impossible with all those brittle bone shards littering the ground. His every step loudly announced his position to the *thing* hiding in the flowers.

Somehow, their slow march through the field seemed to be working. After a dozen cautious strides, they had just about cleared the spot where the surprise visitor had last made its presence known. Reggie waved to get Chantal's attention. Then he gestured with two fingers at his eyes, silently asking if she saw the *thing* anywhere.

Chantal turned in a slow circle, scrutinizing the flowers all about her. She shook her head at him and shrugged.

A rustling sound prompted Reggie to spin around. Five yards behind him, a clump of flowers was shaking. This became a ripple of movement through the field, like a lone wave racing across the surface of a still lake. Something was coming in a hurry, headed straight for him!

Reggie broke into a run. With his heart walloping against his chest, he made straight for the passageway. Walking on this shifting, bone-littered ground was awkward enough, but running on it was a real feat. He was moving with agonizing slowness, and it felt like he was going to wipe out with every step. Just a few more yards. Then he'd finally be free of this field of nightmares.

Suddenly a tall figure reared out of the flowers, blocking Reggie's path. He skidded to a stop, sending bone shards flying.

Then he gazed up in terror at a ghastly creature somewhere between rodent and human. Its head was that of a horrifically large rat, with furry, sunken cheeks and a bare pink snout. Its eyes were merely empty sockets, allowing a clear view deep into its skull.

The creature's body, on the other hand, was entirely human. Its gangly limbs were skeletally thin, and its rubbery flesh was a mixture of unhealthy colors—deathly grays, gruesome purples, and clotted reds. The creature looked almost as if its skin was too small for its large frame, leaving gaping holes all over. Reggie found himself picturing rotting wedges of Swiss cheese, and he resolved to become lactose intolerant straightaway.

What *was* this abomination? One of the Conductor's failed attempts at magic? A transformation gone terribly wrong? His mind churned with frightening possibilities.

Reggie stumbled backward. The half-formed creature twitched its pink snout, sniffing hungrily at the air, honing in on the boy's scent. It suddenly lunged, reaching out with long, bony fingers.

Reggie screamed and threw up his arms.

That's when blue light streaked across his vision. It was the beetle, launching itself through the air, landing on the creature's furry head. The brave insect turned to face Reggie, flicking its tiny antennae frantically, urging him to flee. Then it skittered down the creature's forehead and slipped inside its gaping eye socket.

A moment later, brilliant blue light shone out from the creature's putrid nooks and crannies, like floodlights being turned on in a derelict building. It clutched at its rodent head, then reeled back, clearly distressed by the beetle's intrusion.

"Come on! Let's go!" hollered Chantal, who had reached the passageway.

Realizing that he had been frozen in fear, Reggie roused himself into motion. He took a few unsteady steps forward, then broke into a full-on sprint through the last stretch of flowers. Just as he reached Chantal, a jarring sound echoed out—the hollow thud of a gaunt body hitting the ground. He faced the field, hoping to see some sign that his beetle buddy was okay, that it had won the battle. But the creature had fallen out of sight beneath the pretty, purple flowers. All was silent and still again.

Reggie and Chantal ducked through the passageway and practically flew up the dirt stairs, not stopping until they had surfaced in the moonlit cemetery.

THIRTY-FOUR
Farewell to the Fallen

"Holy crap! I thought you guys were dead!"

Gareth rushed over to his friends, who had just emerged from the earth. Once Chantal had cleared the last dirt step, Reggie slammed the trapdoor shut and fell back against the stone angel in exhaustion.

"I'd say death was a distinct possibility," uttered Chantal, shivering violently in her thin pea coat. Gareth took off his leather jacket and draped it over her shoulders.

"You've been gone for hours!" he said, throwing his hands in the air. "Did you get lost or something?"

Chantal and Reggie looked confusedly at each other.

"Hours? It's only been, like, half an hour, tops," asserted Reggie.

Chantal gasped and pulled the leather jacket tighter around herself. "Time flows slower in those tunnels, remember? Half an hour down there must be several hours up here!"

Gareth made a sour face. "I'm gonna have a hard time wrapping my head around that. This is exactly why I hate time-travel movies."

The three of them sat down on a large, flat tombstone carved into the shape of an open book. In addition to being a fitting memorial for the "dearly missed" bookworm, Mabel Gunderson, it served as a surprisingly comfy bench. Then Reggie and Chantal breathlessly recounted all they had seen down there in that cavern.

"A rat-headed mutant!" crowed Gareth, once they had finished their harrowing account. "That, right there, is reason number two hundred and thirty-seven why *I'm* the smart one for staying up here."

A lump formed in Reggie's throat as he thought about his beetle buddy's sacrifice. He felt a need to pay tribute to the little guy somehow. When the right idea struck him, he got down on his knees and started to dig into the wet grass with his hands. Once he had cleared out a shallow hole, he pulled the staple box from his pocket and held it up in the moonlight.

"You were the bravest beetle I've ever met," said Reggie solemnly.

"The *only* one he's ever met," quipped Gareth to Chantal.

But she shot him such a dirty look that he had the good sense to bow his head in shame.

Reggie set the box down inside the hole and buried it. Next, he went over to a cluster of dandelions sprouting from the base of a moss-covered headstone. He plucked the tallest one and brushed off the ants scrambling over its fuzzy yellow petals. Then he placed it gently on top of the tiny grave. Because no one should ever be forgotten, not even a beetle.

"It's *my* fault," declared Chantal angrily. "If I'd been braver, if I'd *helped* you instead of running, that brave little guy would still be here!"

"Did you see the size of that rat freak?" said Reggie, shaking his head. "You did the right thing trying to get away."

But Chantal refused to let it go. She scrunched her face up with frustration and balled her hands into fists. "Number twelve on the list: *Laugh in the face of danger.* That's just what my sister would've done. She wouldn't freak out or freeze up. She'd jump right in to help, no matter the risk!"

She turned away and added quietly, "I failed her...."

Reggie opened his mouth, ready to disagree. But he could see from the pained look on her face that it would be useless. For whatever reason, she was determined to shoulder the blame herself. On some level, Reggie understood. He knew what it was like beating yourself up over something that's not your fault. After all, he sometimes wondered if *he* was somehow to blame for his world falling to pieces. Had he angered the gods? Was that why the universe took his dad away from him?

Silence settled over the three kids as each of them sank deep into the valleys of their own thoughts. It was one of those peculiar moments when the company of other people felt very much like being completely alone.

THIRTY-FIVE

The Offering

"So...this riddle you guys were talking about...think it can help us?" asked Gareth, interrupting the awkward silence.

Chantal slid her journal across the tombstone to him. She'd written out that mysterious inscription from the cube of black stone (though it seemed a whole lot less mysterious in her glittery purple lettering).

> *You Always Have Been. Always Will Be.*
> *Accept Our Gift of Harmonious Wind.*
> *Forgive Us the Cage We Trap You In.*
> *Your Name Is Mightier Than Iron or Stone.*

"You said this part is about the flute, right?" asked Gareth, pointing at the second line.

"Yeah, pretty sure the Pied Piper's flute used to be down there," said Reggie, nodding. "It was a gift, but we don't know for who."

Gareth stared at the words for a while, muttering under his breath, as if he were deciphering a difficult math equation. Then he tapped his finger on the first line of the inscription.

"Always Have Been. Always Will Be," he said. "Sounds kinda like something I'd hear during the Sunday sermon."

"What do you mean?" asked Reggie.

"Well, that's how people talk about God, isn't it? Something that's been around forever, that'll always be around."

Chantal turned to Gareth, her eyes flashing. *"Oh la vâche!* You're right! That cavern wasn't built for a king or a pharaoh, or even a person. It was built for a god. Or at least, something that people *believed* was a god. That place is a temple!"

"So that means the flute wasn't just a gift," surmised Gareth. "It was an *offering!*"

Reggie's mind drifted back to that temple of purple flowers, where columns stood tall and silent, like wizened priests guarding holy secrets. He tried to picture what it had looked like countless years ago. Did torchlight dance across those black stone walls? Did chanting figures in long robes gather around that cube? Did they perform sacred dances to the eerie music of a magical flute?

That's when Reggie's thoughts alighted on a different memory. Another riddle, of sorts. Bright words appearing in the gloom, delivered as a dire warning...

"*The Darkness Is Angry!* That's what the beetles told me," he blurted out. "Now we know *why* it's angry. Something was stolen from it!"

Chantal gasped, both her hands flying up to her mouth. "The Conductor stole the flute from there, from the *Darkness*! That's what the temple is devoted to!"

Reggie was stunned by the thought of people actually worshipping the Darkness. His one terrifying encounter with the creature had left him with the distinct impression that it was more a devil than a god.

"This is good," said Gareth, standing up and punching his fist into his hand. "If the Conductor stole the flute from the Darkness, that means they're not exactly best buds. We could totally use that to our advantage."

Reggie nodded, his eyes wide. "All those bones down there... Something tells me it's a *bad* idea to make an enemy of the Darkness. It's probably not one to forgive thieves."

"The flute is the Conductor's greatest strength," said Chantal, stroking her chin. "That means it's also his greatest weakness. *That's* how we'll bring down that terrible man!"

Gareth wrapped his bare arms around himself, his T-shirt rippling in the chilly breeze. "Then that should be our next step. We have to get our hands on the Conductor's flute."

"But how?" said Chantal. "We don't know where he is."

Reggie rubbed his hands together. "Well, let's focus on what we *do* know."

"For starters," said Gareth, his teeth chattering as he cast an envious glance at his leather jacket, which Chantal was still wearing. "We know the Conductor replaced all the kids in the city with rats. And we know he used his flute to do it."

Reggie nodded. "We also know that all the grown-ups think *we're* rats. I'm sure that's the Conductor's fault too."

"Wait a minute," said Gareth, his freckled forehead creasing with thought. "We don't really know *how* he did that. I mean, we saw him transform those rats into rat-kids, but that's about it."

"If it's really a magical instrument that once belonged to the Pied Piper, then it's probably capable of all sorts of magic," reasoned Chantal. "Powerful spells we can't even fathom. I mean, why else was it passed down through history? Why else was it used as an offering to the Darkness?"

"But something's not adding up," continued Gareth. "My grandpa was *normal* at first. He recognized me. Acted like his same old self. But then suddenly it was like a switch was flipped . . . and he went all stabby on us!"

All three of them fell into silence as they pondered this inconsistency. While Chantal was lost in thought, Gareth crept over to her and delicately lifted his leather jacket off her shoulders. He put it on, did up the zipper, and beamed like someone who had just scored the last slice of pizza at a slumber party.

Reggie thought over those last harrowing moments in the library. What was the first sign that trouble was brewing? At what exact point did Gareth's grandpa switch from *friendly librarian* to *homicidal poisoner*?

The only thing that came to mind was the peculiar change of expression on Mr. Flanagan's face. It looked as if his very soul had slipped out of his body just for a second, leaving the door flapping open, letting in something sinister. Then Reggie recalled what had happened just *before* that moment. Chantal had picked something up off the floor, handed it to him....

"His hearing aid!" he exclaimed.

"You mean my grandpa's?" replied Gareth.

"Don't you remember?" Reggie tapped his ear. "Right after he put the hearing aid in, he started to hum that weird tune. The same one my mom hummed before attacking me with a frying pan."

Chantal gasped. "That tune! *That's* how the Conductor did it! It turned all the grown-ups against us. It brainwashed them. Made them believe *we're* rats."

"Exactly!" said Reggie. "Mr. Flanagan couldn't hear it at first, because he's got bad ears. But once he put his hearing aid in..."

"Wait a minute," said Gareth, holding his palms up. "If it's loud enough to brainwash all the grown-ups in the city, how come *we* can't hear it?"

A sudden gust of wind picked up, whistling through a

drainpipe that ran the length of the cemetery, like the Conductor's breath slipping into the hollow chamber of his flute.

An idea hit Reggie.

"Maybe we're not listening hard enough!"

THIRTY-SIX

Chasing Notes

R eggie needed silence for this to work (or as close to
silence as he could manage). But that would be difficult
with the steady rustling of the long grass all around
him. Maybe finding higher ground would help?

His eyes narrowed on the tallest structure in the cemetery:
the stone angel.

He hurried over to it, grabbed on to one of its outstretched
arms, and hauled himself up. After some awkward maneuvering,
he had climbed up onto the angel's back, placing each foot onto
one of its ivory wings. Then he stood up straight, steadying his
hand on the angel's head. From this added height, he could see
past the cemetery's front gate. The curving stretch of highway
beyond was unusually empty of traffic.

Reggie closed his eyes and listened. At first, there was nothing but the rustling grass and the creak of the rusty front gate, swinging back and forth lazily. He took a deep breath and tried to tune out those sounds—the gate, the wind, and all the noisy worries and fears crowding inside his head. He tried his best to find silence *within*.

Then, just barely, he heard it. The thin, reedy notes of flute song. So quiet, it hardly qualified as sound, more like a half-forgotten memory flitting through his mind. He shifted his footing on the stone wings, and the barely-there tune disappeared. He cupped his hand to his ear, swiveling his head slowly to the left, then to the right. There it was again: flute song as quiet as the whispers of a ghost.

"It's coming from that way," he said, pointing toward the city center. He hopped down off the angel and raced out of the cemetery, with Chantal and Gareth following closely behind.

They chased the wispy tune halfway across town, through dark and deserted streets, like ghost hunters on the trail of a shy spirit. The farther they traveled, the louder the notes swelled, asserting themselves as something very real and not just a figment of their imaginations. Once they reached the theater district, the tune was so loud that it echoed off the handsome brick buildings on either side of the street.

The three kids stopped in the shadow of a grand theater that reminded Reggie of the six-tiered wedding cake in his parents' wedding photos. All the windows of the theater glowed welcomingly, and the front doors were wide open, as if awaiting their arrival.

But Reggie's attention was quickly pulled upward, beyond the theater's blinking marquee and its flat roofline. A blimp hovered high overhead, like an enormous bullet suspended in the indigo sky. Looking more sinister than cheerful, a huge smiley face was painted across its sleek red surface. Suspended from the blimp was a round wicker gondola from which an odd assortment of twisty brass horns jutted out. They looked like instruments from a madman's marching band.

Pouring out of these horns at a deafening volume was the cheery flute song. The same bouncy tune that Reggie's mother and Mr. Flanagan had hummed with abandon.

"The music's coming from that thing," shouted Reggie, peering up at the blimp. He lowered his eyes to the theater and caught a dark shape in one of the upper-story windows—the broad silhouette of a man with a cap on his head. Then, with a ruffle of the curtains, the figure slipped out of view.

"Someone's inside. Watching us," shouted Reggie over the music.

"Was it him? Was it the Conductor?" said Gareth, panic edging into his voice. He followed Reggie's gaze and stared wide-eyed at the now empty window.

"I'd bet my entire collection of *Deep Space Nine* trading cards it was."

"Then let's get out of here!" insisted Gareth. "Before he turns us into toads or something."

"No, we can't keep running," said Reggie, sounding much braver than he actually felt right at that moment. "You said it yourself—we gotta get our hands on that flute."

Gareth had gone pale as a sheet. But after considering Reggie's words for a few moments, he grunted his support.

With her eyes fixed on the blimp overhead, Chantal spoke up. "We also have to silence that horrible music." Her mouth was a hard, thin line of determination. "If we don't put a stop to its enchantment, we'll never get our lives back."

"So are we just gonna waltz right up to the Conductor and say *Pretty please, can we have that magic flute of yours?*" asked Gareth dubiously. "And how're we supposed to get up inside that blimp? Fly on a broomstick?"

Reggie sighed, keenly aware that the odds were most definitely *not* in their favor. Suddenly all he wanted to do was lie down somewhere soft and warm, close his eyes, and let sleep whisk away all his worries. He slipped his hand into his right pocket, letting his fingers curl around the bear whistle—a silly, plastic trinket that had once belonged to his father.

A memory rose up in his mind, like a photograph drifting to the surface of a dark, still pond. When Reggie was eight years old, he crashed his brand-new scooter into the bottom of a ravine. It was so mangled that he had to drag it all the way home like a farmer pulling along a stubborn ox. He cried when he showed it to his parents. There was no way they could afford to buy him another one. But his dad had given him a big hug and said, "Don't you worry, boy. Nothing is unfixable with smarts and a bit of elbow grease."

This memory shone so brightly that all Reggie's anxieties slithered away, fleeing into the shadowy parts of his imagination, where his fears of sharks in swimming pools and monsters under the bed resided. He looked up with renewed determination at the floating blimp overhead.

A plan started to take shape in his mind—a small, flimsy idea sprouting up into a scheme as stout and impressive as the maple tree in his old backyard. It wasn't a perfect plan, though; it would be dangerous, and super hard to pull off. But with the right amounts of luck, bravery, and smarts, it just might work.

"Team huddle," announced Reggie. He crossed his arms over his chest and hiked one foot up on the curb, mimicking Cristiano Ronaldo's heroic pose from the poster in his bedroom. "Listen up, guys. I've got our game plan. . . ."

THIRTY-SEVEN

Preparing for Battle

R eggie, Chantal, and Gareth stood before the doors of a department store. Even here, three blocks away from the musical blimp, they could hear the jaunty flute song echoing up and down the shadowy street.

"Throw it good and hard," said Gareth, passing Reggie the brick they'd stolen from a construction site.

Reggie nodded. He took a deep breath and pitched the brick like he would a baseball. It collided with the glass doors, and the sound of shattering glass rang through the night air. He tensed, readying himself for an alarm or approaching police sirens. But after the sound of falling glass subsided, everything was quiet and calm.

The three of them stepped through the doors, broken glass

crackling underfoot. Only some of the track lighting overhead was on, so the store seemed as vast and mysterious as the Cave of Wonders from *Aladdin*.

Reggie turned to Gareth and said, "We need flashlights. And a suitcase. Make sure it's big enough."

Gareth gave a salute, spun on his heels, and marched toward the travel section at the back of the store. He called over his shoulder, "This plan of yours better work!"

"What should I do?" asked Chantal, nervously eyeing a clown mask hanging from a Halloween costume rack.

"I need duct tape, rope, and meat hooks. Oh, and a backpack to carry the thingamajig in," he said, thinking through the plan in his head.

She nodded and hurried off.

Reggie climbed up the stilled escalator to the second floor, where the toy department was located. He walked down an aisle of superhero action figures, and down another filled with glass-eyed dolls. Then he saw exactly what he needed. Radio-controlled helicopters. He ran his eyes along the shelf until he spotted one that was red with a gold stripe running across it, sort of like the team crest of Manchester United. He plucked this one off the shelf and returned downstairs.

As he waited for the others to return, he took the helicopter out of its box, popped in some batteries, and flipped through the instruction manual. When Chantal appeared, she was lugging a full shopping basket in her hands.

"Awesome, I think I can get started now," said Reggie as he began rifling eagerly through the contents of the basket.

He nodded approvingly when he found the meat hooks, each one a thin piece of metal that curved to a point as thin and sharp as a needle. He arranged them around the helicopter in a circle. After thinking it over a bit, he repositioned the hooks in different configurations to see how they would fit together. When he was pretty sure he'd gotten it right, he reached for the duct tape.

Chantal watched him the whole time, making little murmurs of appreciation every now and again, as if he was doing something miraculous, like performing brain surgery.

"You're really good with your hands," she said as Reggie flattened a strip of tape down on the helicopter.

"Not as good as my dad," he said with a shrug. "He could make practically anything out of nothing."

"Well, he must've rubbed off on you," remarked Chantal with a knowing smile.

She ambled over to a full-length mirror hanging on a pillar. After gazing disappointedly at her own reflection for a few moments, she let out a long sigh. Then she slowly extended one arm toward the mirror, as if reaching out to someone who looked exactly like her, as if reaching out to a twin.

"I wish more of my sister had rubbed off on me."

"I thought you were identical twins," said Reggie, measuring out a length of tape.

"Yes, we *looked* the same. But we were very different people."

"So, she was a dog person, and you're into cats?" joked Reggie.

"No, I mean the important stuff. Our personalities...our *essences*."

"Your what?"

Chantal held her arms in a circle before her, like a ballroom dancer about to begin a waltz. Her reflection did the same. "Let me put it this way: My sister was like the Bastille Day fireworks at the Eiffel Tower. Big and loud and bright and *spectacular*. But I'm..."

She stared stormily at her reflection.

"I'm a peppermint-scented candle on a window ledge. Small and nice, but completely forgettable."

Reggie put down his project and glanced over at Chantal. Her shoulders drooped, and her knees buckled inward, as if she were that hypothetical candle melting into the floor.

"Now, that's just a bunch of bull," he responded, raising one eyebrow. "A bit annoying, yeah, but you're definitely not forgettable."

A smile broke across Chantal's sullen face. She turned away from her reflection and crossed her arms. "Annoying? That's funny coming from the boy who's always talking about *Star Wars*."

"Star *Trek*! Totally different thing!" Reggie playfully chucked a balled-up piece of tape at her. She caught it and lobbed it right back at him.

He returned his attention to his project while Chantal sat on the floor, watching him work.

After a few adjustments, the invention was finally complete. He'd attached the six meat hooks to the sides of the helicopter, using the entire roll of duct tape. The hooks jutted out awkwardly so that the helicopter looked sort of like a metal spider.

He got to his feet and picked up the remote control. He flipped the on button, and right away, the helicopter's blades spun into action. He gently pulled back on the joystick. The helicopter rose slowly into the air, until it was level with his face.

At that moment Gareth appeared, dragging a wheeled suitcase in one hand and a shopping basket in the other. "Whoa," he said, impressed. "Who would've thought a dweeb like you could come up with something this cool?"

Reggie smiled. Actually, it was sort of his dad's idea. Three summers ago, he'd gotten his soccer ball stuck up a tree in the yard. When he tried to climb the trunk, his father stopped him and said with a sly smile, "I think we can do this a better way." For the rest of the afternoon, the two of them fashioned a bona fide *soccer rescue vehicle* out of a radio-controlled airplane.

Reggie turned his attention to the suitcase Gareth had found and said, "Now we have to make sure that thing's big enough."

Chantal unzipped it, got down on her knees, and started to crawl inside. But then she froze, as if worried something was about to leap out and bite her. She shook her head and got back to her feet.

"What's wrong?" asked Reggie.

"I don't know if I can do it!" exclaimed Chantal, her forehead lined with frustration.

"But you seemed pretty sure you could before," said Gareth.

Chantal pulled her braids over her shoulder and worried the ends with her fingers. "We need someone stealthy, someone graceful, someone *fearless* to pull off my part of the plan. That's not me! I'll only mess this whole thing up! For real, I'm better at *reading* books about ninjas than sneaking around like one!"

"But it *has* to be you!" insisted Gareth. "You're the smallest. We can't fit into the suitcase!"

Reggie flashed an ease-up-buddy look at him and stepped closer to Chantal.

"I know you have it in you," he said gently. "You rescued me from those triplets. And you were awesome down there in that temple. When the chips are down, you get the job done."

Chantal shrugged dejectedly, her eyes cast down to the floor.

"Wait a minute, wasn't there something on your sister's list about a heist?" asked Reggie.

"Number ten," she replied. *"Pull off a daring heist."*

"Well, there you go! That's exactly what this plan is. A daring heist. If we all work together and get this done, that's one more thing you can check off the list."

Chantal smiled, though her eyes still shimmered with anxiety. "Well, Dr. Peregrine does say *it's better to regret the things one has done than regret the things one hasn't.*"

"Um...that your way of saying you'll do it?"

She swallowed and nodded hesitantly. "I'll do my best."

"Your best is all we need," said Reggie, smiling back at her.

"Cool, cool, cool!" declared Gareth, clapping Reggie and Chantal on their backs. "Now that that's all settled—look what I got!"

He reached inside the shopping basket, pulling out a bundle of cardboard cylinders with the words *Galactic Whizzers* printed on them.

"What're those?" asked Chantal.

"Fireworks!" replied Gareth excitedly. "There were tons of them in the clearance bin."

"And what exactly does that have to do with our plan?" said Reggie.

"Nothing. They're just totally awesome!"

Chantal shook her head with exasperation, but when her eyes met Reggie's, they both burst into laughter.

After packing up all their gear, they made their way down the escalator toward the front door. Out on the sidewalk, they were greeted once again by the echoing flute song. Reggie faced his friends, took a deep breath, and said with as much bravado as he could muster, "Let's do this thing!"

THIRTY-EIGHT

The Theater

Reggie and Gareth stood side by side before the shining facade of the grand theater. The smiley-faced blimp grinned down at them from the night sky, blasting out its cheery flute song. Yet, somehow, the insistent beating of Reggie's heart echoed loudest in his ears.

"Ready to go in?" he said with difficulty, since his throat had gone bone-dry.

Gareth loosened his shoulders, cracked his knuckles, and nodded. "Ready as I'll ever be."

The two boys walked cautiously through the open doors, Reggie gripping the straps of his backpack and Gareth lugging the suitcase behind him. As they moved into the lobby, golden light from rows of sparkling chandeliers washed over them. They trod past marble columns topped with carvings of dolphins and seashells and walls covered with silken wallpaper patterned like drifting seaweed. Plush carpet the color of sea foam rolled out before them, muffling their slow footsteps. After the gritty darkness of the streets outside, this place seemed like a fluffy daydream one might have after eating too many freshly steamed bao for breakfast.

They paused at the center of the lobby before a pair of curving staircases that swept up and away in either direction. The insistent flute song couldn't be heard at all in here, as if the theater's majesty had bullied the music into silence.

Reggie's stomach grumbled with unease. This place was *too* calm, *too* pleasant, *too* welcoming—like a slice of delicious cake that had been laced with poison.

"Where should we start?" whispered Gareth as his eyes followed the staircases up to the balconied floor above.

Reggie pointed straight ahead at a pair of mirrored doors that reflected their nervous faces. "Through there."

He rested his hand on the silver door handle a moment, listening for any sounds beyond the rapid beating of his heart. None could be heard, so he pulled open the doors and entered the auditorium. Gareth kept close behind him, silent except for the mousy squeak of the suitcase's wheels.

They made their way down a sloping aisle, with many rows of vacant seats spreading out on either side of them. As he walked, Reggie scanned the empty theater, fearful that an invisible audience was watching them, waiting for the right moment to reveal themselves. Murals covered the walls—an underwater scene, with dozens of ghostly-pale mermaids swimming about a painted sea of moody blues and twilight purples. Up ahead, the crimson stage curtains were drawn, like a mouth clamping down tightly on a dark secret.

"Sure you saw him in the window?" whispered Gareth, eyeing the balcony seats behind them.

"I'm sure," said Reggie. "He's here. Somewhere."

As if on cue, a mechanical click-clacking broke through the hush. Then the curtains whooshed open on a darkened stage. A blinding spotlight flashed on, revealing an ivy-covered wishing well, the sort you'd expect a fairy-tale princess to sing a song into. Lounging on the lip of the well, posed like a lazy cat basking in a ray of sunshine, was the Conductor.

Every muscle in Reggie's body tensed, and Gareth let out a sound halfway between a squeak and a gasp.

"I knew you'd find your way here," declared the Conductor, his lips curling like dying worms. "Such clever little nibblies you are."

Reggie narrowed his eyes at the wooden flute dangling from a cord around the Conductor's neck.

"We know what you're up to!" he said, trying to sound bigger and tougher than a twelve-year-old boy shaking like a twig in a storm. "We know you've replaced us with those horrible rats!"

"Yes, indeedy!" replied the Conductor. He fluttered his

eyelashes and put a hand to his heart, as if he'd received a great compliment. "And a much more splickity-lickity place this city is now, don't you think?"

This was good. The Conductor was talking. And the longer he talked, the longer they had to pull off their plan. Reggie elbowed Gareth and shot him a knowing look. As discreetly as possible, Gareth shoved the suitcase out of the aisle and into the row of seats to his right.

"But why?" exclaimed Reggie. "Why would you go through all this trouble?"

"Why? You want to know *why*?" echoed the Conductor passionately. He hopped off the wishing well and stalked dramatically downstage like an actor about to dictate the somber first lines of a play. The spotlight followed him, etching deep shadows into his pallid face.

"Because things are as they *should* be now. I fixed the great, grand order. Made a sneaky switcheroo. Rats above and *brats* below!"

He spread out his hands to encompass the entire theater around them.

"You children had it easy up here," he sneered. "Sitting on your lumpy butts and playing your electric games while Mumsy and Daddy stuffed your frumpy faces with munchies. You knew nothing about hard work, about *surviving*! While down below, in the blickity-black, the noble ratty-tatties had nothing. Had to scribble-scrabble for scraps."

He lifted off his cap, flipped it high in the air, and caught it with a flourish. "And so, it was time to turn the tables. Brought the rats up to the shiny-blimey world above, and I gave all you kiddies a taste of the forever-dark."

The secret flap Reggie had cut into the suitcase flopped open, and out crawled Chantal. Blocked from the Conductor's view by the seats in front, she inched her way across the narrow row on her hands and knees.

"My switcheroo has been such a trumpity-pumpity-triumph that I've got plans to *expaaand*," he drawled, pulling his hands apart as if he were stretching pizza dough. "All across this gumbledy-green globe, there are kiddies who need to hear my melody. And there are ratty-tatties near and far who need to be brought up into the sunbright. From Yellowknife to Yamato, from St. Petersburg to Pittsburgh...I won't stop until there's no more puffity-puffin left in my lungs!"

Reggie felt like he was going to be sick. It was too terrible to fathom—the thought of the Conductor visiting children all over the globe, like some sinister version of Santa Claus. But instead of toys wrapped in pretty paper, he'd deliver *misery* sheathed in empty promises. Reggie felt the weight of all those countless children on his shoulders. It was more important than ever that their plan worked.

"But you're a human! You're one of us!" exclaimed Reggie. "Why do you care so much about rats?"

An odd look came across the Conductor's face, a tremor of

uneasiness like a ripple through a greasy puddle. "Yes, I was *once* like you. A child. A grubby-flubby little thing. Pampered and cuddled and coddled by my mumsy."

His gaze became distant, like he was watching a film projected on the back wall of the theater. "But one day, Mumsy's squishy-wishy love ran out. She abandoned me. Left me for dead on the clickity-clackity tracks of St. Paddy's. But then *they* found me. The rats. They showed me how to find food in the inky-blinky blackness. Showed me how to find light in the dark. *They* became my family."

Gareth took a hesitant step forward and called out, "And that's where you found that flute—the *Pied Piper's* flute. Down there, in the tunnels."

The Conductor nodded, impressed. "Clever little nibbly. You did your research, I see. There I was, nubby nose to dribbly dirt, crawling through a tunnel I'd never explored before, looking for munchies to fill my belly. That's when I stumble-bumbled across it. *The Darkness.* A forever-dark so thick it has hands to grab you, teeth to chomp you, a mouth to swallow you whole. And it was just lying there like a snoozin' dragon, curled around something I could hear but couldn't see. Something that made pretty sounds when the breeze guster-blustered through the tunnel."

The Conductor's eyes became dreamy. "The prettiest music I ever heard. Like Mumsy singing me lullabies while I blinked 'n' nodded."

His gaze hardened, and his sharp grin returned to his face.

"Whatever it was, I had to have it. So I snitchy-snatched it. The Darkness rip-roared like a blustering beast. Came after me, fast and angry. But I was faster than it, *smarter* than it. I slipped away before it could gobble me up."

He took a moment to rub the flute lovingly between his fingers before continuing. "Took me many moons to learn how to make this sing like a birdy. But once I did ... oh, my thumpity heart ... it was even more splendickity than I'd hoped. It can do amazing things. *Magical* things."

Chantal had made it to the end of the row. She got up from the floor and crept toward the stage. After taking a few careful steps, she treaded right onto a plastic water bottle. The crunching sound echoed through the theater like a gunshot.

Just as the Conductor's eyes flicked in her direction, Reggie called out frantically, "You're a thief!"

The man's gaze slid back to Reggie. He narrowed his cold, beady eyes at him and hissed, "What did you say?"

"You stole that flute just like you stole us away from our lives," said Reggie, breathless with relief that Chantal hadn't been spotted. "You're nothing but a sad little man who steals things. Pathetic!"

Chantal had reached the low set of wooden stairs leading up to the stage, but the Conductor still seemed completely unaware of her presence. She took a deep breath before mounting the first step.

"You dare call me a thief?" roared the Conductor. "*You* are the thief! All you little bratties. Taking everything and giving nothing back. Gobbling up all the goodies in the world while the ratty-tatties starve beneath your feet!"

Chantal was onstage. She tiptoed farther in, keeping to the shadows, well beyond the white glow of the spotlight. And as the Conductor ranted and raved and gestured angrily at his audience of two, she moved stealthily toward him.

"You're a liar and a loser!" shouted Reggie, following Chantal's progress with his eyes.

She stood right behind the Conductor now, contained and exposed within the circle of light. And as Reggie watched with his breath held and his hands clenched, Chantal fumbled for something inside her coat pocket.

Come on, willed Reggie. *Do it now!*

She finally managed to extract a pair of scissors. They glinted vividly in the spotlight. She glanced up, meeting Reggie's gaze.

"You got this," he mouthed to her.

With her whole body stretched out like a ballet dancer performing a pirouette in slow motion, she raised the scissors up toward the Conductor. Her hand was shaking, making the scissors flash a staccato rhythm, like someone signaling SOS with a piece of glass in the sun. She eased the scissors ever so slowly forward, until the points were nearly touching the Conductor's neck. Then she deftly slipped one blade beneath the leather cord from which the flute hung.

Reggie held his breath, his fingernails digging into the palms of his hands. Chantal had nearly done it! One quick snip, and the flute would be theirs.

The Conductor was about to launch into another tirade, but then he blinked and looked more intently at Reggie. The man's eyes widened with realization, and he whirled around, just in time to smack away Chantal's upraised arm. The scissors clattered to the stage floor.

"Naughty, naughty, little nibblies!" he admonished, flashing Reggie and Gareth a razor's-edge grin. "Trying to pull a tricky snippy on me, eh? Well, I think I've chitter-chattered long enough. On-with-the-show time, don't you think?"

He raised the flute to his lips, took a deep breath, and began to play.

THIRTY-NINE

Siren Song

The Conductor was playing a *new* tune, different from any of the others. It trilled up and down like crazed laughter, reminding Reggie of red-mouthed circus clowns who were always grinning, even when they weren't remotely happy.

Chantal fled from the stage, joining Reggie and Gareth in the aisle. The three of them huddled together in terror as the giddy music filled the theater, like helium puffing out a birthday balloon.

"We need to get out of here!" said Chantal, pulling on Reggie's sleeve.

That's when the walls began to shimmer with light and

movement. The painted murals had come to life, as if they were windows into an underwater realm. The pale-limbed mermaids were no longer frozen in time. They'd begun to move, flicking their green tails and swimming gracefully through the two-dimensional sea.

"This is totally wigging me out," exclaimed Gareth. He watched bug-eyed as the mermaids glided across the walls of the theater like elegant ghosts drifting through the air.

Just as Reggie was about to flee up the aisle, one of the mermaids looked straight at him. She'd come to a stop and was slowly treading the purple-blue water with her thin arms. Her face was beautiful, perfect even, like the carved face of the stone angel in the cemetery. Her eyes were like two emerald sparks glowing in a dark, cold sea.

The mermaid smiled at him, and he was surprised to find himself smiling back. He'd never smiled at a painting before, but he guessed it was probably the polite thing to do. She parted her coral lips in a silent sigh as her long, silvery hair drifted all about her face like a halo made of moonlight.

With a flurry of bubbles, she swam to the back of the auditorium, pausing above the two doors they'd entered through. She held Reggie's attention with those dazzling green eyes for a long moment, as if issuing him a playful dare. Then she flapped her tail, spun around, and struck off into the painted sea, swimming hurriedly until she was out of sight.

She wanted Reggie to follow her, and he was more than happy to do so. And yet somewhere at the back of his mind, it occurred to him that this was maybe a bad idea. But why?

Danger. There was danger nearby. That's why. Reggie held this thought firmly in his mind, like a drowning person grabbing on to a floating bit of wood.

I have to get out of this theater, he reminded himself. *I have to get out of here because the Conductor is . . . is . . .*

The laughing flute song suddenly swelled to a deafening volume. It seemed to be echoing not just off the walls of the theater, but inside Reggie's very skull. All of his worries and fears slipped away, carried off by the rushing tide of music. All that was left in his mind was excitement. He was going to follow that beautiful mermaid. She was going to show him a sunken pirate ship, or perhaps some secret aquatic kingdom. Maybe she'd let him live with her forever, deep underwater, where everything was dark and calm and cool and peaceful.

"Come on, guys," he said to his friends, giddy with joy. "We're going on an adventure!"

Chantal giggled. She was watching a mermaid with long purple braids perform a sort of underwater jig with her shimmering tail.

"She's so graceful, isn't she?" Chantal said, gushing, her eyes glazed over like wet marbles. "And so lovely! I've never seen anyone lovelier."

"She's not as cool as this one," said Gareth, grinning from ear to ear. He pointed at a red-haired mermaid who was zooming about the walls, weaving expertly around sconces like a champion skier slaloming down a hill. "She's so fast. She should totally enter the Olympics!"

The mermaids stopped to give Chantal and Gareth conspiratorial winks. Then they swam off, disappearing into the murky sea.

The three kids exchanged eager smiles before racing toward the doors of the auditorium. The Conductor followed them, stepping down off the stage and striding up the aisle with a gait almost sprightly enough to qualify as skipping. He continued playing his flute all the while, bringing the crazed song to piercing highs and breathy lows. The lights began to flicker, and the air crackled like at the beginning of a thunderstorm.

Out in the lobby, the three kids swept their eyes across the green wallpaper, searching for their new friends. Reggie spotted the mermaids on the wall above one of the staircases. They were holding hands and spinning in a circle, their tales flapping lazily beneath them. The emerald-eyed mermaid looked straight at Reggie and took off, swimming up the wall to the second floor. The other two mermaids followed her.

Reggie, Chantal, and Gareth pounded up the carpeted steps after them, giggling among themselves, as if they were playing hide-and-seek in a schoolyard. They found themselves on a dimly lit balcony with two doors on either end, one shut and the other wide open. They made for the open one. The room was cluttered with dusty old stage props—baskets overflowing with wax fruit, wooden rifles and swords, giant mushrooms, and flowers made of papier-mâché.

On the wall opposite them was a peculiar-looking door. It was perfectly square and set in the middle of the wall, four feet above the floor. Its wooden surface was etched with swirls and eddies that seemed to mimic the churning waters of a whirlpool. A golden knob shaped like an octopus protruded from its center. On either side of the door, green curtains billowed gently, like seaweed drifting in a slow current.

The three mermaids had posed themselves on the bare wall around this door, each of their faces turned toward it. They seemed to be waiting for someone to open it, to reveal what lay beyond.

With excitement fluttering his heart, Reggie hurried toward them. Just as he reached the door, it swung open on its own.

He heard Chantal squealing gleefully behind him and Gareth murmuring in pleasant shock. Beyond the doorway, a glittering underwater kingdom awaited. Small fish darted in and out of coral as colorful and varied as wildflowers. An enormous castle made of sand and shells reared up in the distance. It gave off a beguiling pink glow, like an underwater beacon, welcoming all creatures in the dark sea.

More than anything, Reggie wanted to go there—to explore that underwater kingdom. And yet something scratched at his brain like a cat trapped in a box. Was there something he should be worried about? Something he was supposed to do, or perhaps *not* do?

The Conductor stood behind the three kids, blocking the balcony doorway with his wide body. His fingers continued to dance across the wooden flute as the manic song filled the room, leaving barely enough space for the air filling their lungs.

As the tune slithered its way deep into Reggie's bones, his anxious thoughts dissolved like sugar in water. Smiling dreamily, he reached up, grasping the door frame. Then he hauled himself up onto the jamb. The purple-blue water was only inches from his face now, just beyond the frame. All he had to do was take one step forward. Then he'd be off, swimming toward the shining castle in the distance.

But that scratching inside him had returned. That feeling that something wasn't right. His eyes drifted from the dazzling view of that underwater kingdom to the curtains framing the doorway. Their velvety fabric reminded him of something. A dress . . . pretty and blue . . . with sparkly rhinestone sleeves. His *mother's* favorite dress. She always wore it on date nights with his father. All at once a series of images flashed through his mind—his dad's smiling face; his mom setting the bear whistle down on his bed; rats transforming into grotesque children as the Conductor played his flute in the shadows. . . .

Fear rushed back into Reggie's body like ice water putting out a flame. And suddenly that insistent flute song was *outside* his head, where it belonged, not echoing loudly inside him. He had to act fast before his thoughts went hazy again, before it was too late. He pulled the bear whistle out of his pocket and blew on it as hard as he could. The shrill note pierced through the air, drowning out the Conductor's jaunty tune.

The view beyond the door transformed before Reggie's eyes. Like a painted backdrop flying up into the rafters above a stage, the underwater kingdom disappeared. It was replaced with city lights twinkling against the night sky, and just below his feet, a two-story drop down to the sidewalk. This wasn't a door...it was a window! One step forward, and he'd tumble through the air, plummeting to his death.

He reeled away from the open window, falling backward into the room. He collected himself and turned to Chantal and Gareth. He could tell from the confused looks on their faces that the flute song's glamour had been lifted, but probably only for a few moments. The Conductor was still frantically playing, and any second now, the music would sweep away their thoughts, sweep away their reason.

Chantal had clearly been thinking the same thing. She charged at the Conductor and pounced on him with the ferocity of a Klingon warrior. Unprepared for this attack, the man let out a creaky cry, and they both toppled over onto the floor.

They thrashed about, knocking over stacks of boxes, scattering props all over.

Reggie and Gareth rushed forward to help, but Chantal was suddenly on her feet. She raised her hand triumphantly in the air. Dangling from her fingers was the wooden flute.

FORTY

Up, Up, and Away

The three kids raced out of the room and onto the darkened balcony as the Conductor's voice rang out behind them, shrill and squeaky with rage.

"I'll wring your squawky little necks! I'll chop you into itty-bitties and feed you to the alley cats! Give me my flute back!"

They burst through the closed door at the other end of the balcony and flew up two flights of narrow stairs. After shoving through the metal door at the top, they found themselves on the roof. It was flat and empty, except for a crumbling chimney at its center and a rusty ladder leading to a fire escape.

The musical blimp floated above them, almost as high as the skyscrapers rising up on either side of the theater. It blotted out the moon and stars like a low-hanging cloud. Reggie couldn't shake the feeling that the smiley face painted on its underside was laughing at them, delighting in their fear.

From here, he had a good view of all the twisty horns poking out of the blimp's gondola. Flute song gushed out of these strange instruments, as dangerously sweet as scorpions covered in chocolate sauce.

"Hurry!" shouted Chantal over the music.

Reggie shook off his knapsack, got down on one knee, and pulled out the helicopter. He placed it on the graveled rooftop, careful not to prick himself on the sharp hooks jutting out from it. He retrieved a coil of rope from his knapsack and tied one end to the helicopter's landing skids.

"Think that will hold?" asked Gareth nervously.

Reggie didn't answer, but he tied a second knot, just in case. Then he picked up the remote control and brought the helicopter to life. As soon as he pulled back on the joystick, the small, whirring machine rose up toward the blimp. The helicopter was tiny in comparison, like a hermit crab taking on a beluga whale.

The length of rope rippled as it rose up into the air, rapidly unwinding from the coil on the roof like a stream of water pouring in reverse. By the time the helicopter had reached the blimp, all the slack had gone, and the end of the rope hung a foot above the rooftop. Reggie narrowed his eyes at the car-size gondola suspended from the bottom of the blimp. All he had to do was land the helicopter inside it. The six pointy hooks would do the rest of the work.

He flicked the joystick to the left, and the helicopter responded in kind. But he'd misjudged the distance. It smacked against the side of the gondola and fell out of the air, somersaulting as it dropped toward the roof.

Chantal gasped, and Gareth let out a cry.

Reggie pulled back hard on the joystick. Miraculously, the helicopter righted itself and began to rise up again.

"Our plan isn't going to work if you wreck that thing!" exclaimed Gareth.

"I'm not gonna wreck it," said Reggie tensely. "Just let me concentrate."

With his eyes fixed on the helicopter's wobbling tail, Reggie readied himself for another try. He held the remote control out before him and pulled on the joystick, guiding the helicopter to the underside of the blimp. This time, he made sure to steer it a few feet higher. He flicked the joystick to the left, and the tiny helicopter disappeared into the top of the gondola. He clicked the off button, shutting down its blades, and dropped the remote control.

The rope dangled a few feet above the rooftop, a straight line leading up into the blimp overhead. Reggie gave it several hard tugs. It held firm, so he knew the hooks were doing their job well.

"It worked!" cried Gareth, smacking Reggie on the back. "I can't believe it actually worked!"

Reggie didn't smile, though. He knew the hardest part was next. "I'll climb up, get control, and bring it down for a landing. Then you two can get in."

"Be careful," said Gareth, shaking his head solemnly. "And don't look down. Well, that's what people always say anyways."

Chantal peered up at the blimp overhead, then down at the frayed end of the rope. Her huge, shimmery eyes said it all. She was terrified for Reggie's sake. She opened her mouth to say something but thought better of it, and simply gave him an encouraging nod.

"I better do this right now, before I chicken out," said Reggie, looking up at the blimp's grinning face.

He did a few jumping jacks to loosen himself up, just like he always did before soccer practice. Then he leaped up and grabbed hold of the rope with both hands. He hung there a moment, the tips of his shoes dragging clumsily along the gravel. Then he pulled himself up and wrapped his legs around the rope. Gareth and Chantal backed away, watching him anxiously.

Reggie looked up, way up, his eyes traveling along the length of the rope. Forty feet, give or take. That wasn't too bad. Just like climbing the practice rope in gym class. As his PE teacher, Ms. McGregor, always said, *Don't think about it. Just do it.*

With a grunt, he hauled himself up higher, brought his knees up to his chest, and pinched the rope between his feet. Hands pulling, feet pushing. He repeated this two-step process again and again, pretending he was in gym class and not dangling precariously in midair like a spider on a thin web. He soon climbed so high that he could practically reach out and touch the shiny glass windows of the skyscrapers around him.

He tried to block everything else out—the sound of Chantal and Gareth shouting their encouragement; the hot cramping in his legs and arms; the way the rope rippled and swayed with every move he made, as if it wanted to shake him off.

It was nearly impossible to ignore the music, though. It grew louder and more chaotic the higher he climbed. The notes fluttered about inside Reggie's skull like a hundred trapped moths trying to escape.

That's when he heard shouting from below. He looked down and saw the Conductor in the doorway to the rooftop. The man's broad shoulders were squared, and he was glowering at Chantal and Gareth, evidently unaware of Reggie's midair acrobatics. Then the Conductor charged toward them. The two kids fled to the edge of the roof and started to climb down the fire escape on the side of the building.

Reggie felt a heart-thundering jolt. To his horror, he realized that the blimp had begun to drift away from the theater. His fingers slipped, and he was suddenly sliding down, rushing toward the rooftops below. His heart flew up into his throat, and he let out a strangled cry. He tightened his grip, the rope slicing hotly into his fingers. It was only when he squeezed it between his thighs that he came to a stop. Reggie let out a shuddering sigh of relief as cold wind ruffled his hair and tickled his sweaty forehead.

He was desperate to find out what had happened to his friends, but he couldn't think about that right now. He had to focus on getting up into the blimp first.

He took a deep, steadying breath and continued climbing. Pulling up with his hands, pushing down with his feet.

Ten pulls later, he allowed himself to look down again. He'd drifted far away from the theater, and he was shocked to see how high up he was. Below him, the city was made up of broccoli trees, matchstick lampposts, and dollhouses giving off puffs of gray-blue smoke. Toy streetcars zipped along streets as narrow as Reggie's shoe. And all over, tiny fairy lights in red and orange and white blinked against the shadows.

Reggie's head began to spin, and he forced himself to look up. He swelled with hope when he realized there was less rope above him than there was below. He was almost there.

Don't think. Just do it.

He pulled up with his hands and pushed against the rope with his feet. Over and over, he made himself repeat these motions, until his head knocked against something hard. It was the bottom of the gondola. He hauled himself up a few more feet, until he was right below the row of twisting brass horns. They were all different sizes and made up of various metal objects welded together—tin cans, pipes, copper pots, even a rusty horn from a very old record player.

The flute song was so loud here that his ears had started to ring. He reached up with one hand and grabbed on to the largest horn. With a loud grunt, he pulled himself up and swung his legs over the top of the gondola. He toppled forward, landing inside with a soft thud.

FORTY-ONE

Helping Hand

I t was dark inside, but Reggie's eyes adjusted quickly. He got to his feet and swept his gaze around the grayish gloom.

The walls were made of wicker, so it was like being inside a giant Easter basket. Stuck into the wall next to him was his helicopter. Its blades were bent out of shape, and its tail fin had snapped off. Three of its hooks had pierced right through the side of the gondola, latching the helicopter firmly in place. Reggie felt a small surge of pride. If his dad were here, he'd clap him on the back and congratulate him on a job well done.

Up above, too high to reach, was the curved, shiny surface of the blimp. Good thing he hadn't flown the helicopter too close to it. The whole thing might've popped like a balloon.

Dozens of brass pipes poked through the woven walls, each

connected to one of the strange-looking horns that adorned the outside of the blimp. These pipes corkscrewed all around the gondola, like highways of glinting metal. The chaos of piping all joined to a leather tube as long and thin as a finger. Affixed to the end of this tube was a chunky silver microphone. It pointed directly at the speakers of an old-fashioned music player, the same sort Reggie had once found in a dusty corner of his granddad's closet. The reels of a cassette tape spun on the inside.

He stepped over to it, reaching out toward its red stop button. But then he froze. Under the blaring music, there was another sound. A steady clicking, like gnarly toenails scraping against a subway platform . . .

Reggie spun around in terror.

At the other end of the gondola, a wooden steering wheel rose out of the floor. It was the kind you'd see on a sailing ship. An utterly unremarkable hand was attached to this wheel. And this hand was attached to an utterly unremarkable arm, one that was hairy and wouldn't look out of place on a man called Rocco or Brutus. The arm was attached to a grease-blackened box that was ticking loudly, like a clock winding down.

Reggie yelped when he spotted the severed limb. But he reminded himself that it was just a machine, like the clockwork version of his father down in the tunnels.

He crept toward it, keeping his eyes on those thick fingers.

Every now and then, the hand would tug the wheel a few inches left or right, making minor little adjustments in navigation. Once Reggie was standing over it, he took a few deep breaths to calm himself. Then he slowly reached down.

He grabbed hold of its wrist and tore the entire limb off the steering wheel. Its fingers waggled and twitched in protest like an angry spider. Reggie threw the grotesque contraption down onto the floor. But it righted itself on its trembling fingers and scurried toward him, the metal box dragging behind like a freakish tail. The hand latched on to his ankle, squeezing tightly, threatening to crush his bones.

Reggie screamed and stomped hard on it with his other foot. He didn't stop until the robotic arm had disintegrated into a heap of useless cogs and gears. A line of small black shapes streamed out of the mess. Cockroaches. They scattered to the corners of the gondola, disappearing into the shadows.

The blimp suddenly tilted forward. Now Reggie was sliding down the wicker floor, like a puck across pristine ice. He scrambled clumsily against gravity, making for the steering wheel. Once he grasped firmly on to it with both hands, he sat down and wrapped his legs around its base. Then he craned his neck forward, peering through a rectangular cutout in the wall before him. Down below, a network of winding highways was getting bigger, hurtling toward him. The blimp was nose-diving!

He pulled back hard on the wheel. At first, nothing seemed

to happen. But after a few heart-stopping seconds, the blimp began to right itself. Reggie wiped at his sweaty forehead with relief.

He was suddenly at a loss. Their plan had fallen apart. What should he do? Steer this thing back to the theater? Try to find Chantal and Gareth? What if the Conductor had gotten hold of them? What if that nasty man had done something horrible? No, he couldn't think that way. Gareth was fast on his feet. And Chantal was tough. Tougher than she'd given *herself* credit for.

Yes, that's what he had to believe—that his friends got away, that they were safe. He should continue with the plan. If Chantal and Gareth were really okay, then they'd know exactly where to meet him. At the very place this whole nightmare had started.

He gave the wheel a full turn to the right. The air around him shifted, and the scenery swung sideways like the flat background of a cartoon show. He aimed the blimp at the CN Tower, which was all lit up in purple lights like an electric Popsicle.

Except for the big landmarks—City Hall, TD Tower, the Royal Ontario Museum—Reggie had no idea where anything was. So he stayed the course, scanning his eyes over the twinkling city below, searching for anything that might show him the way. After ten minutes of circling around aimlessly, he was starting to lose hope of ever landing this thing. Then he spotted it. Green sparks exploding in the distance, followed by blooms of red and blue. Fireworks!

Reggie's entire body went limp with relief. It was them! It *had* to be!

He spun the wheel to the left, aiming the blimp directly at the crackling fireworks. He soon arrived at a wide avenue of tall glass buildings. Down below, he spotted the illuminated sign for St. Patrick station. Next to it, hopping up and down in the middle of the street, was Gareth. He waved a pair of sparklers over his head and hollered up at the blimp.

Reggie noticed, for the first time, a metal lever sticking out of the floor next to him. On a hunch, he ratcheted it forward. A loud hissing sound issued from overhead, like air leaking from a tire. The blimp began sinking quickly. As the ground below rushed toward him, Reggie white-knuckled the steering wheel and held his breath. The blimp touched down on the pavement about as smoothly as a city bus speeding over a shopping cart.

Once Reggie had resumed his breathing, he shakily got to his feet. He hurried over to the music machine and knelt down before it. Inside, the cassette tape continued to spin, churning out the cheery flute song that polluted the air like smog on a hot day. He pressed down on the stop button.

The music immediately ceased. Everything went jarringly still and quiet. Quieter than Reggie thought possible. Even the air *felt* different—lighter, cleaner, easier to breathe.

After letting out a long sigh of relief, he clambered out of the gondola onto solid ground. Straightaway, Gareth pounced on him, giving him a rib-crushing hug. He lifted Reggie right off his feet, spinning him around a few times.

"Admit it. I'm a genius!" crowed Gareth as he set Reggie down again. "These fireworks sure came in handy, didn't they?"

Reggie smiled and nodded. "Yep, you're way less of a fool than I thought."

Gareth laughed. "And you're less of a dweeb than I thought. Can't believe you had the nerve to climb all the way up into that thing!"

Chantal joined them, an unlit firecracker in her hands. She gave Reggie a quick smile and said in an oddly formal way, like she was a grown-up talking to another grown-up, "You were very brave up there, Reggie Wong."

"Nah, that was a piece of cake," responded Reggie, grinning. "*You're* the brave one! You tackled the Conductor like a Klingon warrior at the Battle of Binary Stars! And you did it! You got the flute!"

Chantal beamed as she patted the coat pocket where her journal was stowed. "I've already checked off number ten on the list."

Gareth whooped and hollered gleefully up toward the dark sky, "Pulled off a daring heist like a boss! Achievement unlocked, baby!"

"Wait, where's the Conductor?" asked Reggie, the smile leaving his face.

"Lost him a few blocks back," replied Gareth. "But he was

angrier than a bear in a hornet's nest. We better hurry before he figures out what we're up to."

"So, that should do it, right?" said Chantal hopefully. "The tune was enchanting all the adults, making them think we're rats. So that means everything's back to normal now, doesn't it?"

"Almost," replied Reggie, fanning his rope-burned hands in the air. "We still have that pesky rodent infestation to deal with, though."

Chantal retrieved the wooden flute from her coat pocket and passed it to him. Up close, it looked as ancient and gnarly as a witch's finger.

Reggie peered into Gareth's freckled face and held the flute out to him. "It's all up to you now, maestro."

FORTY-TWO

Performance Anxiety

Gareth stood in the middle of the street, which was empty of traffic, except for the hulking form of the now silent blimp. He held the flute before his eyes and squinted at it, as if trying to decipher any clues that might be hidden on its knobby surface. Then he took a deep breath, pressed the end to his lips, and blew. A harsh, grating note blared out of it, sounding like a sparrow being stepped on.

He cleared his throat, closed his eyes, then tried once more. Another earsplitting shriek rang out.

Gareth held the flute away from him, glaring stormily at it, as if it had just insulted him. Then he turned to his friends and shook his head. "I can't do this."

"You barely even tried!" exclaimed Reggie, walking up to him.

"I'm done trying. One of you do it instead."

"But you're the only one who knows how," said Chantal.

"Well, that's not my problem!" erupted Gareth, tossing the flute to the ground. He stalked away from them up the street, eventually disappearing around the corner of a deserted intersection.

Chantal was about to chase after him, but Reggie stopped her. "I'll talk to him. I've been his lightning rod since second grade. That sort of makes us old friends, right?"

Reggie picked up the flute. Then he jogged up the street, keeping his eyes peeled for either Gareth or the Conductor. At the intersection, he raised his eyebrows at the mess of overturned shopping carts, abandoned baby carriages, and flattened tin cans that littered the road. *Something* had clearly happened here. He found himself picturing an epic brawl between grocery-toting grandmas and snaggletoothed rat-kids. He hoped the grandmas won.

When he rounded the corner, he saw that Gareth hadn't gone very far. He was sitting on a bench inside a glass bus shelter.

"I thought *I* had the market cornered on angry tantrums," said Reggie, poking his head into the shelter.

Gareth hastily turned his face away and flipped up the collar of his jacket. Reggie was pretty sure from what he glimpsed of his red, splotchy cheeks that he was crying.

He stepped inside and sat down next to Gareth. "I know

we're not exactly BFFs, but we've escaped death together, like, a bunch of times now. That means I got your back. You know that, right?"

Gareth shrugged and sniffed wetly.

"So, what's up?" questioned Reggie. "Why the freak-out?"

Gareth cleared his throat and spat onto the ground. He answered without meeting Reggie's eyes. "Did you see my grandpa's face back in the library?"

"You mean when he put his hearing aid back in?"

"No," said Gareth, leaning forward, resting his forearms on his knees. "When he saw me holding my grandma's clarinet."

"Oh…yeah, I did," said Reggie quietly. He recalled how familiar Mr. Flanagan's devastated expression had seemed. How it had looked just like his mom's face when she was at her lowest.

"He *loved* hearing me and my grandma play together," said Gareth. "Whenever she got back from a performance with the symphony, I'd haul out my clarinet, and we'd perform an encore together for Grandpa. Right there in the kitchen." Gareth breathed in the cold air and squinted hard, as if to prevent any tears from leaking out. "But after Grandma died, it all changed. Our place wasn't filled with music anymore. 'Cuz if Grandpa heard even the first few notes of a clarinet piece, he'd get that look on his face. And it would be *my* fault for dragging up all that sadness."

Gareth turned and locked eyes with Reggie. "I never want to hurt my grandpa like that again."

Reggie nodded, taking in his words. Then he looked up at the night sky, searching for the moon. He was disappointed to find only the blinking lights of a passing plane. "My mom gets like that too. That's why I don't really talk to her about my dad anymore. It makes her so sad and scared and quiet. It just doesn't seem worth it, you know?"

Reggie thought about how angry he got at his mom the other day for missing his dad's birthday. He hated losing his temper like that, but it *did* feel good letting out the words he usually kept locked inside his heart.

Chantal's advice suddenly came to him: *The only way to tame a problem is to name it.* And for the first time ever, he felt like he actually *could* name his problem.

"We can't go on like this," he declared, suddenly filled with the confidence that comes from taking hold of something solid and true. "You shouldn't stop playing the clarinet just because it makes your grandpa sad. Just like I shouldn't stop talking about my dad just because it reminds my mom of what we've lost."

Reggie put the flute down on his lap and took out the bear whistle. He held it up to examine it. Orange streetlights glinted off its plastic muzzle and paws.

"Because that's even worse than losing them," he continued. "That's like pretending they never existed. And once they're gone from our heads, they're really gone for good."

They sat in silence for a while. Then Gareth scooted over on the bench and bumped Reggie's leg with his own. "Promise you won't tell anyone I cried at a bus stop?"

"Only if you promise to save our butts."

Gareth smiled at him and held out his hand. "All right, pass that flute over."

FORTY-THREE

Summon Song

G areth stood in the middle of the street, in the shadow of the parked blimp. He was loosening up his shoulders and shaking out his arms, like a soccer player readying himself for a penalty kick.

Perched on the edge of two newspaper boxes were Reggie and Chantal. They watched their friend with the hushed anticipation of a concert audience, moments before the curtain goes up on a very tricky performance. Which was appropriate considering this was the most important piece of music Gareth had ever been tasked with playing.

He looked to his friends for support before slowly bringing the flute up to his lips. He positioned his fingers over three of the instrument's six holes, then took a quick inhalation of breath. This time, a clear and bright note slipped out. As his fingers fluttered across the instrument, a lovely tune took shape, one that made Reggie think of cold lemonade on hot summer days.

The indigo sky suddenly brightened, and Reggie was sure that something magical had happened, that Gareth's tune had cast a spell over the heavens. Then he realized it was only the first light of dawn streaming between the skyscrapers in the distance.

"Think he'll pull it off?" said Reggie to Chantal.

"He'll come through for us," she replied confidently, her eyes fixed on Gareth's fingers sliding up and down the flute. "I believe in him."

Despite her confidence, Reggie was nervous. Could Gareth really remember the song the Conductor had played down in the tunnels? The one he'd used to summon the rats? That tune was the key to their entire plan. The key to ridding this city of its dire infestation. The key to finally getting their lives back.

As the sun rose higher in the sky and morning spread across the city, Gareth played the enchanted flute. He tried out bits and pieces of melodies, stringing bouncy notes together. Slowly, but surely, he inched closer to something that sounded familiar.

Reggie had begun to pace up and down the sidewalk, listening anxiously to the snatches of flute song. Chantal, on the other hand, seemed surprisingly mellow. She now sat cross-legged on the curb, her journal open in her lap, tapping a pen against her chin thoughtfully.

"What're you doing?" asked Reggie, peering over her shoulder.

"Trying to figure this out," uttered Chantal frustratedly. He saw that she was puzzling over the mysterious inscription from the temple of purple flowers.

"We already know what the first two lines mean. But I simply can't decipher the last two. *Forgive Us the Cage We Trap You In. Your Name Is Mightier Than Iron or Stone.* What cage? And what does the Darkness's name have to do with anything?"

Reggie sat down next to her on the curb.

"Cage...cage...cage," he said, frowning. "Well, maybe it used to be trapped inside that temple? Maybe *that* was its cage?"

"But I don't see how anyone could've trapped such a big, ferocious monster inside that place," said Chantal. "The trapdoor in the cemetery didn't even have a lock."

Reggie shifted his gaze to the last line, and he muttered it under his breath a few times. "Maybe this last bit is about how *strong* the Darkness is. That time it attacked me was super intense. Like being pounced on by a hundred rabid dogs. Thought I was a goner. And did you see all those bones down in that temple? I'd say that makes it *mightier* than iron or stone."

Chantal pressed her lips together, seeming unconvinced. "Maybe...but I just can't shake the feeling the answer is right here in front of us, and we simply can't see it."

"Don't worry," reassured Reggie. "We already have all the info we need. Let's just stick to our plan."

Chantal looked all around her, as if worried someone might be listening. Then she leaned in closer and said, "There's something else I've been wondering. . . . What do you think the Darkness is? I mean, is it a spirit? A shape-shifting beast? The bogeyman?"

Reggie thought back to his encounter with the entity. His blood ran cold as he recalled those many spectral hands snatching hold of him. He'd tried his best to block it from his mind. But he realized there was something in that terrifying memory that needed to be examined, like a glinting penny poking out of a mud heap.

"That time the Darkness attacked me . . . there's something I haven't talked about."

"Yeah? What is it?" asked Chantal, narrowing her eyes at him.

"While it was happening, I was scared, yeah. But I felt something else too. A feeling I haven't had since the day my dad died." Reggie shifted away from her uncomfortably. His throat was suddenly bone-dry.

"When I found out my dad didn't make it through his surgery . . . it was like a bomb went off, and my whole world was blown to bits," he continued, his voice thickening with emotion. "All that was left was nothingness. Like I'd been sucked into a black hole, and I'd never find my way out. That was the worst I've felt my entire life. Up until the Darkness."

Chantal closed her journal and hugged it against her chest.

"I felt the same way after my sister died," she said, nodding. "But I hated myself for falling apart like that. I mean, feeling sad was just something in my head, right? Why couldn't I just ignore it and move on?"

Chantal peered across the street at the window of a shuttered pub. She and Reggie were reflected in the tinted glass, a pair of ghostly children sitting on a gum-caked sidewalk.

"But Dr. Peregrine told me something I'll never forget. She said the grief I was feeling was as *real* as any beast. And in order to fight it, in order to defeat it, I'd have to look it straight in the eyes and get to know it first." Chantal cocked her head and wrinkled her chin. "Hmm . . . Maybe that's what the Darkness is."

Reggie frowned at her, not following.

"Maybe the Darkness is *grief* that's come to life."

He raised his eyebrows dubiously. "Really? A living emotion?"

"It's not as silly as it sounds," reasoned Chantal. "Think of all the people who've lost somebody. All those people who walk around feeling sad and hopeless. Those terrible feelings don't just disappear into thin air. They have to go *somewhere*."

Reggie thought of all the people who ever lost someone they loved. He thought of the tears they shed. So many tears. More tears than there were stars in the sky. He pictured all that salty liquid seeping down into the ground, like dirty rainwater. Flowing into those wild, winding tunnels beneath the city, pooling in the velvety dark—a toxic swamp of sadness. Then the impossible happens. A spark of powerful magic. Colliding with the noxious brew, mutating it into something with shape and form, something that's *alive*. . . .

Reggie let out a long breath and ran his shaking hands through his hair. "Whoa . . . maybe you're right."

"Or maybe it's just the bogeyman," remarked Chantal lightly. "Who knows?"

He chuckled and smiled at her. "Or that, yeah. Come to think of it, who even came up with that name? *Boooogeyman*. So not scary. Makes me think of boogers."

Chantal's head jerked up, her eyes wide and her mouth hanging open.

"Oh la vâche!" she exclaimed.

It took Reggie a moment to clue in, but he finally turned his attention to Gareth. There he stood, in the middle of the street, a wedge of sunshine picking him out like a spotlight. His eyes were shut as his fingers danced nimbly across the wooden instrument. He was swaying slightly, lost in the music unspooling like spider's silk from the flute. It was a fluttery, flowy sort of tune, like clear water rushing over pebbles in a stream.

Every inch of Reggie's skin was tingling. He'd heard this song before. Down in those dark, twisting tunnels.

"You did it!" he said excitedly. "That's the tune!"

Gareth stopped playing. The last few notes drifted into the wind like sails that had been cut loose from a ship. He held the flute away from him and stared at it in astonishment, as if he couldn't believe his own abilities.

"I was worried I'd never get there," he said, shaking his head. "But then I got into a good riff, and it started to feel right."

"It's time," said Chantal significantly, getting up off the curb. "We have to do it now. Before the Conductor finds us, before he can spoil the plan."

The two boys climbed into the blimp. Reggie looked around the cramped, gloomy interior, at the mass of pipes corkscrewing around the wicker walls. The Conductor had made this contraption. Just like he'd made those roach-bots down in the tunnels. They were all parts of his maniacal plan. Now they were using the Conductor's own creation against him. This made Reggie smile.

He moved the clunky cassette player aside. Then he sat Gareth down, right under the silver microphone.

"Do your thing," said Reggie, squeezing his shoulder.

Gareth played the Conductor's summoning song, his fingers moving up and down the wooden instrument with confidence. The tune slid out of the flute, into the microphone, and up through the brass pipes, growing louder and louder as it coiled around the walls. Then came the sound of groaning metal—the prelude to an eruption. The music blasted out of the blimp's many horns, like cannon fire from a pirate ship. It echoed loudly off the tall glass buildings, sounding like a half-dozen flutes playing slightly out of sync with each other.

As Gareth continued to play, Reggie climbed out of the blimp and joined Chantal. They peered up and down the empty avenue, keen to spot any signs of life.

"Do you think they'll come?" asked Chantal, pulling her pea coat tight.

"I hope so," said Reggie. "We just have to wait."

* * *

The music traveled far and wide across the slumbering city—an enchanted arrangement of notes so light and airy that it floated on the chill morning breeze like pollen in the spring. So sprightly and limber that it could squeeze through the tightest of nooks and crannies—easily slipping down chimneys, under door cracks, between heavy curtains meant to shut out the world.

The music was tireless, determined. Not stopping until it had found its target. Soon, in every corner of the city, small eyes sprang open and whiskered noses twitched with recognition. The melody tugged at their sense of loyalty like a hand on a leash. It coaxed them out of their warm beds and into the dawn-bright streets.

FORTY-FOUR

The Rodent Stampede

"I don't think it's working!" hollered Chantal over the blaring flute song. "Shouldn't they be here by now? What if they know it's a trick?"

Reggie glanced at the blimp and its assortment of strange horns, which rattled and shook as music poured out of them.

"Gareth's only been playing for a few minutes," he replied. "Give it some time."

"What if it's not loud enough?" asked Chantal anxiously.

Reggie listened to the flute song echoing back from every direction, the notes overlapping like frenzied chirping. "I'd say it's plenty loud."

"Well, maybe we should get the blimp up in the air," she suggested. "Maybe they'll hear it better if—"

"Shhhhhh!" interrupted Reggie, holding up his hand. "Do you hear that?"

"Hear what?" said Chantal, confused.

Reggie tilted his head, listening for a moment. There was something *under* the flute song, a sound he could feel inside his very bones—a deep, low rumbling. And it was getting louder, growing in intensity, like an approaching tornado hell-bent on destruction. He peered off into the distance, toward the end of the avenue. Something was moving down there.

He climbed up onto a newspaper box and shielded his eyes against the rising sun. His breath caught in his throat when he saw it—a sea of bodies filling up the width of the avenue. It was getting closer, flooding toward them like a low tidal wave.

Chantal gazed into the distance. "What is it?"

Too terrified to reply, Reggie grabbed on to a light pole to keep from falling off the box. It was a massive stampede. Thousands of rat-children, heading straight for them.

The flute song took a sudden turn, plummeting from high, fluttery notes into a low, plodding tempo, like an old horse struggling through a snowdrift. It was no longer the Conductor's summoning song; it was a new composition altogether.

"What's Gareth playing?" asked a bewildered Chantal.

Reggie shook his head, his eyes wide.

Then an unseen force swept through the horde, causing each of those rat-children to lose their footing, tumbling to the pavement. . . . No, that wasn't it. Something *else* was happening, something much stranger. Reggie squinted into the distance, trying to make sense of what he was seeing. His mouth dropped open. The rat-children weren't falling down; they were *shrinking*, collapsing in on themselves like sand castles hit by a swift tide.

Even as this astonishing transformation was happening, the horde continued to barrel forward. Only, it was no longer a mob of rat-children; it was now a vast mischief of rodents. Countless furry little bodies surging ahead—a lumpy stew coating the entire avenue.

"They turned back into rats!" exclaimed Chantal, blinking in awe.

"I need the flute!" yelled Reggie. "They're coming!"

The music stopped abruptly. Gareth hopped out of the blimp, hurried over, and passed the flute up to him.

"So. Many. Rats!" he choked out once he spotted the approaching herd.

"Was that you? Did you do this?" asked Reggie.

"Yeah, I think so," replied Gareth, shrugging. "I was thinking how they'd be easier to outrun if they were just little rats again. And my fingers took over, like they were doing their own thing. It was awesome. Sort of like that time I played jazz with my—"

"We should run!" interjected Chantal. "We should run... shouldn't we?"

"No," said Reggie firmly. "We have to make sure they see us first. We need them to follow."

His heart pounded furiously as he watched the rats drawing nearer. They were an unstoppable force, streaming over cars, knocking over parked bicycles, clambering over one another to reach the front of the herd.

"Hold steady," shouted Reggie, his voice shaking with nerves. "Just a little closer..."

The advancing rodents were only forty yards away now. He could make out their many beady eyes, their twisted snouts, their snarling mouths.

It was time. Reggie jumped up and down on the newspaper box, waving the flute wildly in the air. At the sight of their master's instrument, the army of rats slowed to a halt. They cocked their tiny heads suspiciously at Reggie, unsure if he was friend or foe.

"Looking for your master?" he shouted. "Well, you're not gonna find him. We dropped that sucker in the middle of Lake Ontario! Yep, he's sleeping with the fishes now. Bet that makes you real mad at us, huh?"

"Think they'll buy it?" said Gareth, his eyes fixed on the mischief. "What if they know you're lying?"

The front of the pack let out a series of stuttering squeaks that sounded like violins being tortured. The ranks behind them echoed this strange call. Then they spilled forward, goaded on by the promise of revenge, the promise of blood.

"Pretty sure they bought our story," said Reggie, jumping down off the newspaper box. "Run!"

FORTY-FIVE

Return to the Tunnels

Reggie, Chantal, and Gareth raced into St. Patrick station. The man in the booth didn't even glance up from his sudoku puzzle when they hopped over the turnstiles. They flew down the stairs to the subway platform below, skidding to a stop at the far end.

"They're super mad!" wheezed Gareth. "Five-alarm, nuclear-meltdown mad!"

"Well, it worked, didn't it?" said Reggie. "That's all that matters."

Gareth puffed out his cheeks and shook his head. "Better hope those vermin don't catch up with us!"

They turned their attention to the walls, searching the many curved green tiles. Each one was large enough to function as a toboggan for either a small child or a few dozen subway rats.

"Here it is!" Chantal called out, pointing at the tile with *S.S. Enkrad* scratched into one corner. She reached up toward it, but then paused. She tipped her head to the side and stared curiously at the jagged writing.

"Hurry up and open it!" insisted Gareth, peering anxiously down the platform.

"Darkness!" declared Chantal, her eyes wide with realization. "*S.S. Enkrad* is 'darkness' spelled backward! That's why we keep finding it on doors leading into the tunnels. It's to warn people about what's inside. It's to warn us about the Darkness!"

"That's nice and all, but this isn't really the time for word puzzles!" shrieked Gareth, pushing past her. He reached for the tile, wedged his fingers through a gap in the grout work, and gave it a firm tug. It popped open, revealing the secret passageway. Cool, fishy-smelling air rushed out.

Then came a clattering crash overhead—the sound of countless rats invading the station.

Reggie climbed up inside the rectangular opening first. Then he stuck out his hand, helping Gareth and Chantal clamber up as well. Now it was just a matter of retracing the path they'd taken before.

After ducking through a small red door, they found themselves once again in the now familiar tunnel of pebble-flecked dirt. It stretched dizzyingly before them, disappearing into blackness. Reggie had a moment of doubt. Was it really a good idea to plunge back into this forever-dark? What if they weren't so lucky this time?

"Non, non, non!" uttered Chantal, panicked. "I left the knapsack up on the street! Our flashlights are in it!"

Reggie shook his head. "Don't worry. I got this."

He fished out his bear whistle, took a deep breath, and blew into it. The piercing tone reverberated through the tunnel. He squinted into the gloom, hoping desperately that this would work once again.

Sure enough, a glowing green dot appeared far down in the darkness. It grew bigger and bigger, until the balloon was bobbing right over Reggie's head.

"It's real good to see you," he said, patting its rubbery surface.

There was a cacophony of angry squeaks from behind. Reggie turned to see a river of ravenous rats streaming into the passageway. When the rodents spotted the three kids, they hissed and bared their teeth at them.

"Let's bounce!" exclaimed Gareth.

They ran pell-mell into the velvety darkness as the balloon kept pace overhead, casting its thin green glow upon them. The rats weren't far behind. Their vicious squeals and clacking teeth echoed loudly through the humid air.

The deeper they ventured into the winding tunnels, the easier it was to lose all sense of distance in this perfect, pitchy blackness. Reggie couldn't gauge just how far behind the rats were. One moment it sounded like they were breathing down their necks, the next it was like the mischief had detoured into a distant passage.

The three kids eventually reached a split in the tunnel. And since they could no longer hear the pursuing rodents, they stopped to get their bearings. The balloon wobbled frantically overhead, urging them to continue moving.

"I can't do this," said Chantal breathlessly. She collapsed against the dirt wall, which was veined all over with thick roots.

"Too late to back out now," responded Gareth, doubled over, trying to catch his breath. "Those rats aren't just gonna let us stroll out of here."

"I can't do this!" repeated Chantal, her voice high and frantic.

Reggie looked into her terror-filled eyes. "The plan's working. All we gotta do is keep ahead of the rats. Just until the Darkness finds them."

"No, you don't understand," she said, tears streaming down her cheeks. "I'm not brave or strong or special. My *sister* was. It was okay when she was alive. She could be all those things for the both of us. But she's gone now. And I'm just... just... me!"

"But that's not true," protested Reggie. "Look what an awesome job you've been doing with her list."

Chantal let out a stifled sob and slumped down onto the ground. "But it doesn't matter, does it? Even if I finish every last thing on that list, I'll still never be as amazing as she was. She's gone... forever! And nothing I do can make up for that!"

She began sobbing in earnest. Reggie got down on his knees and put a hand on her shoulder.

"You're nothing like your sister . . . so what?" he said, shaking his head. "You're smart, you're not afraid to talk about feelings, and you don't take crap from anyone. That's all *you*, and that's pretty amazing in my book."

Chantal searched his eyes to see if he was telling the truth. "Think so?"

"Totally."

"I second that," added Gareth, saluting her awkwardly.

"You don't have to *become* your sister to carry her memory," Reggie said softly.

She nodded and wiped at her cheeks. Then a wide smile appeared on her face. "That was surprisingly insightful of you."

"I'm a quick study," said Reggie, winking.

After composing herself, Chantal got to her feet and dusted the dirt from her pea coat. She glared defiantly into the tunnel ahead. "Come on, boys. We've got a mission to complete."

FORTY-SIX

Relative Fear

They pushed on through the gloom, trying to retrace their route from the night before (or was it *three* nights ago? This whole slippery time thing made Reggie's head spin). Since one stretch of tunnel was nearly identical to the next, navigation was a real struggle down here. But that all changed once Gareth made his discovery. He halted midstep, gasped, and pointed down at the ground. Imprinted into the soft dirt were three sets of distinct footprints. They were all headed in one direction.

"Wait a minute!" breathed Gareth. He raised up his foot, comparing the sole of his shoe to one of the prints. Under the balloon's green glow, it was clear that they shared the same honeycomb pattern. "This is mine! Which means these are *our* footprints! From when we escaped to the surface!"

"That's brilliant!" exclaimed Chantal.

From then on, the three kids simply followed their own footprints in the opposite direction, certain that they were heading deeper underground.

The farther they traveled, the more a sense of unease crept over Reggie. That unease soon swelled into full-fledged fear when the realization hit him: The Darkness was following them. Reggie was sure of it. He could *feel* it stalking them every step of the way, like a hungry panther cloaked in night. It was simply waiting for the right moment to strike. Sure enough, as they filed silently down a narrow passage, shadowy hands appeared at the edges of the balloon's protective glow, testing the limits of their reach. Their thin, impossibly long fingers scratched at the circle of green light cast onto the ground, as if it were a bubble that could be popped.

Reggie peered up at the balloon, suddenly hyperaware of how fragile it was. It wouldn't take much to pierce its thin, rubbery membrane—just one determined rat leaping out of the gloom, swiping at it with its sharp claws . . . and *pop*.

"You okay, buddy?" asked Gareth. "You don't look so good."

"Yep. Fine. Totally cool," said Reggie, his voice an octave higher than usual.

The surrounding gloom thinned, as if a choking fog had

lifted ever so slightly. The balloon's green glow traveled much farther now, reaching a fair way ahead of them.

"I think it's gone," said Reggie, looking around warily. He could no longer feel invisible eyes on him, stalking him.

"You mean the Darkness?" whispered Chantal, casting her eyes about.

"Yeah. It's left us alone . . . for now."

Reggie surveyed the familiar corridor stretching out before them. All along its length, on either side, dirt staircases curved up and away to unseen doors. He knew that each door opened onto a space that was perfectly ordinary—a kitchen, a bedroom, even a backyard with a big maple tree growing at its center. . . .

But something was different about the corridor. Something that Reggie couldn't quite put his finger on. When he finally noticed what had changed, he gasped and stopped abruptly. Figures stood at the bottom of each staircase. Silent and unmoving, like statues in an unlit museum. All at once, their heads turned in unison toward the three children. A sudden motion that made Reggie's heart drop to the floor.

"This seems like a super-bad idea," said Gareth through clenched teeth.

"Let's keep walking," whispered Reggie. "And don't make eye contact. They'll probably just leave us alone."

The kids moved slowly down the corridor, between the two rows of twisting staircases. As they passed each figure, its face was revealed by the balloon's pale glow, like a ghost appearing out of thin air. A stooped old man in round spectacles smiled blankly at them. On the other side, a snub-nosed boy glared as he puffed out a huge bubble of chewing gum.

"Have you seen my Horace?" called out a lady in a bee-hive hairdo. She held a tray of blackened cookies in her hands. "Horace is never this late getting home. His choco chippies are getting cold."

A mustached man in a wrinkled suit stared mournfully at Chantal and begged, "Where's my Selimah? Are *you* my dear, sweet Selimah?"

The three kids picked up their pace, hurrying past these sad characters, each calling out for a missing loved one. Reggie reminded himself that they weren't real people. They were mechanical, no more alive than his alarm clock.

Then a familiar voice called out, "There you are!"

A girl in a polka-dot dress ran up to Chantal, taking hold of her hand. It was her identical twin sister, or at least, a convincing version of her.

Chantal pushed her away and shot back, "You're not real! You're simply a bag of bolts."

The twin's face bunched up, and her lower lip began to wobble. "*Je ne peux pas le croire!* Why would you say such a horrible thing?"

Chantal's expression softened, and she started to reach out to comfort her. But then she shook her head and crossed her arms.

"I'm not falling for it this time!" she said angrily.

The twin ran forward and threw her arms around Chantal's waist. "Don't be cross, sister! I have so many things to tell you! So many things to *show* you!"

This set off a dangerous chain reaction. One by one, the mechanical people left their posts and lurched toward the terrified children.

"Come and try a choco chippy," insisted the woman with the tray of cookies. She strode right up to Reggie in chunky high heels that sank into the ground with each step. A too-big smile appeared on her face, as she tossed the tray behind her and grabbed firmly on to his shoulders. "You can play in Horace's room until he gets home from school."

Reggie tried to shake the woman off, but her grip tightened like a vise. She drew him toward one of the staircases, like a stern mother marching her son to bed.

"You look a lot like my Bryan," boomed a deep voice into Reggie's ear. He turned to see a lumbering man in a plaid shirt following right behind them. The man sniffed accusingly at the air. "You sure *smell* a lot like him too."

He took hold of Reggie's hand and yanked hard. This prompted the cookie lady to squeeze more tightly on his shoulder, hauling him off in the other direction. A crazed tug-of-war started up between the two confused automatons, with Reggie as the hapless prize in the middle. He wondered if it was possible to be torn in half, like a teddy bear being fought over by feuding toddlers.

All around him, more figures were shambling out of the gloom. They reached for him desperately, their eyes bulging with misplaced hope. Soon he would be completely surrounded.

Reggie called out for help, but his friends were in no position to rescue him. Chantal was being dragged one-handed down the corridor by her twin, as if she weighed nothing. Gareth wasn't doing much better. He was pinned to the ground by a lady in a nurse's uniform who was trying to wind a knitted scarf around his neck. Even the glowing balloon was in a tizzy. Seemingly unsure of how to help, it zipped frantically up and down the corridor, causing elongated shadows to lurch all about the dirt walls.

Reggie redoubled his efforts, trying to thrash free of his captors. Displeased with his struggling, the cookie lady used her free hand to pinch his ear.

"Stop being such a stubborn goat," she said cheerfully. "Come with me, and I'll fix you one of Horace's favorites. Egg and soldiers on toast, maybe? Peanut butter brownies?"

She yanked violently on his ear, and Reggie howled in pain.

"Okay, okay, lady. I'll come with you!" he croaked.

She smiled and released him. "Good boy! I can't wait for Horace to meet you."

Reggie had no intention of following her. He elbowed the man in the plaid shirt and wrenched his arm away from his meaty grip. Momentarily free, he lunged at the cookie lady and grasped either side of her head with both hands. He ran his thumbs over her forehead, feeling for a seam. Sure enough, he found the thin indentation, located exactly where it had been on his mechanical father. He slotted his fingernails into the seam and flicked his fingers up.

There was a mighty *pop*, and the top of her head launched into the air, landing on the other side of the corridor. Reggie watched disgustedly as cockroaches skittered out of the spinning cogs and dials inside her head. The lady's eyes went blank, then she keeled over, clattering to the ground.

Reggie felt thick arms close around his torso. The plaid-shirted man had pulled him into a bear hug, squeezing the air out of his lungs. He stomped hard on the man's foot, causing those pythonlike arms to loosen. Then he spun around and reached up toward the man's bald head. He found the seam even quicker this time, digging his nails inside. Another satisfying *pop*, and a colony of cockroaches trooped out as the man tipped over like a felled tree.

Reggie raced down the corridor, dodging dozens of mechanical people reaching out to him, trying to claim him as their own. Then he heard Chantal's terrified screams echoing through the tunnel. He spotted her up ahead, being dragged up one of the staircases by her twin. Chantal was fighting back as best she could, kicking her feet and clawing frantically at the steps.

Just as Reggie was about to rush over to help, someone clamped on to his arm and wheezed hotly onto his neck. It was a wild-eyed lady in a red kimono.

"Come home with me, Kentaro," wheedled the lady through yellow teeth. "I need your help in the garden."

"Get off me!" shouted Reggie, trying to pry her bony fingers off his arm. But her grip was too strong. She used both her liver-spotted hands to tug at him, compelling him farther up the tunnel.

Even more figures were stumbling out of the gloom toward Reggie, like a pack of wolves closing in on a wounded animal. Panic welled up inside of him. How was he going to get out of this mess?

The tunnel was suddenly filled with music—flute song cutting swiftly through all the chaos. It was a simple tune, small and quick, made of only five notes played over and over. But it had an amazing effect. All up and down the corridor, the mechanical people stopped their frantic efforts. They went stockstill, like windup toys whose motors had stopped spinning.

Reggie was finally able to wrench his arm free of the lady in the kimono. He backed away from her, just as hundreds of cockroaches burst from her mouth and scurried down her body to the dirt floor. The same fate awaited the other robots in the corridor. Cockroaches began erupting out of their heads—from their noses and ears and eyes and mouths. They spread across the ground, moving en masse toward the middle of the corridor, where Gareth stood playing the flute. These countless cockroaches pooled around his feet, like a thick spill of molasses.

Gareth's eyes were closed as he played, and he was swaying

slightly. He teased the song out for a few more bars before ending it with a flourish of his fingers across the wooden instrument. Silence returned to the tunnel. No longer in the melody's thrall, the cockroaches scattered, disappearing into the shadows.

Reggie and Chantal exchanged astonished expressions, before hurrying over to Gareth.

"That was amazing!" Reggie said enthusiastically, shaking his head.

"How did you do that?" questioned Chantal.

"Same way I turned the rat-kids back into rats." Gareth looked down at the flute in his hands. "I totally get it now. With this flute, it's not just about finger placement, it's also about where you put your *mind*!"

"I don't get it," said Reggie.

"What you picture in your head while you play. That's the key."

"Really? That's all it took?"

"Well, I couldn't have done it without my grandma's advice," replied Gareth, his eyes bright with amazement. "She was always telling me to relax, to let a tune go where it wants to go. So, that's what I did. And then the notes just sort of fell into place. It was amazing. Like the music was coming out of *me*."

"Your grandma would be so proud of you!" cried Chantal, throwing her arms around him.

Gareth chuckled bashfully and ran a hand through his curly hair. "Yeah, I guess she would."

FORTY-SEVEN

The Feast

The three friends resumed their trek down the long corridor, stepping carefully over the many fallen robots. Reggie paused at the sight of Chantal's robo-twin, lying motionless on her back. A rigid grin was stretched across her face, and her big brown eyes stared lifelessly up at him. He knelt down, reached out to her waxen face, and closed her eyelids.

"What's that sound?" asked Gareth, stopping in his tracks and turning around.

"I heard it too," responded Chantal. "It sounded like—"

A great hubbub of earsplitting squeaks suddenly filled the tunnel. Chantal yelped in alarm, and Gareth let out a curse.

Reggie peered behind him. The rats had burst through the other end of the corridor, flooding toward them like a force of nature—a snarling, snapping, shrieking tsunami. They galloped ahead, their furry bodies filthy with dirt and grime.

"Run!" shouted Reggie.

The trio bolted down the corridor, away from the menacing mischief as the glowing balloon kept pace overhead. Reggie glanced over his shoulder, horrified to see that the rats were gaining ground with frightening speed.

"We gotta go faster!" he shouted frantically. His legs burned with the exertion, and his lungs were on fire. He couldn't keep this up for much longer.

An earth-shuddering growl echoed through the tunnel, announcing the arrival of the most fearsome beast of all: the Darkness. The gloom around the kids suddenly thickened, becoming as impenetrable as a wall of black marble. It was as if everything beyond the circle of green light had simply ceased to exist.

"Stay in the light!" warned Reggie, sprinting even faster. "It's back! The Darkness is back!"

Barely-there hands skittered in and out of view at the edges of the penumbra, like wisps of smoke materializing and dissolving in a stiff wind. The Darkness was stalking them, *hunting* them.

"I can't keep running!" shrieked Chantal, her gait slowing.

"Just a bit longer!" urged Reggie, trying to ignore the cramping in his legs. "Our plan's gotta work. Just keep going!"

The rats were in close pursuit, just beyond the circle of light.

Reggie couldn't see them, but he could *hear* the patter of their tiny paws against the ground. He could even hear the wet flick of their tongues and the clickity-clack of their small, sharp teeth.

Then *new* sounds reached his ears. Sounds so unsettling that it took everything inside him to keep running rather than freeze in terror. It was the sickening symphony of a predator feeding on prey.

Behind him, panic spread through the pack of rodents, like fire sweeping across a parched wheat field. They let out squeals and hisses at the realization that it was now *their* turn to be hunted. These frantic noises eventually died down as, one by one, the rats were devoured by the Darkness. Soon there was nothing at all. Just silence.

Reggie, Chantal, and Gareth stopped running. They turned around, peering wide-eyed into the solid gloom. There was nothing to see. And yet terror still twisted like a knife in Reggie's gut. He knew very well that the Darkness was there, watching and waiting, wanting to feast on *them* too. But he reminded himself that the three of them were safe so long as they were bathed in the balloon's green glow.

"I think I'm gonna hurl," wheezed Gareth. His knees buckled, and he dropped down onto the ground. "That was a whole other level of nasty!"

Chantal looked about her in a daze. "It ate them. The Darkness actually *ate* them!"

Reggie reached up and gave the floating balloon an appreciative pat.

"We better get moving," he said, his brow furrowed. "I get the feeling the Darkness still has room for dessert."

FORTY-EIGHT

Tunnel of Light

R eggie, Chantal, and Gareth staggered back the way they
had come. The Darkness followed them every step of
the way, growling and bristling, sending out shadowy
hands to menace them. The kids were careful to keep well within
the balloon's protective glow, keenly aware that there was quite
a ways to go before reaching safety.

The ground underfoot crunched and popped, just as it did
in that temple of purple flowers. Reggie kept his eyes up, not
wanting to see what remained of the Darkness's rodent feast.

Before long, they arrived at the corridor of twisting staircases, where dozens of motionless bodies lay. Reggie had to
remind himself that they were just a bunch of busted-up robots,
as harmless as discarded shop mannequins.

"So, what happens now?" asked Gareth as he stepped carefully over one of the felled automatons.

The sharp *snick* of a match being struck was quickly followed by an orange flame roaring to life. A man stood at the foot of the nearest staircase, holding a lantern aloft. Then he was racing down the corridor toward them, his broad body moving with the speed and menace of a charging bull. It was the Conductor.

Before the kids had time to react, he snatched the flute right out of Gareth's hand. Then he swung his other arm out, striking his lantern against the trusty balloon overhead. It popped, and the two glow sticks inside dropped pitifully to the ground. They flickered a moment before going dark.

The Conductor backed away a few steps, far enough to keep out of the children's reach, but near enough that they were still within the flickering glow of his lantern. The Darkness grumbled and growled around them, anxious for a taste of whoever was first to leave the safety of that orange glow.

"My dearest toot-toot," cooed the Conductor soothingly to the flute, holding it up to the lantern to examine it. "Did the nasty nibblies hurt you? Did they put their grubby-stubby fingers on you?"

Satisfied that his precious instrument was intact, he narrowed his cold eyes at Reggie and snapped, "Where are they? Where are my ratty-tatties?"

The three kids looked wide-eyed at one another, unsure of what to tell him.

"Where. Are. My. Rats?" thundered the Conductor.

Reggie gestured at the seething Darkness that coiled around them like an invisible anaconda. "They're gone," he said somberly. "The rats are all gone."

The Darkness emitted a low gurgle that sounded almost like a burp. The Conductor flicked his eyes wildly about him, as if trying to catch sight of the recently fed monster. Then his round face went slack as he realized what had happened to his comrades, to the rats of St. Patrick station.

"My ratty-tatties! My noble rodents! Gone, gone, gone!" he wailed, falling theatrically to his knees and raking the air with his fingers. "Gobbled up by the forever-dark! Munched on like nummy-nibblies!"

Then, like a dull knife being sharpened to a point, his show of sorrow turned to rage. His head snapped up, and he aimed the flute menacingly at the three children. "You will pay the price for their lives, nasty nibblies! You will pay dearly!"

He raised the flute to his lips, sucked in the fishy-smelling air, and began to play. As his fingers flew up and down the instrument, a strange tune spooled out. It was a jarring mixture of melodies, as if a handful of pretty songs had been smashed to pieces, then cobbled together into a Frankenstein tune that sounded more creepy than beautiful. The discordant notes filled the tunnel, and even the waiting Darkness seemed to take notice. It purred deeply, seemingly in appreciation of what it heard.

The three kids huddled together, terrified of what was to come.

The tunnel began to shake violently, and dirt rained down from overhead. Then a mighty tearing sound rang out as an enormous crack appeared on the wall next to them, zigzagging up the crumbly dirt like a lightning bolt. The crack expanded, bursting open, until it grew into a tunnel—big enough for three people to walk through shoulder to shoulder. Dazzling white light poured out of this newly formed passageway, as if the most brilliant, sunshiny day waited at the other end.

The seismic rumbling ceased, and the only sound left was the creepy flute song.

Reggie, Chantal, and Gareth stared in awe down this dazzling tunnel of light. A figure was emerging. It was just a silhouette, so Reggie couldn't make out a face, but it looked like a girl walking toward them. She stopped halfway down the tunnel and waved excitedly.

"That looks like my sister," said Chantal warily.

Another figure stepped out of the light, striding up the tunnel toward them. It was the shape of a woman in a flowing dress, with a mass of wild hair on her head. She too stopped halfway down the tunnel and waved.

Gareth shook his head in disbelief. "Grandma?"

Then one last figure came through. A man with his hands in his pockets. He was ambling casually up the tunnel, like someone on an after-dinner stroll in the park. Something about the way he moved, about the way his shoulders bounced loosely with every step, was very familiar. Reggie's mouth dropped open. He'd recognize that silhouette anywhere.

"Dad?"

The three figures stood waiting, halfway down the tunnel, like black cutouts against the blinding light. It was clear that they couldn't come any closer. It was up to Reggie, Chantal, and Gareth to join them. All they had to do was step into that tunnel and move toward the incredible white light....

Reggie glanced over at Chantal. He could tell from the scowl that had appeared on her face that she wasn't falling for another of the Conductor's false promises. And neither would he.

"We're not fools!" he shouted. "This is just more of your lies. More of your illusions!"

"Not at all, little nibbly," replied the Conductor with eerie calm. "I've opened a tunnel between *this* life and the *next*. Parted the veil, lifted the curtain."

He held the flute up and gazed reverently at it. "This tooty-flooty can do splendickity things, *powerful* things. More glorious than your tin-toony head can fathom."

Reggie started to doubt himself. What if the Conductor was actually telling the truth this time? He'd seen that flute transform rats into children, seen it control the minds of people and insects alike. So maybe it really could bridge the chasm between the living and the dead? Maybe being with his dad was as simple as walking into the light....

He took a step toward the tunnel, his eyes dazzled by the brightness.

"No, we don't need this!" implored Chantal, cutting in front of Reggie and taking his hands in hers. "Even if they're real. Even if that's really them. We don't need this!"

"What are you talking about?" Reggie asked angrily, trying to brush past her. "Of course I need my dad! He's all I think about. I need him back!"

"But don't you see? We have them already," insisted Chantal, tears leaking from her eyes. She held firmly on to his hands, keeping him in place. "I can feel it every time I write to my sister in my journal, or when I cross something off her list."

"And I feel it when I'm playing the clarinet," whispered Gareth. "When the music's moving through me, it's almost like she never left, like she's still here, y'know?"

Chantal looked at Reggie, her face shadowy against the heavenly light spilling out from the tunnel. "I've never met your dad. But I bet he was real good at making things, right? And I bet he was super creative. I know all that because *you* are. Don't you get it?"

Reggie gazed into the tunnel of light, at the silhouette of the man who'd taught him everything he knew.

He found himself thinking of his father's hands. Rough and callused, and lined with thin scars, they somehow reminded Reggie of his own. Because they were always in motion, always itching to create something out of nothing. Like sculpting a starship out of clay or crafting a grappling hook from a toy helicopter and duct tape.

Reggie thought of all the times in the past two years when he'd conjured up an idea and brought it to life. Those were the moments when his dad had felt close, his dad had felt *real*. More real than mossy tombstones in cemeteries, or robots filled with roaches, or whatever waited for him now in that tunnel of light.

"Yeah, I get it," he said softly to Chantal. "I totally get it."

They turned away from the blinding light. The Conductor was watching them with devious interest, like an arsonist waiting for a house to go up in flames. But his face went purple with rage once he realized that his honey trap had soured, that he no longer had any power over these children.

The man's dark eyes became as dead and glassy as a shark's. Then he brought the flute to his lips once more.

FORTY-NINE

Rat Rage

A different tune filled the air, one that sounded like the frightened shrieks of dying rats. It was a chaotic series of notes more *murderous* than musical. The sound was so earsplittingly terrible that Reggie clamped his hands over his ears, desperate to block it out.

"We have to get out of here!" cried Chantal, her eyes wide with terror.

Something was *happening* to the Conductor. He'd turned away from them and was doubled over, as if in pain. Then he collapsed onto all fours, dropping both the lantern and flute to the ground. Reggie was about to attempt to snatch them, but a horrible sight made him freeze in place.

The Conductor had started to swell up, every inch of him

bulging outward like a balloon being inflated. His blazer tore down the middle, as did his pants, before all the fabric finally gave way, flapping to the ground. Then his skin ruptured all over, splitting apart in the most revolting fashion. It slid wetly off him in irregular swathes, like an overripe banana shedding its peel. A *new* body emerged—one covered in bristly white fur. Finally, a long pink tail sprouted from his backside, like a length of hose unraveling. It thudded up and down against the dirt, stirring up a cloud of dust.

The Conductor wheeled around on his four paws, showing off a brand-new *face* as well—a whiskered snout twisted into a permanent sneer; yellow teeth as sharp as glass shards; and those familiar beady eyes. His red cap somehow remained atop his head, wedged between two triangular ears that flicked back and forth with predatory alertness.

The Conductor had *transformed* into an enormous white rat, the size of an overgrown grizzly bear. And from the looks of the fleshy bits and bobs littering the ground, it was a transformation that couldn't be undone.

He raked his narrow tongue over those rows of razor-sharp teeth and focused his ratty gaze on Reggie. The meaning of his leer was quite clear: The Conductor was hungry, and the only thing on the menu was three meddlesome children. . . .

Gareth shot a freaked-out look at Reggie.

Then Gareth let out a battle cry and darted forward, reaching for the flickering lantern on the ground by the Conductor's back paw. But the newly minted rodent wheeled around, lashing his fleshy tail at him. It walloped Gareth's chest with the heft of a fire hose, sending him arcing through the air. He landed with a thud just outside the lantern's glow.

Gareth groaned and got unsteadily to his feet, but ghostly hands reached out, taking hold of his ankles. The hands tugged mightily, and Gareth crashed back down to the ground. He clawed at the dirt as the Darkness pulled him deeper into the gloom.

Chantal charged at the Conductor next, making a play for the lantern. But he lunged at her, cracking his mouth wide open. He chomped onto her arm and thrashed from side to side, tossing her about like a rag doll. She let out an agonized scream that echoed up and down the tunnel.

"Let her go!" hollered Reggie.

He joined the skirmish, punching and kicking at the Conductor's wide, furry body, though it didn't seem to have any effect. That's when he spotted the lantern lying on its side. He swept it up off the ground and gave it a good swing, bashing it over the Conductor's head. The Conductor let out a distinctly ratlike squeal and reared back, loosening his grip on Chantal. Reggie yanked her out of the way just as the Conductor rebounded, snapping at the air where her head had just been. His teeth clattered together with the force of a guillotine.

Reggie and Chantal raced down the corridor toward Gareth. He was sprawled out on the ground, still being dragged by his ankles across the dirt. But as soon as the lantern's orange glow washed over him, those wispy, not-quite-hands dissolved like smoke.

"Took you guys long enough!" he shrieked as he was helped up by Reggie.

The battered trio fled up the nearest staircase. The Conductor bounded after them on all fours, his hulking mass shaking the walls of the tunnel. They burst through the door at the top and slammed it shut behind them. All three of them fell back against it, bracing it as best they could with their small bodies.

FIFTY

Caging the Beast

The entire door rattled in its frame as the Conductor threw his sizable bulk up against it from the other side. Again and again, he crashed into it, causing the wood to creak worryingly and dirt to sprinkle down from overhead.

"We can't hold him off!" shrieked a terrified Chantal.

"Maybe the Darkness will get to him!" exclaimed Gareth, pushing against the shuddering door with both hands.

Reggie's eyes dropped down to the floor, and he uttered a curse. There was a sizable gap between the bottom of the door and the floorboards. The lantern light seeped easily through it, protecting the Conductor from the Darkness's vengeful hunger.

"I don't think we can count on that!"

Reggie twisted around, keeping his back wedged against the door, trying to get a better sense of his surroundings. He held the lantern out before him, casting its firelight across the tidy, sleek surfaces of this darkened room. They were in what looked to be a fancy kitchen with marble countertops, gleaming silver appliances, and a glass table set for breakfast (golden pancakes topped with whipped-cream smiley faces). Yet another one of the Conductor's deceptively comfy traps.

"There's no way out!" wailed Gareth. "What are we gonna do?"

The door shook again, and a zigzagging crack splintered down the center. Reggie clutched at his chest as he started to hyperventilate. Fear had taken its icy hold of him, squeezing all the air out of his lungs. He just might suffocate right here, in this fake-homey kitchen, like a zoo penguin keeling over on a Styrofoam iceberg. Then there would be no more Reggie, no more anything....

But he refused to give up that easily. He reminded himself that there was *always* a way out of every problem. That's what his dad had taught him. He just had to keep his wits about him.

The best way to tame a problem is to name it.

There it was again, Chantal's helpful psychiatric advice, echoing through Reggie's head like the catchy slogan of a breakfast cereal. It was a silly thing for him to think of, since no amount of *naming* would tame the rapacious rodent trying to bust its way through that door.

Naming . . . That reminded him of something. . . . Something that had to be solved . . . A word puzzle . . .

And then, it was like a glittery curtain lifted up in Reggie's mind, revealing an exciting grand prize, like on a TV game show. Except the prize wasn't a high-tech dishwasher or a shiny new car; it was the *key* to getting out of this place alive.

He looked excitedly at Chantal, blurting out, "Forgive us the cage we trap you in. Your *name* is mightier than iron or stone!"

She shook her head at him, confused.

"The name! The name is how they trapped it!"

"You tripping or something?" exclaimed Gareth.

"Don't you see? Chantal was only half-right!" continued Reggie excitedly. "*S.S. Enkrad* is *Darkness* spelled backward. But it's not a warning. It's a cage!"

Chantal's mouth dropped open in awe, and her eyes were shining. She'd finally clued in. "*Oh la vâche!* You're right!'

Reggie knew exactly what needed to be done. But they had to act fast or their bones would soon be scattered up and down these winding tunnels, like all those poor souls who never managed to escape.

"Check my left pocket!" he called out to Chantal as the door jolted violently, nearly knocking all three of them over.

"Are you sure you two can hold it?" she said anxiously.

"We have no choice!"

Chantal broke formation, pushing away from the door. She came over to Reggie and stuck her hand inside his jeans pocket. She extracted something short and thin, and held it up for examination. Pinched between her fingers was a stubby piece of blue chalk. The same one Reggie had swiped from his robot-dad's toolbox earlier.

"Go, go, go!" he urged.

Chantal raced over to the middle of the kitchen, got down on her knees, and began to write on the wooden floor planks.

The Conductor rammed again. But this time the door buckled in half, ripping clean off the hinges, sending Reggie and Gareth tumbling inelegantly to the floor. They scrambled to their feet and hurried over to Chantal. She was still on her knees, scribbling away.

The Conductor thrust his head through the door frame, then proceeded to twist and writhe awkwardly, squeezing his expansive width through the opening. Once he was entirely through, he stalked toward them slowly. His white fur bristled all over, and his whiskered nose twitched with fiendish excitement. He was taking his time, relishing every moment of their terror.

Reggie's hand shook as he held the lantern aloft. Its flickering flame was the only thing keeping everyone in this room safe from the waiting Darkness. Having finished her task, Chantal stood up, pressing close to the boys. They stood shoulder to shoulder to shoulder, a united front against the gargantuan white rat creeping toward them.

"Don't you dare come one step closer!" warned Reggie.

The Conductor let out a series of short, sharp shrieks that could almost pass as breathless laughter.

"I mean it!" shouted Reggie, straightening up to his full height.

The Conductor bowed down low, leveling his beady eyes at the boy. He slid his front paw forward and thrust out his rear. That long, fleshy tail rose up, forming a question mark behind him. It was the pose of a predator about to pounce upon its prey. Then the Conductor sprang forward.

As if in slow motion, Reggie hurled the lantern to the ground. He stomped on it over and over again, glass shattering underfoot, until the flame finally went out. The room was plunged into pitch-blackness.

The three kids huddled together, unable to see anything but solid gloom. A low, throaty purr signaled that the Darkness had entered the room. The air thickened like greasy smoke as the invisible monster circled them. Reggie held his breath. He could feel Chantal's shoulders quaking against his, could hear Gareth gibbering in fear. Seconds passed, and yet nothing happened. No skeletal hands reached out to snatch them.

Reggie felt the air lighten ever so slightly as the Darkness moved on, seeking a different victim.

Somewhere close by, angry squeaking and hissing sounds cut through the silence. Although Reggie couldn't see a thing, he *imagined* the scene unfolding before him: the Conductor snapping defensively at the air, trying to fend off an ancient creature that was coiling around him, trapping him in place, readying itself for the kill.

The Darkness roared—a sound best described as a freight train crashing into hundreds of brawling lions. In response, there were scuffling sounds, like large rodent paws trying in vain to flee. Then came a bloodcurdling squeal of terror that made every hair on Reggie's head stand on end. It was the scream of a creature about to meet an unpleasant end—the sound of the Conductor getting his comeuppance.

Finally all was still and quiet once again.

A strong draft ruffled Reggie's hair as the Darkness whooshed out of the room.

Moments later, from the tunnel below, flute song rang out. A joyful tune. The notes swooped playfully up and down, like sparrows in spring sunshine.

Reggie smiled. The Darkness finally had its cherished flute back. The melody drifted away, deeper into the winding tunnels, growing fainter and fainter, until the only thing left was silence.

FIFTY-ONE

Homeward Bound

R eggie blinked anxiously into the dark for a long while,
listening for any hint of lingering danger. When he was
sure the battle was over, he finally let out a sigh of relief
and relaxed his tense shoulders.

"Everyone good?" he whispered.

"I almost wet myself...but yeah, I think I'll survive," said
Gareth.

"Did we do it?" asked Chantal hopefully. "Is it safe to go
home now?"

"Yeah, I think we actually did it."

Gareth put on a deep, gravelly voice and intoned, "In a world
where bloodthirsty rats roam the earth...humanity's only hope
is a trio of fearless warriors in the seventh grade...."

Chantal and Reggie burst into laughter.

Blinding blue light suddenly whirled out of the gloom, a dazzling combination of color and movement, bringing the world back into existence. The swarm of beetles swooped down toward Reggie, swirling around his body, then flew off to investigate Chantal and Gareth.

A few of the beetles broke off from the swarm. They fluttered right up to Reggie's face, hovering inches from his nose. At first, he thought it was a trio of beetles flying in tight formation. But when he peered closer, he realized it was two beetles lifting a third one by its periwinkle wings. This flightless beetle looked about as familiar as an insect could look to a human— one of its wings was bent in half, and its back leg dangled limply.

A joyful gasp escaped Reggie. It was his beetle buddy.

"You're alive!"

He held out his palm. The beetles flew over to it, gently setting down their passenger before flitting off to join the others. Reggie's beetle buddy frolicked all over his hand like a puppy trying to impress its owner. Then it waggled its antennae happily at him.

"I missed you too, little guy!"

Reggie glanced over at his two friends. They were covered from head to toe with shimmering beetles.

"They're so beautiful!" gushed Chantal. She was waving her uninjured arm before her eyes, watching the insects form ever-changing patterns across her skin like a miniature version of the northern lights.

"Hold up!" said Gareth as his gaze dropped down to the floor. "Is *that* why the Darkness left us alone?"

On the floorboards, encircling them in blue chalk, was a name written over and over again. *S.S. Enkrad.*

"The Darkness's name is the one boundary it can't cross," explained Reggie, smiling knowingly at Chantal. "It's the only cage strong enough to contain it."

His mind drifted to whatever mysterious sect had built that temple of purple flowers. The same folks who branded all those doors with *S.S. Enkrad,* he figured. If not for their efforts, the Darkness would be free to leave these endless tunnels, free to terrorize the world above.

The beetles took flight all at once, spiraling off Chantal's and Gareth's bodies. The swarm flew in a rippling column out the door, like a sun-dappled stream flowing in midair. The three kids followed, trooping down the stairs to the tunnel below. The beetles affixed themselves all over the dirt walls, making the tunnel as bright as a summer's day.

Reggie's beetle buddy climbed onto his shoulder. He reached up with his finger and gently stroked its wings, which were smooth and cool to the touch.

"You guys ready to head home?" Reggie asked, smiling.

"But there's one more thing," responded Chantal, gazing at

the winding staircases that lined the tunnel in either direction. "All those kids the Conductor lured down here..."

How could he have forgotten? This was the most important part of their plan. There were a lot of children who needed their help.

Reggie turned in a slow circle, addressing the glowing swarm. "Hey, guys, think you could help us with a search and rescue mission?"

There was a tickly flutter of wings as the beetles rearranged themselves into shimmering blue words.

BOY HELPED US

WE HELP BOY

"Great," said Reggie with a resolute nod. "Let's get to work, then."

The glowing swarm accompanied the three friends as they scaled each of the dirt staircases and ventured into the rooms beyond—convincing replicas of bedrooms, kitchens, backyards, even classrooms, anywhere that a heartbroken child might think of as *home*. In most of these rooms, they found terrified kids huddled in corners, hiding under beds, or holding on to mechanical loved ones that could never love them back. It didn't take much to coax these poor kids out of their hiding spots and lead them to the corridor below.

In short order, the tunnel was filled with throngs of children who were hungry and dazed, but in surprisingly good spirits.

The rescue mission didn't go off without a hitch, though. Some of the rooms had no one in them, like stage sets waiting for the actors to appear.

"What do you think happened to them?" whispered Chantal, so that the kids around them wouldn't hear. "The missing ones."

"I don't know," said Reggie, shaking his head sadly. He thought of how angry the Darkness had been, how it had devoured everyone in its path. "I guess not everyone's gonna make it home today."

Chantal held herself and shuddered. "That could've been us."

As the procession of lost children made its way through the winding tunnels, the swarm of beetles circled them protectively, making sure no one strayed from the group. At one point, two of the youngest children broke into tears from exhaustion and refused to walk one step farther. The three friends begged and pleaded and even tried to calm them down with camp songs, but nothing worked. They finally came up with a solution: carrying the little ones in their arms.

After a long and exhausting march, they reached the small alcove with two doors.

"This is it!" announced Reggie. "We're almost home!"

Home. That word was like a brilliant spark, setting aflame the hearts of all the many children. Suddenly the tunnel was filled with their happy chatter and hoots of excitement.

"Are we there yet?" asked the tiny, red-haired boy in Gareth's arms.

"Almost!" replied Gareth, tousling the boy's hair. "I bet your family will be real glad to see you, eh?"

Reggie turned the brass knob on the small red door and pushed it open. Fluorescent white light spilled over him, making him squint. Just beyond the passageway, he saw a train pulling into St. Patrick station.

Satisfied the children were out of danger, the beetles spelled out parting words on the tunnel walls.

EVER CAUTIOUS, EVER SAFE

Reggie's beetle buddy darted from his shoulder to his outstretched hand. It flapped its one, functioning wing slowly, and pulsed its periwinkle glow in farewell.

"Take care of yourself, little guy. Try not to get into any more fights with mutant rats, okay?"

The beetle took a leap of faith off his hand. It was caught midair by two helper beetles that ferried it back to the swirling swarm.

"Looks like you've made a new BFF," remarked Chantal, nudging Reggie with her shoulder. She winced and grabbed her left arm, which was bloody and torn up from her showdown with the Conductor.

The swarm corkscrewed three times around Reggie's body— an acrobatic adieu—before trailing off into the tunnel.

"Ready to get back to our boring old lives?" he asked.

"Are you kidding me?" responded Gareth. "I'm even looking forward to math class!"

FIFTY-TWO

Lost and Found

Outside of St. Patrick station the sun was shining bright, and a brisk wind swept through the canyon of glass buildings. The big red blimp was still there, parked in the middle of the avenue, like a parade float that had lost its way.

Although it was only midmorning, the streets were jam-packed with people. Hundreds of men and women milled about, seeming anxious and confused, unsure of where they were headed and what they had lost. Having rushed out of their homes in a hurry the day before, many were still in their rumpled pajamas and bathrobes.

Up here, in the world above, an entire day had passed since the flute song's enchantment had been lifted. One full day of

318

utter confusion and desperate searching. All the while rumors had spread, whispered from one bereft guardian to the next: *Something strange was going down in St. Patrick station.* Maybe this *something* held the answer to all their questions?

Then it happened. The thing that transformed their worries and confusion into pure, candy-sweet joy. Children streamed out of the subway station, scores of them, blinking into the sun and smiling at the wide blue sky overhead. Cries of happiness and relief rose up from the crowd as men and women spotted their children. They ran up to them, pulling them into tight hugs that wordlessly said, *I love you, I missed you, don't ever disappear on me again.*

Reggie, Chantal, and Gareth stood by the entrance of the station, taking in the happy reunions popping up all around them. The little boy in Gareth's arms suddenly let out an elated squeal when he spotted his parents. Gareth set him down and watched him scamper off.

"We saved the city, maybe even the world," said Gareth, squaring his shoulders. "But no one's ever gonna know, are they?"

"Yeah, probably best if it stays our little secret. Wanna know what's even funnier?" asked Reggie, raising an eyebrow.

"What?"

"You and me—friends," he said, punching Gareth playfully in the shoulder.

"Well, you gotta admit: We make a pretty good team!"

Gareth put his arm around Reggie's shoulders. Then he looked over at Chantal and put an arm around her too. "The three of us make an *awesome* team!"

Gareth's eyes grew big as saucers when he spotted someone in the crowd.

"Grandpa!" he shouted, rushing over to Mr. Flanagan, whose face somehow managed to appear both tender and grumpy at the same time. "I thought I'd never see you again!"

After watching Gareth and his grandfather disappear into the crowd, Reggie leaned toward Chantal and said, "By the way, thank you."

"For what?" she asked, buttoning up her pea coat against the wind.

"For your super-helpful advice." Chantal seemed confused, so he added, *"Best way to tame a problem is to name it."*

She wrinkled her chin, impressed. "Dr. Peregrine would be proud."

Then she squinted into the crowd at two people who stood out from all the others—a man and woman dressed to the nines, as if they had just come from a fancy shindig somewhere. They were drifting through the throng, searching around worriedly.

"Maman, Papa!" cried out Chantal. She raced toward them, but stopped and turned toward Reggie. "You should come meet my parents."

"No, it's cool. Maybe later," he said, rubbing his neck.

Chantal nodded and gave him an encouraging smile. Then she ran to her parents, who enfolded her in a double hug.

Reggie stood there awhile, watching all the happy people with smiles brighter than the morning sun overhead. There was so much joy and excitement bubbling up around him, and yet he felt like a goldfish observing a birthday party from inside a tiny fishbowl.

There was no point hanging around here. Not like anyone was coming to find him. He should probably head home and check on his mom. He wondered if she'd even noticed that he was missing.

He started to walk away, up the avenue, when a familiar voice reached him from the cheerful hubbub.

"Have you seen my son?" asked a woman anxiously. "He's about this high, has spiky hair, and always talks about *Star Quest*... or is it *Star Wars*... I'm not sure...."

Reggie stopped in his tracks. He turned around, running his eyes over the scene, until he spotted a woman at the edge of the crowd. Her long black hair was tied back in a ponytail, and she was wearing a silk robe that was being tossed about by the wind. She was bending over, peering into the face of every boy who passed by, hoping to find someone she knew, someone who belonged to her.

Reggie gaped at her, wondering if his eyes were playing tricks on him.

"Mom!" he shouted, his voice catching with emotion. "Mom, over here!"

She looked up, searching around for whoever had called out to her. Then her eyes locked on Reggie. A mixture of warmth and relief swept across her features, smoothing away the worried creases of her face. She raced over and pulled him into a hug so tight that he could barely breathe. Being in her arms felt so good, so *right*, that he didn't want her to ever let go. He felt safe and warm and loved.

"I was so worried," she gasped into his hair. "I thought I'd lost you!"

He pulled away and looked her up and down in astonishment. He'd seen plenty of extraordinary things lately— roach-filled robots, magical flutes, rats masquerading as children—but all of that paled in comparison to seeing his mom out and about.

"You left the apartment!" he exclaimed. "You actually did it!"

"I know!" said his mother, seeming just as gobsmacked as him. "I didn't think I could do it. But then I woke up yesterday, and you were missing! I was so scared. I didn't know what to do."

She peered into Reggie's eyes and nodded. "But I was sure of one thing: I couldn't just wait around in that ratty old apartment, doing nothing. And so, I did *something*: I came out to look for you. It was hard. Took me about a million tries to even walk through that door. But here I am!"

With tears streaking down her face, she pressed her forehead against Reggie's. "That's when it hit me: The thought of losing you is way scarier than anything I might find out here."

"I'm proud of you, Mom," said Reggie, hugging her even tighter.

"Not as proud as I am of you, little man."

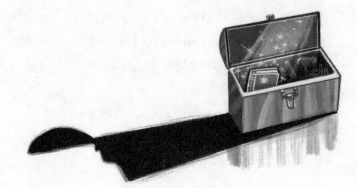

FIFTY-THREE

The Toolbox

R eggie slept well that night. Tucked safely under the covers of his bed, he had airy dreams about picnics and
birds singing sweetly from tree branches. But his eyes
flew open just past midnight. He sat up in bed, looking around
confusedly at his darkened room. He couldn't shake the feeling
there was something he'd forgotten, something he had to do.

He switched on the bedside lamp and scanned the familiar
contents of his room—the shelves lined with mystery books and
Star Trek action figures, his ever-messy desk, his smelly soccer
gear piled in the corner behind the door.

That's when he noticed it—something gleaming at the bottom of his closet.

He climbed out of bed, crossed the room, and knelt down

on the carpet. He stuck his hand into the dusty shadows of his closet and fished something heavy out from under a heap of rumpled clothes. It was a shiny red toolbox. His father's toolbox. After the funeral, Reggie had packed this away in storage, because it had hurt too much to look at. Yet here it was. His mom must've unpacked it for him.

He unlatched the box. As expected, it was filled with all his dad's greasy tools. He lifted off the top tray, and his breath caught in his throat. At the bottom of the box was a familiar black sketchbook. He'd forgotten this was in here.

He picked the book up and flipped through it. Pages and pages of his dad's sketches greeted him—elaborate drawings and schematics, accompanied by instructions in his dad's particular style of chicken scratch. Each one was the start of a project that had yet to be built. He hugged the book to his chest and smiled. He could finish these projects for his father; he could bring all these ideas to life.

Suddenly his dad didn't seem quite so far away. He was as close as the pages in this sketchbook.

Acknowledgments

First and foremost, I need to thank all the people who read my story when it was merely a Word document attached not to a publisher but to a wing and a prayer. Without exaggeration, I am astonished every time someone is willing to read my make-believe tale, let alone offer feedback. First on this list are my remarkably creative and supportive loved ones, who also served as great beta readers—Jamie Venn, Rosena Fung, Mila Jarecki, Aaron Jarecki, and Robert Pinet.

My agent, Thao Le, who was the first person in the publishing industry to convince me I was capable of writing books that people just might want to read. Without her encouragement and incredibly clear-eyed feedback early on in my process, I don't believe anyone other than the millipedes who reside in the bottom of my closet would be aware of Reggie's story today.

My editors, Kieran Viola and Cassidy Leyendecker. They have made what could have been an overwhelming process incredibly joyful and fulfilling. I have zero doubts that my book has reached its full potential through their stellar guidance.

All the editors I worked with on various anthologies—Allison O'Toole, Merissa Tse, Mark Foo, BC Holmes, and Phillip Joy. Every single one of their notes and suggestions pushed me to do better, to craft the best stories I possibly could. I've never taken a writing class, but I consider all of them my teachers.

Those editors and publishers who brought the anthologies to fruition, giving voice to so many creators (myself included): Steven Andrews, Malcolm Derikx, Nelson Da Rocha, Aaron Feldman, Stephanie Gauvin, Matthew Lee, Nicole Marie Burton, Joamette Gil, and Andrew Wheeler.

The Ontario Arts Council for a grant that propelled me to the finish line of my writing process.

My mom for always being there for me.

Finally, my eternal gratitude goes to Jamie Venn, the love of my life, and the one person who keeps my world spinning on its proper axis.

ONTARIO ARTS COUNCIL
CONSEIL DES ARTS DE L'ONTARIO

an Ontario government agency
un organisme du gouvernement de l'Ontario